THE DARKER SIDE OF HENRY VIII
BY HIS QUEENS

Dorothy Davies

THE DARKER SIDE OF HENRY VIII
BY HIS QUEENS

INTRODUCTIONS

From Katherine to Katherine – the ladies have their say
about Henry:
the lies, the facts, the reality of being Queen of England
and consort to His Majesty King Henry VIII.

"I have no fear but when you heard that our Prince, now Henry the Eighth, whom we may call our Octavius, had succeeded to his father's throne, all your melancholy left you at once. What may you not promise yourself from a Prince with whose extraordinary and almost Divine character you are acquainted? When you know what a hero he now shows himself, how wisely he behaves, what a lover he is of justice and goodness, what affection he bears to the learned I will venture to swear that you will need no wings to make you fly to behold this new and auspicious star. If you could see how all the world here is rejoicing in the possession of so great a Prince, how his life is all their desire, you could not contain your tears for joy. The heavens laugh, the earth exults, all things are full of milk, of honey, of nectar! Avarice is expelled the country. Liberality scatters wealth with bounteous hand. Our King does not desire gold or gems or precious metals, but virtue, glory, immortality."
Lord Mountjoy to Erasmus, 1509

It follows that the one thing we should not do to the men and women of past time, and particularly if they ghost through to us as larger than life, is to take them out of their historical contexts. To do so is to run the risk of turning them into monsters, whom we can denounce for our (frequently political) motives—an insidious game, because we are condemning in their make-up that which is likely to belong to a whole social world, the world that

helped to fashion them and that is deviously reflected or distorted in them. Censure of this sort is the work of petty moralists and propagandists, not historians.
Lauro Martines, Fire in the City: Savonarola and the Struggle for Renaissance Florence

Dedication:

This book is dedicated with many thanks and considerable affection to Henry's queens for sharing their secrets and opinions with me. It is also dedicated to Henry VIII, King of England, Supreme Head of the Church of England, Fidei Defensor or Defender of the Faith.

And to Terry Wakelin, my rock and anchor, who passed to spirit during the writing of this book. He, like Henry, lived life to the full and he, like Henry, has left a huge hole in many lives, especially mine.

Katherine of Aragon

Henry's wives, divorced, beheaded, died, divorced, beheaded, survived

Katherine, the first of Henry's wives. (Divorced)

I know well this is a book which gives Henry's queens a chance to talk about Henry as if he were not there. I also know well he is supervising; reading over the shoulder of the channel but that makes no difference to the words I will give. I apologise to the reader for taking time to talk of my first husband, but if I did not set it down plainly, my statement that I was virgin when I went to Henry would not be something they could understand and accept. It is my hope, my wish; my prayer that they will accept it, for it was and is the basis of my stance that I was Henry's lawful wife. In turn, that was the basis of one of the major problems to torment Henry's life. The choice of his second queen was the basis of the major problem to torment Henry's life. And so, much as we wish to talk of the king himself, of necessity what happened to us and how we reacted has to come into it, to make sense of all that is written in your history books – mostly falsely but then the historians did not and do not have the advantage of talking to the people who lived the life. I believe it is called primary sources.

The primary sources here are the queens themselves.

Herein lies the truth about the reign of Henry VIII as told by his six wives. Herein is the man at the centre of the many controversies and tyrannies, let us not blind ourselves to his nature, who took England in a new religious direction which in itself caused even more problems, ones he - for once - did not foresee.

In truth, it is women who were Henry's 'downfall' and two women, both resulting from his loins, who tormented England with their religious beliefs when he was no longer there. Mary took the land in one direction, Elizabeth reversed it and chaos ensued, whilst Henry, in the realms, raged impotently at his inability to do anything about it. But England survived as a Protestant country and, some would say, was the better for it. Certainly it made England different and that was ever Henry's intention. England stood proud in his time and it has many times since.

Henry Tudor, the great king, is seen by many as the overweight red-faced man depicted so accurately by Hans Holbein. They forget, or cannot accept, that long before the portrait was painted Henry was first a youth, then a young prince, then a young king. He was charming and handsome, someone who attracted women as if he was made of honey and they were all worker bees buzzing around him. He had everything you would now call charisma, you would have fallen over yourselves to see him and talk with him, just as you do your celebrities and movie stars now.

This is the man at the centre of this book, the man at the centre of all our lives, often our hearts, too. I have sympathy for those for whom he was not the centre of their hearts, for he was not at any time an easy man to live with. If there was no love to provide an easement of the days, it was much harder for them than it was for us who adored him. Love makes a cushion for the bad times, a filter for the evil times and a mirror for the good times, when we could reflect the sunshine we felt back into his life so he could bask in it.

This is the man I was - and still am - proud to call my husband. For me the divorce never happened, I was and am his Queen even now.

***

There is one question everyone asks, that is, every historian and historical fiction author, so I begin this part of my narrative with the statement which I declare on my immortal soul to be true.

I was virgin when I went to the bed of King Henry VIII. I say this with honesty and truth and swear to its truth on my immortal soul and that of my husband the king, because it is a truth: his brother Arthur, Prince of Wales, was 'impotent'.

Now let me tell you how this sad situation came to be.

I left Aragon with a very heavy heart. Despite all the assurances of Sir Edward Woodville, King Henry VII's emissary and negotiator at the court of King Ferdinand and Queen Isabella, that I would love England and its beauty and its people, nothing on this earth could or would match the sun baked beauty of my homeland. The English weather made it worse, we had a terrible crossing and arrived to fog, rain, mud and more grey clouds than I thought possible.

I found my prospective father-in-law, the king, to be dour and mean with money for the palace was shabby and cold. I found my future husband to be everything I hoped he would not be; thin, bookish, uninteresting. He looked at me with what I took to be longing. I wanted to say to him, it will not be long now before we are one and then we shall have no secrets from one another, but I did not say it for I did not believe it.

And then I looked at his brother and all was instantly lost.

11

Henry was then a young man, as tall as his brother but wider in the body, a sturdy person with intelligence and learning showing in his eyes. He was not someone to trifle with or attempt to hide anything from, for I knew he would see through any deception.

I also knew at that moment I was there to marry the wrong man - as far as I was concerned. The world knew that I had been betrothed to Prince Arthur for a goodly number of years. The world did not know that Arthur's brother was charismatic and handsome and I would have preferred him but my life was rigidly bound by the agreements signed by both sides in the negotiations.

I recall Sir Edward standing by and smiling, this being almost the culmination of his diplomacy. The marriage would conclude that for him. I wondered what reward he would receive for his work.

Having made my obeisance to the king and queen, having acknowledged the Prince of Wales, having sat through a small meal and some difficult speeches and courtesies, my ladies and I departed, we went back to my suite of rooms where my ladies chattered and giggled and talked of –

Henry.

Like me, they had found him of great interest. I did not hear them speak of my husband-to-be once. I did not blame them. Once you had looked upon Henry, no one else in the room mattered. It was a blessing and a curse. A blessing that he came to be mine for some years; a curse in that others found him as fascinating as I did. But at the time, those early heady days when I first met him, I had no idea that life would turn as it did. All I knew then was that I was madly in love with a man I was not to be married to and that life stretched out before me as a long empty path of grey clouds and mud. It was a vision I could not lift from my mind. I have no doubt this had been generated by the storm which disrupted the crossing of the Channel and the lengthy wet muddy inordinately dull journey to meet my husband to be. Whatever the reason, I could not have been more unhappy if I had actively worked at making myself so.

I found it hard to adapt to the English buildings, with their narrow windows, heavy wooden doors that clanged so miserably when someone shut them, as if they were to keep out the very world itself, their cold damp walls inadequately covered in tapestries and the fire in what everyone said was the Great Hall, no matter where we were, which was never big enough for everyone to huddle round and get warm. The buildings proved to be cold in the summer and even colder in the winter and no dividing line between the two, except the need for more clothes, more cloaks, thicker boots and strong mulled wine to keep heat inside the clothes, cloaks and lined boots.

In Aragon the buildings were light, airy, with huge windows and wide open doors and archways so the air could circulate freely all the time. We were never aware of the damp cold which England seemed to be made of and which got into the bones and stayed there.

It was a good thing my husband to be did not understand Spanish, especially my accented Aragonese Spanish, for most of my sentences began 'in Aragon we...' but I found this only added to my intense and overwhelming homesickness.

I did not know then that Henry spoke Spanish – among other languages. I did not know he oft overheard my bewailing the English way of life and was amused by it. These are things he talked of when we were married, much later in our lives, when so much had happened for us to endure. We were very different people by then and yet he remembered everything, the way I looked the first time he saw me – sick to my stomach from seasickness and endless swaying travel on horseback and homesick too – the first words we exchanged, the way he said my face lit up when I met him, the longing he swore he saw in my eyes when he had to move on from me, for diplomacy called for him to talk with those who had escorted me there.

All of that surprised me when we spoke of it for it had been as deeply engraved in my heart as it had his.

I believed then that we had a marriage made in heaven and blessed by the Virgin herself. Would that it had been so.

What then did I see when I looked at Henry? A handsome face, almost adult in its shaping and in its ability to keep one mask in place for a long time. That mask was not quite indifference but it was no more than a whisper from it. Then a smile would come, suddenly, a flash of sunshine on one of those dark dreary days which persisted throughout that winter. A smile that did, sometimes, lift the sombre look in his eyes. A smile that transformed his face and made me see the younger man who was beneath the stern upbringing that so regulated and informed Henry's life.

And never did that smile appear in his father's presence. That I noted well. He had smiles for his long suffering mother, a woman I felt right sorry for. She seemed to me to be living as dull a life as I foresaw for myself. There was beauty beneath the sorrowing which I detected but it was fast disappearing in the overwhelming drear of the paucity of wealth shown in the buildings I visited.

In my long lonely empty nights I saw that smile of Henry's and wondered at the youth beneath the rigid man suit he seemed to have to wear. I dreamed of him turning that smile to me all the time and my responding to it, to my realising that England could be a place for me to live – but ever did the face of my chosen agreed on and signed for husband intervene and spoil the dream. As it should, for I was bonded to another and naught could be done of it.

Think then of my wedding day. Henry escorted me down the long endless aisle of the cathedral they said was dedicated to St Paul. It had its glories, high sweeping soaring roof and incredible carvings but for me it was desolation. A huge tomb, a mausoleum, anything but a place of rejoicing. Before all the people who had gathered in their fine robes, I walked alongside a young man of radiant looks and golden hair who was wearing cloth of gold slashed with scarlet and looking every inch the perfect Prince who then ceremoniously handed me over to a thin, insipid, indifferent Prince who had managed to lose the look of longing he gave when we were first met and now – did I not see it already – turned that look onto others who surrounded him. But he was as bonded as I and as Henry stood back and allowed his brother to take me to wife, I wondered where and when and if this nightmare would ever end.

I was virgin when I married Arthur, Prince of Wales. I knew what married people did for my nurse had explained to me, as best she could, what happened between two people in one bed. I had no way of knowing what to do if that did not happen, if the part of the body which should be firm was not so firm and could not stand up by itself. I could not begin to understand why this was and what I should do about it.

He came to my room, shy, diffident, uncertain, halting in speech and hesitant in manner. His hands fluttered uselessly as he tried to untie my gown which I had left loosely knotted to make it easier for him. My heart was pounding but with the wrong emotion, this verged on hatred as I looked at the thin body and pouting face, which pouted even more when he realised he was making a considerable mess of it. I realised in that moment he was a spoiled boy who was used to his own way. In normal circumstances he would have called for someone to untie the ties for him but this was different, this was his marriage night and he should be capable of doing it himself.

Finally the strings fell free and he pushed the gown from my body. I hoped my shape would please him, it was womanly enough and I had enough knowledge of other women's bodies, from being with my ladies, to know I was well endowed enough to please any man. It seemed not to please my new husband. My heart sank even further at this realisation.

Arthur, with one hand on my breast and the other working hard to make his soft piece stand up by itself, looked at me with such intense sadness and longing it near broke my heart. I had insufficient English to try and console him; he had insufficient Latin, our only common language, to make himself understood. I believe even if he had, nothing would have been said. We came to the marriage bed as strangers and strangers cannot communicate their innermost desires and feelings in that moment. It takes time – I was later to discover – to break down the barriers of morality and formality to speak the words that change duty to pleasure, change inability to ability. But then, I had no problems with 'inability' with my second husband.

What Arthur did that night was lay himself upon me, half firm, half not and whispered to me, with difficulty, that he was sorry. I gathered from his broken speech that he would try harder. He would say that he had laid with me – which in truth he had. I was shocked to think they would ask but it was part of my education that, being royal, nothing was private. I understood that, he did not want to be seen a failure, he the heir to the throne, the one tasked with bringing his heirs into this world from my body.

Another night I did not sleep, for I felt I had failed him in some way. Was I not alluring enough for him? Did I not arouse his interest in my body? What had I done wrong? I was lonelier that night than I had been the entire appalling journey to England, the long trek from the coast, the elaborate reception and then the wedding – all took their toll on me but I managed to get through with smiles, nods and limited Latin. But this, this terrible failure on my part to consummate our marriage on the very first night, left me desolate, aching, lonely and utterly helpless. I had no one to discuss this with, none of my ladies were – how can I say this without being snobbish? This is a word I learned later, it summed up the way I felt but at the same time denigrated the way I felt. It was wrong, I should be treating my ladies the way I treated the staff my new husband had arranged for me. But I had always treated them as friends. I could not suddenly distance myself from them, and at the same time, I could not tell them of the failure to consummate. It was personal, embarrassing, humiliating for Arthur and I did not dare tell a soul about it for fear of it getting back to him and making a bad situation worse. A new land, a new life, a new husband and very much a new situation for me. All I wanted to do was arrange for my possessions to be packed into saddlebags, to leap onto a horse and ride for the coast. At that moment even the thought of the golden Henry could not stop me from wanting to go home.

I wonder now what might have happened had I done just that.

Instead I laid awake all night, hearing the sounds of this new to me land, the haunting cry of the night hunting birds, the scuffle as small animals lost their lives to another's hunger, the rustle of grass as the wind passed over it or something scoured the landscape for its evening meal. These were all strange to me; I tried to divert myself from thoughts of Arthur and, naturally, of Henry, wondering how he would have coped with this situation – as if I did not know.

Someone told one of my ladies of Arthur's boast to his staff the next morning 'this night I have been in

Spain' but it was a boast for he knew as well as I that we had to put a brave face on what did not happen and hope that it would happen when we got to know one another better.

But could we get to know one another better when information or even idle chatter had to be relayed from one of his gentlemen to one of my servants who told one of my ladies who told it to me? No common language meant difficulties in communication. My husband seemed to make no effort to learn Spanish and I found English exceedingly difficult to comprehend. Everyone appeared to speak the same words in a different way which confused me.

The wedding feast went on for days. I will not recite them for you, they were dull for all but those who took part, those who wished to drink and dance each day. I found time for my daily prayers and meditations, found time to be polite and converse, in stilted Latin, with those in the court and longed for the end to come so that life could begin to settle down to the one I believed I would be living for years to come.

Henry was there, day after day, through the wedding celebrations, through the feasting, through the jousting and all the events staged to make our celebrations even better. I felt I had no part in it; I was a mere bystander watching something that had no meaning. Jousting seemed nonsensical to me but I was expected to applaud and shout encouragement. I found I could do neither. I sensed too that my husband had no interest in the goings-on of the feasting. He ate little and drank much, he smiled often with his mouth but not his eyes and his hands never strayed to me once. And yet, there was a longing in his look which I observed and could do nothing about. It was as if he wanted a friend and I could not be that friend as we could not converse together.

I had three problems. One was that I did not and knew well I could not love this person, my husband, who was bookish, withdrawn; incapable of speaking for very long and who only wished to retire quickly to his book-lined room if he was not drinking with the gentlemen of his household, 'celebrating' our wedding. The other was that I was not sure what to do about the lack of what I might call our relationship. Should I ask someone, his physician, his father? What did I do? Who could I turn to? It was an embarrassment to him and to me. I walked the gardens in a fret of anxiety. I had no way of knowing what he expected of me, what he thought I could do about it. I thought he might seek help for the problem, for surely it would be a serious humiliation were I to broach the subject with anyone. I sat in my room for an age and prayed to the Virgin for just as long, asking for a solution to my nightmare. I was trapped in a marriage with a man who could not consummate it and who appeared not to want to be with me.

I worried that he would become king and I be queen and unable to bear his children, the heirs to the throne of England, and that it be believed I was barren when I never had the chance to even try and conceive.

The third problem was the biggest one – for me, anyway. Henry was the man I wanted, desired, yearned for, the man who filled my dreams at night and my thoughts during the day.

And there I say the word I should not, for he was not then a man, but a boy, but being bigger, stronger and more handsome, leaving aside more intelligent and charming, than anyone else in the court, he attracted women as a plant attracts butterflies. It was clear he revelled in this but to my astonishment, ever did his eyes seek me, ever did he come to talk to me, ever did he bring me sustenance when my husband had – dare I say flagrantly?- ignored my needs. We ate at table together but he would make his escape – there is no other word for it – as soon as he could.

I could do nothing about the constant presence of him, the one man I did want; the one man I could talk to; the one man I longed to take to my bed and show him what a Spanish woman could do, given the opportunity.

Shameless thoughts. I prayed long to the Virgin Mary to forgive me the sin of carnal thoughts that were not directed to my husband and pleaded with Her to understand that my husband had no thoughts or feelings for me. The sense of grace which came over me at those prayer times said She did indeed understand and I felt forgiven if not justified.

Around and around went my thoughts, for there appeared to be no way out. They were moths battering themselves to death against the light of my anxiety.

Then everything changed. Did I want that change? Yes, for London was not good for me, too many people who mostly came to stare, especially at my servants. I was finding the English an unforgiving people who only grudgingly accepted those from other lands. Did I want that change? No, for it would take me from Henry but that in itself was good, for it was an ongoing sin that I should desire him so.

I already knew we were going to Ludlow, a castle situated somewhere on what the people called the Marches. I had already, in my heart, bidden goodbye to Henry for he would not make the journey to see us; he had no need to do such a thing.

I already knew that heart would break the moment we set out on our journey.

Packing seemed to take an age, had I really acquired so many new things? I did not think so, it was just that the roads – as I knew well – were unbelievably bad and everything had to be made secure not to be damaged or damage something else or lost on the journey.

Finally the day came to leave. No family member set foot in the courtyard as we set off. Part of me cried bitter tears at the parting, the other part of me rejoiced; would I now be free of the conflict which had so tormented my first weeks in my new land?

Ludlow. It almost seemed a mystical place; we took so long to get there I began to believe it did not really exist. I have to say that winter in England is not pleasant, nor is travelling roads which are rivers of mud, which bogged down the horses and mules, wearied the armed guard, splashed everything that it could and generally made us all feel cold, aching and utterly sick of England. If it were not for my wifely duty I swear I would have demanded a return to London, a return of my dowry and my body back to Spain. I longed for sunshine so much it hurt.

The journey showed up something I did not expect: Arthur was a different person away from the influence of his father the king. He was more confident, more capable of giving orders, more the sort of person I felt I could turn to, had I the ability to speak with him. It changed the way I looked at him – for a while.

By some miracle we arrived at a beautifully maintained, solid, comforting castle. Ludlow welcomed us with warmth, good food, secure stabling for our vexed wearied animals and a good deal of curiosity from the servants for my entourage, some of whom were dark skinned, but I knew they would be used to us after a while.

Whether I would be used to them is another matter entirely, I thought, as I felt the heat from the fire in the Great Hall at long last. There were ladies to talk to, servants to scurry hither and thither, maids to see to my wardrobe and my needs and if I had not been countless mud-strewn miles and endless days from London, I would have been content. In London was Henry. Here was Arthur. I wished, beyond all sense and reason, I had wings and could fly back there to be with Henry and not here with the man I married. I told myself at prayers that night to stop being foolish and immature, this was reality; this was life as it was to be lived for the remainder of my life. I had no way of knowing whether Henry wanted me as much as I wanted him. It could all have been a fantasy in my head, a fantasy born out of my dislike – by then I admitted it – for my husband.

It was time for Katherine to face up to reality.

Reality was a sense of hostility and hatred from some of the women who eyed me as if I was some kind of monster, or a creature from another planet. It took me some time to work out, with the help of my perceptive ladies; that they were intensely jealous and feared for the affections of their men who openly admired me and vied for my attention. It worried me, I did not anticipate this reaction and I did not know what they had in mind. Did they wish me gone? Were they out to damage me in some way?

Reality was kindness from Margaret Pole, for whom I held great affection, from a servant girl called Ann who claimed my heart from the start with her gentleness and her fierce loyalty and from the Welsh notables who came to greet their Prince and whom I could not understand. For all our lack of communication, they made their feelings clear; I was welcome as Princess of Wales. Without them, I cannot begin to imagine how my life would have been.

There was intense loneliness. I could not understand the legends, the ballads or the talk of those who gathered at our hearth of an evening to discuss matters relating to the land in which we lived. That was in addition to the talk during the day. It was endless, dull and incomprehensible. It gave me time to think, observe; come to my own conclusions about people.

One thing became very clear, so clear it cut like the very knife it resembled in my mind.

My new husband preferred men. Therein lay the secret of his inability to consummate our marriage. He simply could not react to me, no matter how he tried.

And therein lay another secret, one not spoken of until now: he did not try very often. Oh, he came to my bed to keep the pretence going that we were a married couple in every way but as soon as he could reasonably do so, he would escape. Literally. He would shout for his squire, dress hastily and be gone without a word to me. It could not go on forever this way, I told myself, but it looked as if it might do just that. I spent nights crying into my pillow, crying for the man I wished I could have, for the man I did have, for the life I had which I resented and wished I could change. I wrote letters in my sleepless hours, begging my parents to rescind the marriage agreement and send guards to escort me back to Aragon, there to find me a Spanish prince who needed a good wife, one who knew what she was doing, one who spoke the language and understood the ways of the court.

It would also take me far away from the man I longed for and that would remove all temptation from me. For that in itself was a sin. I was a married woman, I should act as such.

The days in Ludlow were interminably long. We rose with the dawn and bedded with the darkness. In between were bad half-cold meals, bitter ale, water that had a strong taste of earth and stone; and endless meetings with this one and that. I sat as often as I could with my ladies and stitched and embroidered tapestries and warm clothes, for the chill was all pervading and I was never warm enough. Arthur scorned layers of clothes but I needed them, for I was not ready for the dampness of the Marches and the biting coldness of an English winter.

By distancing myself somewhat from my husband, not a difficult thing to do for he made little attempt to bind himself to his wife, I could see clearly how he touched hands with this one, held the arm or the shoulder of another of his gentlemen, how they would look into one another's eyes and give smiles which were not the type men would normally share. I had seen and heard of this in Aragon; I was not naive enough to think it would not happen here. I just did not expect it to be the man I married. Foolish thought, I could not have known. I despaired of bearing a child, an heir to the Tudor throne. I prayed to the Virgin for a solution to my problem, my need to be fertile, my need to prove my worth as a wife and consort to a future king.

I had my answer in a way I did not expect, not for a moment. Arthur took sick. I had an illness too, resembling the sweating sickness, but was capable of moving around. For all that, the Welsh doctor associated with the castle was in constant attendance and I was banned from Arthur's rooms, for fear of the illness being contagious. I was ill, they didn't see it; they thought I would catch his illness. Mayhap I would, but my life stretched out before me as an endless series of days I did not wish to live anyway.

I sent messengers regularly to ask after my husband's health, receiving in reply answers that told me nothing, nothing at all. 'He is resting'. 'He has taken sustenance this day.' What did that tell me of his health? I knew it was serious, the amount of activity around his chambers told me that, but no information was given to me until the day in April when the chamberlain came to tell me he had died.

I am relating things here that I never told my confessor at the time – or since. I am fooling myself if I say I ever confessed to this. I found it too difficult to say such things then, for fear of it being passed on. Oh, we are taught to confide all in our priests, that the confessional is sacred but men will do anything for the right price. I did not know the man well enough to entrust him with my innermost thoughts.

And so I say it now. My first thought on hearing the news about Arthur was relief. Overwhelming shocking relief that my burden had been taken from me. It was all I could do not to say 'Thanks be to God' out loud for that would have been traitorous in the extreme. Instead I invoked God's name by crying out 'Oh my God!' instead and let them take the exclamation any way they would.

They said it was the sweating sickness that took my husband. They said that was why they kept me from him. I understood that but sorrowed I never got to say farewell to the person who brought me here to England and to Ludlow. The fact I had been ill myself had bypassed them, for the Prince of Wales was the great concern, the overwhelming worry, the heir to the throne and they were fighting for his life.

The fact is: Arthur was no robust Henry, not strong in body and heart. An illness such as that could not be withstood by someone with no strength in him. It is not a surprise he died, the surprise is that he lived as long as he did, for his dissolute lifestyle, his disregard for eating well, he picked at his food as if it would poison him, whilst being free with mulled wine, does not build up a strong constitution.

I never got to say farewell and replace in my heart the memories of the person who stood beside me at my wedding and who gave me in marriage to the vulpine Prince of Wales. An odd description, you might think but consider this: no one in any history book I have seen has spoken of my husband's 'tendencies' or his inability to think sensibly about diplomatic matters, something which would have been a considerable disadvantage to him as Prince of Wales and later as King. He was clever in a different way, a conniving craftiness that somehow convinced people that he knew more than he did, as if he was concealing great secrets and abilities. I saw this in him from the start and despised it. I would not have had a happy marriage. But then… but I get ahead of myself and that will not do.

***

Almost immediately the discussions began on my future. For a time I was moved to a beautiful home in London, warmer and safer than Ludlow, for very quickly the parsimonious king reduced the amount of money available to me, sent most of my ladies away, including Margaret, which sorrowed me deeply. The house was warm but not home. Only one thing got me through the endless worrying days, the agreement that Henry and I would be married at some time.

At some time. it was enough to light a fire that sustained me through the long period of isolation and more loneliness than I ever envisaged one heart could carry. The day that Henry would marry me was so far in the future, farther again than I could ever envisage, that it reached the point when I believed it would never happen; that I would return to Aragon and be a widow for the rest of my life. At times that seemed a better option for me.

We had no news of Henry for a long, long time. It was only when his father the king died and he was released from what was essentially imprisonment, that we realised why we had not heard anything. Shut away with limited companions, what sort of life was that for a young man? What possessed the strange person that was Henry VII to do such a thing? These were thoughts that I longed to discuss with Henry but he never spoke of it. He put a lock on the door of those memories and kept them there, silent, in darkness. We spoke of everything there was to speak of during our long marriage, but not that.

But again I divert myself.

I remember well the day the new King came to me at the court, for it was in truth still a court, albeit a small one. It was in mourning for His Grace King Henry VII, news of whose death had been brought by a weary messenger. None of us were in black, for we had no money with which to buy the material and order the seamstresses to make gowns and doublets and tunics of the right colour. We had scarce enough to live on; the deceased King had kept us short of finances for a long time and there was often talk of the dowry being repaid and my return to Aragon. I wanted it and did not want it. I had somehow grown used to the people and the land and – let me be honest, existed for the time when I might see Henry again.

In the times of the late king's generosity, the monies we received – I say we, for my Seneschal and clerks had care of the day to day outgoings – went to pay off debts rather than give us anything new. The home had become shabby and tired, the tapestries worn and threadbare, the candle stubs melted and renewed and the plate was in dire need of replenishment. I had on the darkest clothes I could find, something in purple as I remember and that in itself was old, tired, fit to be used for nothing more than rags.

For all my need of finance to keep my household, my ladies and myself in good state, I felt the day to be fine, with clear sunshine, unfurling leaves, unfolding flowers and, in the distance, a dust cloud that spoke of riders, shards of light from arms which spoke of guards and in that instant I knew his Grace King Henry VIII approached and I had nothing to offer him. No food, no decent wine, no well-dressed widow.

I stood as if turned to stone, shaking inside, sick with apprehension and anticipation both, watching from the window in the room where I had been at prayer. I stood so until a tremor shook the stone from my body and I ran from the room, gathering up my skirts, hurrying down the stairs; shouting for servants, for grooms, for anyone to come and help me welcome His Grace. In a moment the place was a seething mass of people rushing here and there, as if his coming had disturbed an ant's nest. It was like that in my mind, anyway. As they hurried to do my bidding, my stomach quieted and my heart beat a little less fast, although it still leapt wildly into my throat and scared me.

Somehow the place became tidy, wine and fine goblets were produced from somewhere and just as I ran my hands over my skirts to smooth them, he was there, in the courtyard. I hurried out to greet him and saw him looking at me with a smile that was both tender and kingly. I curtseyed low and he lifted me up, looking at me, the golden prince, all strength, handsomeness and presence.

I murmured, "Welcome, your Grace," and saw the eyes I loved so much twinkling at me.

"Thank you, Katherine." Then he looked round at the servants, the state of the place, took it all in and shouted to his men for a bag of gold. Suddenly there were people rushing hither and thither on different errands, buying food, calling a seamstress, settling bills. In that moment life was transformed.

"Come." He said it all in that one word. He gestured to me to take his arm and we went into the gardens. At least they were tidy and cultivated, I was pleased to note. They did not require money, just tending daily and there, in the midst of the spring blooming flowers and sweet smelling shrubs, he asked me to marry him. No matter it had been arranged these years since Arthur died, he had come and he had asked me himself.

It was all I could do to say yes in a calm way, for my body was on fire and my heart was leaping with excitement and relief. I was not to go to home after all. I was to stay with the man I cherished above all others. I could not believe it. He swung me round, presenting me to the courtiers he had brought with him, strangers to me but obviously his favourites.

"Acknowledge my Queen!" he bellowed and they did, going down on their knees in the dust and the dirt and sweeping their bonnets from their heads. I smiled and asked them please to stand. As they were busy getting up again, dusting their hose and boots and replacing their bonnets, Henry whispered words to me which I found passing strange.

"Remember this moment, Katherine. In five hundred years' time you will write the story of your marriage to me and this will be the start of it."

I must have looked startled if not bemused, for he quickly added: "I know the art of scrying; I have looked into the future. Say nothing."

How could I? What strangeness was that? How could I say anything to anyone without looking the fool I felt I was at times? Ah but how many days, weeks, months and years did I cling to that moment, holding it as close as I held my dead children to my breast before they were taken from me to burial places unknown?

And here I am, five hundred years on, writing my story - and his. 'Tis truly passing strange.

After a meal, we sat by the unlit fire. There was no need of heat, not really, for all was being said in his look and I do believe mine in return. There was fire between us, unspoken, but sensed and acknowledged. How long had I loved this man, this Prince, this King! I must not forget he was now king and ruled everything, including me. We talked of nothing much, of his journey, of his feelings about the state of the house, which he deplored, of his father's meanness in keeping me without funds, of his favourite horse and his favourite hound and his favourite hawk. I listened and heard the sound of his voice more than the measure of his words. They consoled me, they comforted me and they lifted me. I basked in his attention and his choice of me as Queen. I had rooms made ready for him and his entourage, knowing he would stay but the one night for there was much to do. Knowing too I had much to do, for I had to pack and travel to be with him. I would do so on a cloud of pure, pure happiness.

Would that it had lasted longer than the time it took him to discover other women. Would that he had not an overwhelming taste for other flesh, other voices, other faces and, in doing so, managed to create an ongoing problem – what to do with them when he cast them aside. For many of them, once loved by Henry they were smitten forever and difficult to remove, limpets had nothing on the discarded lovers. They cost a good deal in titles, property, allocations of money – I despaired at the cost and I know well those who handled the accounts did too. And ever did Henry need money to ease the way of his life; one of unashamed luxury. Without that, what king could call himself king and live up to all that his people expected? At least, that was his reasoning and who could argue with that?

Kiss and tell. So I will tell you of our wedding night. How Henry came to me, bathed and freshened with oils that made him glisten in the candlelight. How he held me so tenderly and was gentle and understanding that I had no experience and if he had any, I knew not of it for he seemed to fumble and be embarrassed at being over so soon, before we began, almost. So I considered him as virgin as I and told him that together we would learn. So we drank wine and nibbled comfits and touched one another in every place we could and we began again and in that time we achieved what we should, the way lovers should be.

He was big, bigger than I expected and able to last a long time, which was wonderful for I could not always respond as fast as I would have liked. Such talk from our bedchamber, such words as I thought I would never have given in public in this way but why not? Every other part of our lives has been turned over a hundred or more times, usually wrong or, even worse, badly done. I will not have Henry denigrated in that way. He was a considerate and careful lover and together we made magical times that we shared with none but each other.

That night I lay in the heat of the room, wishing I could have the cool night air flow over me from an open window. I could not call anyone, they had been sent away as they always were when the king came to me. I could not rise from my bed and open the window myself because – because I wanted to become pregnant as soon as possible and prove to the world and my husband I was a fit queen to bear his children, his heirs, his sons. I wanted his seed left inside me as long as possible. So I lay still and sweated and felt the water drip from my body into the sheets and remembered the heat of Aragon and how much drier it was than this water laden air of England. For a moment I was consumed with homesickness such as I had never felt before. It was a physical pain coursing through me and I almost cried out. I bit hard on my lip and stopped the cry before it left me. No one should know of that particular heartache. Instead I concentrated on thinking of my new husband and that which we had just done together.

He told me he was virgin when he came to me. I believed it but oh, he learned fast how to please a woman and himself! He learned fast where to touch and where not to, what was good and what was not, he led me rather than my leading him, not that I could have done such a thing. I knew nothing of this lovemaking, for Arthur had no interest in females and had no idea of their anatomy, if I can be that crude. I ask myself, why not? In the many years since my adored husband walked the earth, book after book has depicted him as all controlling, all powerful, which he was, all demanding, which he was, but never anywhere that he was a considerate and caring husband, that our first years together were all that any woman could ask for. It was true, I admit, that there were days he could not come and talk with me or just be with me, for the demands of parliament and envoys and knights and whoever else needed his attention, his signature, his judgment, everything but let him live the life he really wanted. And that was: to hunt, to hawk, to joust, to bowl, to play tennis, to write music and songs, to play musical instruments, to dance, to study the night stars, to study learned books… there was so much he wanted to do and somehow, some inconceivable how, he managed to do most of that and still find time to rule the country, make decisions and finally, spare time for his loving ever patient wife. And so I do describe myself for I was ever waiting on his tread on the stones, his voice echoing from the walls, his booming laugh at something someone said. He had a Fool in his employ but Charles Brandon had the sharp sarcastic tongue that Henry loved and the liberty and the courage to use it. So many others did not, afraid of his caustic moods. Charles simply didn't care about that, he made Henry laugh and Henry loved him for it. I do believe, as much for Charles' courage, too, that he would say such things against and about his liege lord and hope to get away with it.

It is said a Fool has that liberty but Henry's Fool, someone I disliked intensely, did not have the nerve to say the things he could have said. Oh he came close at times but Charles always had the edge, accordingly he was the one who had Henry's true friendship and equally, mine, for he was a good companion for my husband, someone who could take some of the stresses from him.

I divert again but I am attempting, in my own poor way, to show you every aspect of the great king and that includes the people who pleased him, who were able to cope with his strong willed hot headed ways – at times – whilst Cromwell and others had to cope with his administrative ways and needs, his every whim and wish. They could not take to the hunt with him as Charles did, or wrestle him to the ground and hold him there. Oh, how difficult it is to express in words the complex, larger than life, larger than any existing person, was my husband.

And yes, my love was and is that huge even now. He is everything to me.

Now, to resume the secrets of our bedchamber. He taught me much, how to pleasure him and what to do. Inventive, virile, strong, romantic, in the height of passion he found words of love to murmur and caresses to bind us together. He wound my hair around us both, trapping us in its web of curls and waves. He told me he loved the colour, how it shone in the candlelight. I admired his hair, so light, so golden; I could see why he was admired by many. Tall, slender, handsome, charming, radiating goodwill to all, but ready to turn at a moment if he thought he was being deceived or slighted. Nothing got past him, nothing. Those who thought they had managed to conceal something from him were sorely often sadly mistaken and paid the price, often the ultimate one. He would not be deceived; he would not be betrayed by anyone. He was the supreme ruler of England and all should know it.

And I lay with his seed inside me and prayed to the Blessed Virgin that it would find its way to my womb and there create the new life he wanted, even though he never said it to my face. Then. The demands came later, after the first stillborns. The ones which tore the heart from me and brought out the bitterness of disappointment in Henry, the bitterness which grew into an acid that killed his love for me.

One night Henry asked me to talk to him of Aragon. He lay beside me in my bed, content, replete, gazing up at the ornate hangings. He spoke in Spanish, our private language of love. His Spanish was accent free, pure, clean; he often smiled at my pronunciation and tried to copy it.

We had been married for some weeks by this time. I was beginning to know the real Henry, the one hiding beneath the golden exterior, the ebullient monarch, free with money and favours, provided he got what he wanted in return. The hidden Henry was the one to watch. The other was easily catered for, flattery and more flattery. The hidden one demanded more of people; it demanded total commitment even unto death. No hint of deceit, betrayal, underhand dealings, even innocuous ones. I think now of the stillborn children that slid so reluctantly from my womb. To Henry they were a betrayal, destroyers of the dream he held of a dynasty of fine children to fill the nursery and ensure the Tudor line. To me they were a constant reminder of my inability to be the queen he wanted.

I would not wish anyone to think I did not love both Henrys, I did, in every way, completely, totally and absolutely. I never knew it was possible to love someone so much and still breathe.

That night I recall well, the night he mentioned Aragon. I asked what it was he wanted to know whilst trailing a long strand of hair down his chest. Lean, hard, muscled as it was, he still flinched from its touch.

I still remember his reaction: "Don't torment, Katherine!" It was almost a groan. He told me he could not, not that night anyway. I tormented him by asking if I had exhausted my much loved husband, so he sought stories instead, as Scheherazade did.

His great laugh rebounded from the panelled walls as he told me I was so clever with my words and wished he could be as good. This was a clear invitation for flattery to be heaped on his head. I didn't disappoint him, telling him how he spoke so cleverly to those around him so that they knew not whether he was serious or fooling, whether he ordered them or asked, whether they should walk or run to do his bidding. I spoke of his favourites, of course, not the servants, who did everything at high speed. They had to.

There are special moments in a marriage, no matter how long or short it might be. I recall how he raised himself on one elbow and looked at me in the flickering candle flame that illuminated his sweating flesh. The night was close and the window shut fast against the vapours that might bring pestilence. I knew well that he had a fear of that, I had been told of it by his closest advisers so I would never make the mistake of leaving a window open.

Henry asked if I had seen all that, the way he spoke to his favourites, seen the underlying thinking. I could not read his expression and took a chance. It was always a chance; everyone had to be very careful what they said to him. I was still new at it but learning fast. I said of course I had but hadn't everyone else realised it too? In this I disseminated, for I knew well he had many of them in such a state of confusion they had no idea what they, or Henry, was doing.

He said no. I stopped to consider. In the short time we had been together I had learned that it was dangerous to have the king think you knew more than he did. I had to cover myself as fast as I could. So I told him I felt as if I was linked to him beyond that of being husband and wife. That I felt as if I knew him, had known him all my life, not just the few days we had been together. I reminded him he spoke of scrying when he came to me as king and asked: Do you not feel we have a link?

He frowned, the handsome face falling into hard lines that could – and had – scared many a courtier in the days I had been at court. It was something we all had to remember; this was no boy uncertain of himself. He was born to be king and he was king. He was young but experienced, determined, hardened by hatred and imprisonment; honed by piety and determination.

The face softened and he leaned down to kiss me. He told me I was right in how I viewed his words. He mused that it was a pity that they didn't see it that way and were left in utter confusion how to react. I knew it amused him. He went on that I was right that we were linked, that he had loved me from the moment I arrived in England and how it broke his heart to hand me over to his brother. He went on that it broke his heart into smaller pieces when I was taken to Ludlow and out of his life. He reiterated that he had never stopped loving me, never stopped thinking of me, never stopped hoping something-

It was then I caught his hand in mine and held it tight. I told him not to think on it, that he had done nothing wrong. That what was to be had to be. That Arthur was not destined for the throne of England. The crown was for him.

It was then he said, "I never thought it would be the death of my brother which gave you to me, Katherine. Never."

"The thought must go. The thought must be dismissed. The thought is not worthy of you," I insisted.

In English he said, with sorrow and so soft I scarce heard it: "Would that I could take it from my mind."

Henry roused himself and called for his men. "I will leave you now, Katherine, to sleep and rest and make yourself calm for the morrow." As the door opened, he leaned over me, kissed my temple and murmured, "Right glad I am to have you as wife."

The bed creaked and he got up. A cloak was draped around him, his feet thrust into silken slippers and my husband was able to leave the room.

I recall I let out my pent up feelings with a long heartfelt sigh. It was like walking on glass, I thought, having to watch every word for fear it would be the wrong one. He was a loving man, a virile man, a determined man but he resented anyone having more than he or thinking they knew more than he. I had to watch my tongue for fear of upsetting him. His wrath was not to be incurred. It was frightening. One of his rages could destroy much, including the person who had upset him. In every way he was what I had been led to believe, a true king. I had heard enough tales and seen just a hint of the anger when things were not as he expected them to be, or someone did not obey as quickly as he wished. He was a man with a quick temper and all should know that by now. He took his role as king very seriously and they should know that, too.

And, though I loved this husband of mine with all my being, sometimes he was too much for me and I needed rest to allow my body to recover. I believe we were both virgin when we coupled for the first time; even if this were not so, he was larger than I expected and larger than I could take easily, so there was blood from both of us. Tis this which confused my husband the King into thinking I was not virgin when in God's truth I was.

I have to say we were both innocent but we learned fast, exploring each other's bodies in ways I had never dreamed of. My upbringing in Aragon forbade any such erotic talk; I had the facts and naught more than that. Now I had an exciting and passionate lover and I knew, from the looks of the other women, I was envied and even hated at times for Henry walked tall and sure with a secret smile that tormented them all. I wanted to say to them, his body is fine muscled and hard, his assets large and capable of long standing, his touch is sure and sets me on fire. Beyond that, his mind is far ranging and his interests wide and all encompassing.

He is a man head and shoulders, both physical and mental, above all other men.

I said none of this. I felt if he sought the bed of any of the pretty women who looked at him with longing so clear it was as if they carried banners announcing they were available and willing, it would give me rest for a night and I would be better able to soar the passionate heights with him the next time he honoured me with his presence.

For we still had a child to make between us.

Henry thought he had difficulties in coping with his 'I never stopped hoping something…' I had done the same and could not tell him that. I have never told him. He will know now, for he reads the words we write. But then… nothing could be said. How disloyal would that be to his brother? For the truth was, from the moment the tall, handsome young prince greeted me when I arrived in this country, I loved him. I was shocked beyond all sense and reason when I discovered his age. So tall, so well mannered, so assured, so cultivated and clever, to be just ten years old! I walked down the centre aisle of St Paul's on his arm and was given over to be married to his brother, when I longed to push Arthur to one side and grab Henry to put him in his place. I rode to Ludlow with an aching heavy heart and the knowledge that I was married to the wrong brother.

There. It is said. I have admitted it and I am not sorry. It has haunted me these past how many hundred years? I have said it and I at last feel good inside. My channel is not crying. I thought she might. Instead I sense her relief that the words are written, for she knows well the truth of them. She was me in that lifetime. I loved Henry. Jointly, we still do.

I did not, that night or for quite a few nights afterwards, get to speak to him of Aragon. But later, when we lay awake into the night and talked long on many subjects, I spoke to him of my homeland, of my parents, Queen Isabella and King Ferdinand. He knew of them only through Sir Edward Woodville and the portraits I had of them.

I talked of the people and of the court there, how different it was from the English court, how the weather was so different from that of England, how the countryside was baked and brown and parched and unlike the greenness I had come to love and appreciate. But it was hard to talk of such things and bring it to the mind of someone who had only known England. He could not envision the dryness, the rocks, the sands, the strange plants and trees, the buildings which were built to allow cool breezes to enter the rooms by this window and that opening, of the carvings which were ornate and intricate and – some said – were foreign but for all that they were beautiful. Here the buildings were made to keep out the cold and the rain and the carvings were clumsy and heavy and depicted gargoyles and other things which scared me for they seemed like the work of the Devil himself.

London was so different from Ludlow. London was gaiety and music, colour and variations: Henry and I went from this home to that, with our great entourage bringing all that we needed, clothes and musicians, clerks and the ever present favourites. I found I disliked some but liked others very much, Charles Brandon for one. He was the consummate courtier and I discovered he was Henry's most trusted friend. I could see why;

they were as one in their pursuit of pleasures at games and hunts. Charles, when not vowing he had never seen anyone as pretty as I, a blatant lie if ever I heard one but it pleased me nevertheless, was telling everyone the day would come when he would beat Henry at tennis. I doubt it ever happened, any more than any of them could beat him at the joust, at archery, bowls or anything else he decided to do. None could play instruments better than he, or compose finer odes than he.

The reader will now say, 'but of course you say that, Katherine, you were his devoted loving wife and the courtiers knew better than to beat him at anything.'

There is a seed of truth in there but the real truth, the larger one, is that Henry really did excel at all things. His athletic body seemed capable of doing more than the average man, especially at sports. He out-rode his friends at the hunt; he out-hawked them, if I can coin such a phrase, in that his birds were released at precisely the right moment to make a clean kill. He seemed to manage on less sleep than those around him. I knew well that when he left my bed, he did not go to his own but to his observatory to study the stars and planets, to note the movements of the heavens, to extend his knowledge of all things beyond this earth.

I did wonder where he did his scrying. I did not ask, it was against my faith to dabble in such things and I feared for his immortal soul but did not feel I could remonstrate with him on such a subject. I was too new a wife in every way. It should have been against his faith too but I had quickly realised Henry was a man who stood above the rest. Not only in his height, which was ever an amazement to me, but his whole personality. He was just a big man in every way. He dominated every gathering he walked into, was the centre of attention in every room he entered. He was the supreme king.

And no, this is not 'new wife' hero worship. These are my memories, as clear now as they were then. And that after many years of being his helpmate and Queen and then hapless and discarded wife. Nothing has made the memories alter, nothing has dimmed their brightness; nothing has changed my opinion of him. There have been many monarchs; none have dominated the country and Europe as he did.

It is difficult but I wish you to put to one side the Holbein portrait of a big man with a weight problem and the worries of the world on his shoulders. I wish you to see him as I knew him first, the golden prince; the glorious leader, the fit healthy lean man who could do anything – and did.

What I do not wish to do is burden you with my miscarriages and stillborn and living-for-a-few-days babies. This is about Henry and how everything, from the weather to our misformed and unfortunate children, affected him.

This is about Henry and how every single person in existence was there to serve him and him alone. Or so it seemed, from the way he lived his life.

Henry acted as if every single happening, from storms to sunshine, from roast beef that was not as good as the last time it was served to perfect meals which he relished, from hunters which went lame or could not sustain the hunt as he wished to the perfect animals which stayed the course and delivered him to the kill, was there for his benefit or torment - and him alone.

No matter that the kitchens could only cook that which was delivered to them to deal with, that no one could intervene and change the weather patterns to allow him to go hawking if he so chose, that a horse could not help going lame. It discomforted them as much as it discomforted the king himself. He would complain bitterly about the kitchens, threaten to imprison the cooks. He would rant about the wine – which I knew well was the same as the wine he drank the day before but did not dare say so. He would not be gainsayed. He would storm around like a child having a temper tantrum if the weather changed and he could not fulfil his hawking or hunting plans and God forbid a horse of his went lame – unless he had ridden the animal to the point when it could no longer sustain its footing.

His demands on his servants were unbelievable.

His tailor and apprentices were kept busy week in, week out, creating new beautiful clothes for him, the shoemaker, the jeweller... his barber was ever in attendance, his doctor was often there, he being in charge of the king's body under pain of death of anything happening to him that he did not wish to happen, like getting ill, Heaven forefend.

His scribes, clerics and those in charge of the Treasury and other offices were likewise given massive tasks, some of which made The King's Great Matter seem like a small task in an otherwise boring day. The dissolution of the monasteries, for example, and the resulting havoc, but once again I get ahead of myself. I just want to make the point that Henry was one of the most demanding kings England had ever had, I do believe. Others may have made demands but none equalled the quantity that Henry made of everyone around him – including his mistresses. That was one reason none of them lasted very long. A brief fling, a moment of pleasure, if they were fortunate – for there again Henry took his satisfaction without always being aware of the other person's need as well. Not every time but when the mood was upon him to take what he wanted and to the devil with all else, person, animal, object, no matter what, that was it. No arguing for that would prompt even more furious outbursts. It was best to let the storm die down and he find something/someone else to please him. It was at times like these I actually welcomed the mistresses and pitied them for being such.

The early days of our marriage when he was the perfect lover were soon swept away when he realised the extent of his ability to dominate. It was total. It was endless. It was all he had ever wanted. He never said this and I doubt he would ever think it, but Henry was a true controller of all life.

And all life had to submit to his imperious will.

Let me go back to where I was.

Being a Gentleman of the Bedchamber was a high honour but those who achieved that status paid a high price. They had virtually no sleep, because Henry managed on so little. They rode to hunt for hours, even if they could not physically cope with such a strenuous exercise. They had to play tennis and bowls, they had to wrestle and box, they had to joust. Was it worth it? I have to say I doubt it very much but they wanted the position, the power, the wealth and the estates which went with the high honour. They often had to board Henry and his entire entourage when he left London to escape the plague, for example, or any other illness. The sweating sickness regularly came and he regularly ran from its ravages.

It cost them a fortune.

I need to explain that if Henry feared anything at all, it was being ill. He fled London at the merest hint of plague, sweating sickness or any other illness that would or could touch him. He would stand up to any enemy, any country; any force other than that, because he could not control illness, could not smite it and destroy it. He was in the hands of others or the vagaries of disease and that did not suit Henry at all.

My constant miscarriages and stillborns came into that category. He would parade me around during my early days, when the baby belly showed and his prowess as lover and maker of heirs could be seen and appreciated. He showered me with gifts and exotic foods and fruits during that time, he was ever the proud father-to-be. That first pregnancy he could scarce control his anticipation, all but demanding he be there in the birthing chamber but even he would not go that far.

All this made the arrival of our stillborn daughter the biggest disappointment of Henry's life. For a moment, a tiny fleeting moment, I saw a glimpse of the true nature of the king, his rage was barely contained. Two offences: a girl and a stillborn one at that. No matter my tears flowed and my heart all but broke, for Henry the world had something to throw at him: he had not arranged an heir.

But he smiled and it was a real smile, not one of his diplomatic ones, as I thought of them. He said 'we have all the rest of our lives, Katherine. Rest, be well, we will bed again ere long.'

I saw the way he glanced at one of my ladies as he left the birthing room. I knew that he had been bedding her for a while and in my heart had forgiven him, for he could not go without a woman for more than a few days and I had been heavy with child for some time. A child he was afeared I would lose if we were to indulge. The irony of it; we lost the child anyway.

Henry could not control the pregnancies, could not arrange for perfect sons to be born, one after the other. Could not control the lack of breath and lack of life in the hapless babies that came out of my body. After a while he would stare at me, not say a word and just leave, often going to Charles Brandon's home or any other that took his fancy at that time. Leave the sorrow behind. Leave the thought behind. Leave the burying of the dead one behind. Ever did Henry flee from what he could not control and never spoke of it again.

No matter that I was torn apart, physically and mentally, by the loss of the child I so longed for. It was not just the heir he did not have; it was my motherhood which was at stake. I longed and prayed ceaselessly for a chance to hold a healthy living child.

When I gave birth to our daughter, a strong healthy child who howled at the world when she took her first breath, I saw how hope blossomed in Henry's eyes for a few moments.

"A healthy child," he said softly, so low I could scarce hear his words. "A healthy girl. Katherine, the next one will be a fine boy. Hurry and be well again so we can create another child."

We did. It was a boy. It did not survive.

I should have prayed for a chance to hold a healthy living boy. But would the Virgin Mary penalise me for not phrasing my prayers so carefully to her?

Henry did not lie with me again after that last abortive pregnancy. His disappointment was so deep, so all consuming, he could not bring himself to lie with me and perhaps form yet another child which would not and could not live.

I knew not where the fault lie, was it in me? Was I incapable of holding a living child in my womb? I questioned this over and over, crying out to God and the angels to grant me a son but with no husband in my bed, how could God answer my prayer?

Mine was not an easy life. Living with Henry was never easy, never comfortable in any way. If I had been given the gift of scrying and had used it, I would have chosen to be a widow for the remainder of my life. I would have accepted that, despite its inherent loneliness and crushing heartache, if it meant taking from Henry the bitterness and disappointment he suffered through the constant miscarriages, stillbirths and finally giving him a daughter, not the son he so desperately longed for. His heartache was mine. His bitterness burned my stomach. We were as one in those early years. I suffered for him and for me.

But as usual I digress. So many memories flooding in, ones that I would wish at times to lose to give myself some peace. My hope is that creating this book will grant me what I have sought for so long. My hope too is that my beloved Henry will find some peace, for I know many things trouble him even now. Oh he will talk boldly of this and that but do I not know his heart and know he suffers still over the death of Thomas More, for one. So many deaths, so much damage, so much destruction and still his reign went on and on. And his cruelty went on and on with it.

I can see, looking back at our time together, that the seeds of his buried cruelty were there then, he just disguised it well. He was a brilliant diplomat, could talk his way round just about one's argument, no matter which court they came from. He was particularly good with envoys from the Vatican, for his knowledge of all matters religious was equal to if not better than theirs most of the time. The fabulous and fabulously expensive Field of Cloth of Gold is an example of how Henry insisted on impressing those he held discussions with. I was there, I saw his brilliance; I saw how he manoeuvred everything to his advantage, as he always did. The memory of that incredibly elaborate time is one that will never leave me. Henry was bigger in every way after that event; it seemed to almost inflate him physically, such was the effect it had on him mentally. It was the kind of huge showy event that pleased him more than anything else.

We had a long marriage, compared with his other queens, that is. I see in your world today that ours was a long marriage, now you seem to walk away so quickly if something does not feel right to you. If I had done that, if I had walked away when Henry first cast his eyes on another woman, there would have been no queen for him at all. He found every woman with a pretty face and enticed her into bed. He was insatiable, endlessly needing sex, endlessly needing the flattery of another woman telling him how wonderful he was. The two went together; there is no question about that. His ego was already the size of England but it grew even larger as time went on and we all, without exception, bowed to his every wish and obtained for him every single thing he ever asked for. And he asked often, believe me!

Well now, 'asked'? I have to say he was invariably courteous and every order – unless he was in one of his sudden flaring tempers – was couched as a request. We all knew that and we all knew that we dare not disobey.

I watched this golden prince grow from youthful maturity to elder statesman maturity. He was never a youth, never even a child, I do believe. He was aware of everything from the very beginning and all that the years did for him was add to his knowledge, his wealth, his girth and his ego. That is quite aside from his ever-present ability to manipulate, coerce, impose, impress his will upon others and get them to do what he wanted without even so much as a blink of his dark eyes – just with words. He was so very clever with words. In your time he would have been a brilliant writer. Instead he composed music and small songs to entertain us, so we would applaud and tell him how good he was – and of course he was. It wasn't flattery, it was truth.

I watched this husband, whom I adored so completely, grow into a statuesque statesman. I knew from the letters and despatches he received and shared with me that there were few people on the Continent who did not feel the same way. They might have secretly resented his power, his charisma, his total monopoly of England, but none could gainsay his abilities to do just that, have a total monopoly of England, without too much bloodshed. After the endless wars that had plagued the country for so long, after the austerity of his father Henry VII, my husband seemed to bring in a golden time of peace and conscious wealth. He went everywhere in a glorious progress, even if it were only to the next town. It took upward of five hundred people to escort him anywhere he needed or wanted to go.

Needed came if there was any hint of sickness. I have mentioned this; it has to be said again. He was afeared of being ill. A mere cold meant taking to his bed and being doctored constantly, the bad heads were terrible for him, he saw himself with all manner of brain conditions that would terminate his life before he was ready, or so he said. His increasing girth, small though it was, gave him a clear indication that he should be more careful with his intake of food and ale. But as long as he remained a fine upstanding figure of a man – I say this with the utmost care but know that the reader will understand what I mean – my husband would not listen to counsel about such things. He lived his life to the full, no matter what he did during any day, from hunting to sports to meetings with envoys or planning elaborate banquets and balls and allowing people to come and see him.

For a long time I had a vision of us growing old together, the perfect King and Queen in a perfect country, albeit one still recovering in many ways from the terrible battles which had so decimated the working men of the land. For a long time I lived in what I came to realise was a dream, one from which I would have to wake at some time.

It was when I woke up to the new phase of Henry's life that the overwhelming longing for Aragon crashed back into my heart. It took me by surprise: I thought myself long over my need to see and be in my beloved homeland again. But no, there it was, an intense longing that would not be assuaged.

I know precisely the occasion when this happened.

Throughout our marriage I saw how any beautiful woman who caught Henry's eye would soon be in his bedchamber. This could and would happen at any time: a banquet, a formal ball, an evening of music, at meals, anywhere. I became used to it but at first it hurt so much I thought I would physically be damaged by the pain. I never spoke of it; that was not my role in his life, to supervise and regulate what he did and when he did it. I knew well Henry would never tolerate that kind of interference anyway.

Yet he must have known how it affected me, for one night, after some intense loving, he touched my face with the uttermost tenderness and whispered 'they mean nothing, Katherine my sweet love, they mean nothing. They ease an itch, that's all.' In that moment he dismissed all the women of the court, servants or those of a higher standing, as if they were nothing and I do believe to him they were nothing.

But still, being female and very much in love and wishing to hold that love to me exclusively, I would lie awake nights, wondering if they were better than me, if he would ever favour one more than me, if there were ways I could learn new things so he did not have to stray. This was despite my accepting that Henry wanted the different body, the different face; another voice uttering the platitudes of flattery that fed his ego as I sought to feed his soul with faith and the cook sought to feed his body with food. In the end, we were all serving him in some form or another, were we not?

Sometimes in the night I would hear him return to his rooms. I would hear the great booming laugh that meant Charles had said something, that one of his favourites had done something stupid or simply that they had all had way too much to drink and I would wish with all my heart he would divert his course and come to me instead. He never did.

Henry only came to me in the early evening, when he had time, he said, before the night sky drew him to the tower for his studies of the heavens or some pretty face drew him to his or even her room for sex. He never came at any other time for what I thought of as love, not sex. He would sometimes visit me during the day, sending my ladies into a total flutter of excitement and blushing and simpering nonsense instead of just being themselves. He would not stay long, just enough to let us all know he was around, supreme ruler of the country and of us, all of us.

Then he would leave and the light would go out of the day. The golden prince would shine his light on us for a brief time and then depart for places unknown and people unknown. Maybe later he would return with talk of this envoy, this visitor, this letter, this work he had done on his book, for ever was my husband busy with projects that demanded his intelligent view of life – and it was an intelligent informed view of life. For all his profligate ways, his hunting, hawking, gaming, wenching, he found time to read, to discuss, to experiment with scientific things, to create music and songs. I wonder he ever slept. The time he spent away from me stretched out endlessly, the time he was with me seemed crushed into a few seconds.

As the arrival of misformed, stillborn babies went on, he came to me less and less. When he did he was polite and ever was Henry polite, even to the very end, but the loving touch was missing. I was aware of a coldness creeping into our marriage that had not been there at any time. We had surmounted the other losses together, side by side in the chapel asking for their souls to be snatched into heaven by the angels so they did not linger anywhere, those hapless blameless sinless babies, and in each other's arms. He was ever dry-eyed, I confess to sobbing helplessly every time motherhood was once again denied me.

If I had not my daughter to admire and tend, I would have gone out of my mind, I do believe. Henry showed interest in Mary but it was limited, ever was he looking past her and waiting for the true birth, the son he hungered for. I do believe it was more than just the need for an heir for the throne, I believe for him it would be a demonstration of his masculinity. See, I produced a son.

I wondered at times if he would return to me – he never did after the last miscarried stillborn child– and, the ultimate in fear, the one that sent me into cold sweats and more tears than I thought possible, was it possible any one of the dalliances would become serious enough to displace me as his queen.

The mere thought of it was enough to send me into hysterics but I quashed all that, for it was not seemly and my ladies would hear and talk about me and that might get back to Henry and that would never do. I had always to be his regent, his consort, his princess, his queen and rise above everything that was troublesome in life. He asked for nothing less.

Then the Boleyn woman arrived from France and was allocated a place as one of my ladies, despite my desire not to have her there, and I knew my worst fears were about to be made into reality.

It was then my mind and heart fled to Aragon. Then, in my mind I was a young girl again, cosseted and cared for by my nurse and governess and servants, where I was honoured to be allowed to see my parents, where I learned to ride and to be – just be the royal person I was. I went back to a land of sunshine, of parched earth, of wild and exotic plants and where people of different colour skin were welcomed and befriended and not looked upon as some kind of strangeness come among them as they were here.

And where the language flowed soft from the mouth and all was understood.

For even after all those years of speaking English, I found at times some people did not understand me. I mentioned it to Henry once and he said:

"They do understand you, Katherine, but you are foreign and they tell themselves they can't."

Such is the strangeness of the English.

Henry did not know of my thoughts for I never had the chance to speak to him again in a quiet comforting comfortable married couple way. It was all formality and business and indifference, as if he was deliberately moving away from me. All this before She arrived, too. I should have known the marriage was over but I clung to my love for him and his perceived love for me.

And I know I am diverting myself and my thoughts from the Boleyn woman because it causes much pain even now to think on her.

I have to be honest for this is my one chance to be honest. Our marriage was over before she arrived, because Henry had grown weary of the same woman as his wife. It would be good to say the same woman in his bed but as he had by then sampled every woman in court, no matter where we were, and in whose home we were, that could not be said.

And so... I needs must speak of the time when Anne Boleyn arrived.

She was everything I was not. I admit I had not moved with the 'fashions'. I had not given up my traditional dress and ways. I spent hours in prayer and the rest of the time stitching and sewing and being useful. I attended meetings, sat with Henry at meals, listened to his playing, which was a sheer delight, I have to say. I did all I thought necessary. Henry used to tell me he liked the fact I held on to the old ways of doing things, that he wanted a devoted dutiful wife. And so he did until the French whore burst onto the scene and then all his likes went out of the castle door.

The only good thing was, most of his mistresses followed too. He had no eyes for anyone but her.

I could not, at first, understand why he wanted her more than me. I recall the time when I stalked the floor of my chamber, demanding to know why my husband favoured her more than me. I recall my ladies being up against the wall, giving me space to stalk, stamp and rage and not saying a word. What words could be said? He was still a handsome, virile man and a beautiful woman had just arrived in court.

Slowly, it all became clear. She dressed in a strange almost outlandish way. It was not exotic; it was erotic but only in impression, not in fact. It is very hard to describe. It was in the way she changed the look of an ordinary gown by adding a trail of lace or fine netting to it and wearing jewellery in different ways, wound into her hair, for one. The younger women in the court immediately began to copy everything she did, without her success. Most of them just looked foolish. You need to do such things with confidence and flair and most of all, be the instigator, not the fawning copy.

Then I saw how she tantalised and flirted and danced rings around all the men, especially Henry. He could not have enough of being with her. I heard her name everywhere I went, in the gardens, in chapel, in the Great Hall, no matter where we were, someone spoke about her. And every word was a small paring knife cutting away a bit more of my sanity and my peace of mind.

Word soon reached me that she had refused his advances, wanting nothing to do with him that way until she was his legal wife, she said. I knew well the Boleyns were behind all this, power seekers that they were. But I could see, by her attitude, she wanted it as well.

It was then I knew for a certainty that my time as queen was over.

It was then my heart broke. I saw my husband besotted with another woman, saw that he lost all sense of days and weeks, saw him consulting with the learned men in his court, knew that he was looking for ways to put me aside so that he could marry his new love.

The one thing I wanted to ask him but never had the chance, was: have you looked into the scrying mirror, husband, and seen her producing the sons you so crave and giving you the happiness and satisfaction you no longer achieve with me? If you have not, why risk all on a mere whore?

It was in the lonely hours I spent in my chamber, at prayer, away from my ladies, my confessor, everyone, that I wished I had the power of scrying. It was a mortal sin but I longed with all my heart then to look into the future, to see if my beloved husband was truly going to put me to one side, was truly going to end my role as Queen of England. I ask myself, these many years on, did the one mean more than the other?

I can truly answer no; one did not mean more than the other. When I came to England that far off time, I came with the knowledge I would one day be Queen of England and my husband would be King Arthur. I hoped to acquire the skills to be a good queen. This I did through being married to the man I truly loved: his Grace King Henry VIII. So in truth, the two things came together: I was about to lose my husband and my status as queen. Both would tear my heart but again, looking at the situation carefully and as dispassionately as I can, it was losing my husband which would cause the most pain. Not to see him, not to be welcomed by him, not to hold him and hear his voice, no matter the words, would be the end of me.

Sadly that began anyway; I had no choice or chance to do anything about it. As Henry pursued the path that would take England away from Rome, so he pursued a path that included Madame Boleyn and discluded me. She was at his side at meals, he danced only with her, he sang only for her. He had new extravagant clothes made the better to walk with her, she as bright as a garden full of foreign flowers. Lady in waiting to me she might be, but in name only. I had no service from Madame Boleyn during her entire time in court, no matter what anyone might say or even think. I know well who brought my meals and tended to my wardrobe and brought me my thick robes when it grew cold in my chambers. I know who sat with me, who talked with me, who tried to be everything but couldn't for they were not and never would be a replacement for the man at the centre of my life and my heart.

I waited for news that she had given in, that he had taken her; that he had impregnated her, for then my time would be truly over.

I was sure, in my heart, that Madame Boleyn had never been refused anything in her entire pampered life. Because of that, she had held out for a legal marriage before she allowed Henry into her bed, or so word had it. Because she had never been refused anything, it was obvious that Henry would find a way to break that, for he would not allow anyone to have their own way completely. Oh, he would play the game for a while, 'of course we will wait until we are lawfully married, love of my heart' – I can almost hear the words, knowing full well that in the end she would capitulate, they all did. I also believe that his break with Rome, on surface so he could marry the French whore, was for a far bigger and deeper reason than that. I believe he wanted an excuse to break the power of Rome, for with that in place he was ever the servant of the Vatican. Without it, he was supreme ruler of England. He had a God given chance, a God given reason and he took it.

It all went on longer than I thought. I waited and waited on the news she had given way. She held out far longer than I thought. It must have been difficult, for Henry was nothing if not the most persuasive talker I had ever met. But in the end, of course, she succumbed –

they all did - and I saw even less of Henry than I had before.

It was most likely she was pregnant and he hoped for a legitimate heir at long last. Knowing Henry, he would not want a child born out of wedlock. He had enough of those around the court, ones he could not claim for himself.

He sent messages to me, asking if I wanted to go and live in this place or that, we argued about our daughter Mary, he sometimes even consulted me on matters of state when he needed another unbiased opinion, for those who surrounded him were virtually all sycophants by this time. Those who treasured their lives saw what happened to those who did not agree with the king all the time and kept their counsel. I had more respect for those who went against him, even if it meant my being deprived of supporters. I knew too that Henry did not think overmuch of those who agreed with everything he said, just to save their meaningless lives.

Am I wrong to think their lives were meaningless? Should we not all have standards by which we live and work and reason? Are we so weak minded we would give way to someone because they wear a crown and we do not? Those who stood against Henry and paid the price were those he secretly admired, whilst being angry they should stand against him. Ever did my husband have this conflict in his heart and mind and there was nothing he could do about it. He lost fine men from his close counsel through their refusal to agree with him and he would rage about it to me, knowing well I would not say anything to the others. It was for each man to make his own stand. Those who chose to agree, regardless of their own personal feelings, were the weak ones – in my eyes and I do believe in Henry's eyes, too. They let wealth, power, positions and such of the king's 'friendship' as they could obtain take their moral sense from them.

Henry argued with me, too, angry that I would not agree we were illegally married and go quietly away and pretend nothing had ever been between us. I could not do this for I could not accept we were not legally married. I knew well I was virgin when I went to him and all the bible statements in the world could not change that – in my mind. Henry wished to believe otherwise and I could not change his thinking, for he had set his mind on another woman, one I could not outshine and so get my husband back. I have admitted our marriage was over insofar as romance and closeness was concerned, but from the legal point of view, I felt he would have to find another reason to set me aside, anything other than the fact I was his brother's wife.

I wonder even now, these hundreds of years on, if the lingering guilt of wishing his brother were not there so he could have me for himself from the start was the real reason for finally basing the divorce on a supposedly invalid marriage because of my being his brother's wife. That seems a complicated sentence now I have written it, but I needs must consider this and settle my mind.

Henry needed a reason to put me to one side for That Woman. His sorrow was so deep, so palpable that night when we spoke of it, that I remember it well. I believe there was a strong element of guilt there, for Henry had a deeply religious background and a very strong faith. His carnal needs overcame his faith on many occasions, for as I said he was a man of great appetite and zest for life, but beneath it all was the man of faith and conviction. He had what he wanted but the cost to his conscience was high. I am sure there will be those who think they know him better and will argue against this: let them. I make the statement and so it must stand. Of all the Queens, I knew him best for we were married far longer than any of them were, and the hours we spent together were those of true husband and wife, king and consort. We discussed everything.

Again I divert but that had to be written, had to be said, for it is something I truly believe.

I was kept a virtual prisoner in my chambers, not allowed to walk in the gardens if he or she was there, not allowed to be present at banquets if he was there, which was every time, of course. I was not allowed to meet with envoys or courtiers from other countries. The excuse was given I was unwell after the last disastrous pregnancy which had left me weak. It had, that part was not a lie but I would as lief attend a banquet or meet with someone who talked of matters outside the court in which I was confined just to break the monotony of the days. I had not realised how dull life was without Henry at the centre of it.

This part is about me, of necessity. I had little idea of what Henry was feeling at this time, so forgive me for the diversion from the theme of the book. I know he closeted himself for hours with advisers who pored over books with him, who discussed religious and philosophical pathways with him, who put every viewpoint to him. Henry ever was one who wanted to know what would happen if – and the 'ifs' went on and on before he made up his mind. He seemed to do things impetuously but in truth he didn't. Everything was calculated to benefit one person – Henry.

Life became more difficult when Henry issued an order banishing me from court, but having said that, I realise it actually made things easier.

I knew that my husband had married the Boleyn woman supposedly in secret and thereby committed bigamy. As a God-fearing person, this was an abomination to me and although it could have turned me against Henry, all it did was fill me with sorrow that he should put his soul into jeopardy. Being away from court meant I did not have to see the smirking smugness of the woman who had set out – it seemed – to steal my husband from me. My only solace, one which I confessed to my cleric, was in wishing that someone would do the same to her so she would see and know how it felt to be discarded, set aside, unwanted, unloved whilst someone else danced the farandole with him. Having been through the sham marriage with Henry's brother, I had already experienced something of that but this was totally different in so many ways. The deeper emotions are much the same, ranging from utter despair at being rejected, displaced, replaced, by someone you cannot attack to ease your raging hatred, there is no other word for it, to surrender. I did not like Arthur but I hated the effeminate young men who had claimed his affections which he would then never give to me, no matter what. There is embarrassment, when you were someone who commanded a high standing in the land suddenly finding yourself referred to by some other demeaning title, not the one you have become used to, the one that fits like a well worn glove that just slides onto your hand and gives comfort. Surrender, yes, when you know there is no point in arguing, no point in demanding, everything you thought you had is gone and there is nothing left but facing up to a new life in a new place with a new, lesser, title and no person to hold on to in the long dark nights, either in reality or in memory.

A little self indulgence there, I confess, but the time was tumultuous for me, devastating in every way, hurtful beyond all understanding and acceptance, for a very long time.

There was also a sense of relief that I had no longer any need to fight. I attended the 'court' to give my side of the story, the truth. It was dismissed as I knew well it would be. I caught sight of my husband who looked older and heavier than he had when with me. I wondered what the Boleyn woman was doing to him. I felt sadness, overwhelming sadness for a while; it should have been me taking care of him, not some other woman. So the thoughts ran wildly but then I thought, he is no longer my concern.

Then I wondered why it mattered to me.

What I had were golden memories of a golden prince, the exciting young man who handed me over to his brother in marriage, the exciting and handsome young man who rode to Ludlow to ask me to marry him, the golden prince who stood alongside me and took me to wife and cared for me and bedded me and worked with me and made me his regent and trusted me to help with diplomatic affairs for more than twenty years.

I could and did dismiss the memories of the other women and indeed the other men, for such a golden prince attracted the attentions and devotions of those whose interests lie in that direction. Not that Henry took any of them to be his paramour, he was too much the rugged male for such things, but they tried, oh how they tried. I could have saved them weeks of trials and bitter disappointment but none thought to ask me, so I left them to their efforts, knowing they would be in vain.

The most treasured memories of all?

Henry's visit to ask me to marry him. This surpasses even the looks we exchanged at the time I first met the golden prince when I came to England. That time when he came to me, when all his courtiers and retinue went down on their knees before us, when he bid them greet his Queen is a moment that will forever remain pure and so very clear in my mind. The intense love I had for him then swept away all the years of loneliness and poverty and I knew true happiness for the first time since I had left Aragon.

Henry's tenderness the first night we lay together, the look of pure love on his handsome face that gleamed in the candlelight as we climbed to heights of passion I never dreamed of. We did this again and again but the first time is, ever, the most memorable. I will always treasure that look, that time, that feeling.

The walk in the gardens with Henry on a perfect summer day, so clear, so bright, so intense the colours it almost hurt to look. He stopped and plucked a perfect white rose for me, went to hand it over and then took it back and, one by one, he snapped the thorns from the stem so I would not be hurt. 'No one should ever hurt you, Katherine,' he said as he gave me the rose. Would that he had remembered that in later years, but it matters not. In time, all is condensed to memories that can be eliminated – in time – but the gold remains. That is one of the golden times.

Another is the foolish night when we were travelling on the royal barge and, in the middle of a tussle with cushions, I went over the side into the water. I heard his bellow, his yell 'Katherine!' and the way he looked when the bargeman lifted me back in. I was dripping all over everything, the gold embroidered drapes and cushions and was more concerned with that than with myself. He caught hold of me and whispered 'I was afeared I had lost you but you are safe,' and I said 'nothing is lost,' and he smiled a very special smile, one that said more than his words ever would. It said I was his all at that moment.

The look on Henry's face when I gave birth to our healthy daughter after the sad miscarried and stillborn babies. It was pure joy and anticipation and hope that next time would be the boy he so longed for.

It was these memories I took with me to cold, damp, uncomfortable and intensely lonely Kimbolton. They were a comfort in the long empty days ahead of me.

Was there bitterness? Of course, I am but human. There was bitterness that there were other women but that is to be accepted when the man you are married to is the supreme king of England and ruler of all and women were ever an addiction he could not ignore. There was bitterness in the hurt that we gave one another over the stillborn children, for it was nothing anyone could do to change, it was nature, the bodies we had been given, the body I had been given. I often could not give consolation for I had none for myself. Bitterness at the loss of the great men who had been counsellors and comforters and supporters but who stood in Henry's way and that could not be gainsaid.

But the golden memories and the silver ones are ever there, even now. The times we laughed, the times we shared the pangs of sorrow, the times we consulted over matters of state, the times we loved and were one.

And ever did I hold before me the image of the man I loved above all others and in truth, have never changed my mind on that, not all these hundreds of years when there have been stories and rumours and books and films. None of them, not one single one, ever captured the true essence, the true likeness, the true character of the man who ruled England like a Colossus.

Know well that there will never be another like him.

The most treasured memories

The first time I saw him when I arrived at Henry VII's court, standing head and shoulders above everyone.

Walking down the aisle at St Paul's to marry Arthur, longing to turn and run away with Henry.

The moment he came to ask me to marry him.

The first years when he shared all with me, including my bed.

The relief on his face when our daughter was born healthy and strong.

The pride he showed when I acted as regent for him and made no mistakes.

These are the diamond memories, if you like; the rest of our life together was a series of golden memories, interspersed with the sadness of the lost children. If only…

Expressing Henry in one word: Ruthless

Ten questions about Henry:

His favourite colour: gold
His favourite sport: hawking
His favourite animal: hawks
His favourite interest: jousting
His favourite meal: roast pig
His favourite sweet: medlars in syrup and wine
His favourite time of year: Autumn
His favourite home: Grenewich
His favourite gem: emeralds
His favourite musical instrument: lyre

Anne Boleyn

Henry's wives, divorced, beheaded, died, divorced, beheaded, survived

The second Queen – mother of Elizabeth (beheaded)

I am grateful beyond belief to find I am given a chance to put my side of the 'lovers' story, the great affair between the great Henry VIII and myself. So much is read into the notes we wrote, the annotations in books, the special moments we shared, his seeming dismissal of me to the swordsman as he cavorted with Jane Seymour – excuse me, her name does not sit well in my mouth or my mind but that is my problem, not yours – none of which has been explored by the person who suffered so much at the end. I have seen the words His Majesty wrote, that is his interpretation, here is mine.

And again, I need to say how grateful I am to have this chance, God given that it is, to let the world know how much Anne Boleyn loved the king and always will. And that what he believed to be true is in his heart and mind, for he wished me gone and he had no other way to do it. Oh, he will deny this, he has denied this, has said he believed I grew tired of him. Never. Had we been married a thousand years, I would not have tired of him for he was ever enchanting, entertaining, intelligent, knowledgeable and capable of so much. I swear he hardly slept during his early life, he did so much, knew so much, schemed so much... how much will even he never tell! How many state secrets have gone to the Windsor grave alongside 'her'?

The truth is, those of us who loved him did so beyond all sense and logic and even knowing what he was, we loved him still. And what was he? Can I even begin to give you a proper picture of the greatest king England ever had?

The French court had heard stories of the great King of England; some dismissed the tales as fabrications, exaggerations, saying none could be that handsome, that golden, that gifted, that charming, that diplomatic and that learned in the ways of the world and the languages of the world, as were given to this person. Others swore on the Holy Bible that all that was said was true and he was all of those things.

What did I believe? It's hard to remember a time before Henry, a time when he was not in my life, a man to be admired and courted if you could, to talk with if he let you… so I cannot say with certainty that I believed or I did not. I think, if I am to be truthful and there is no reason not to be, it has been these many long years since I walked the earth plane and knew Henry of England, that I was half believing and half disbelieving and wanted to see for myself.

When our time, the Boleyn time that is, was through in the French court, I eagerly awaited our return to England and our presentation at Court. On the journey I listened to others to try and gain more impressions of this king and his opulent glorious court, but none added much to what I already had been told. So it was with impatience and anxiety and anticipation that I settled myself in England once more, gathered a new set of friends around me and waited on the summons to Grenewich, the place everyone said was the favourite home of the King and Queen.

That for a moment brought my musings – and I admit now, fantastic daydreams of captivating this golden prince and making him mine – to a halt for I was too busy with images of Henry to remember that there was a queen at his side, one that had been there for a goodly number of years, too. That was unusual for a king as widely acclaimed as this one, surely he had paramours and mistresses who would be vying for the position of Queen, or did he think so much of his Spanish wife that he did not consider them?

So you see, with your own eyes now, that this Boleyn had made up her mind, long before she saw the glittering figure for herself, that she wanted this man in her life, in her arms and in her bed and to wear the title of Queen herself.

That's an admission that may be a shock for some but for others, they will tut over the words and say 'did we not know this from the very beginning, that she set out to capture the king and that it was not the king setting out to capture the fleeting romance of a Boleyn? After all, he had already taken many to bed and found them wanting, or they would have been Queen by then.'

The question was: what did Henry want? What was it that the Spanish princess had that other women didn't? Did she bring so much Castilian charm to the marriage that he did not think to look elsewhere with any serious intent?

The question haunted my days and nights. Much powder and covering was needed for the black rings of sleeplessness, that sure sign of unrequited love and we were not even asked to London by that time.

Was ever a woman so smitten?

Very likely, but at the time I doubted it. The goal was his body, his love, his bed and his crown for me.

My next serious thought was: would I love him as much in person as I did in fantasy and thought?

That was dangerous thinking and I had to avoid it. Having set my mind to get something – someone, if I am to be correct, I could not allow myself, for my own sense of honour, to fail in that quest. Determination was everything. Determination is everything, even now. Picture what you want and hold it, no matter what the cost.

And then we were invited.

It had rained consistently, as it does in England, tis that which makes it a green land. But I wanted to go to Grenewich in sunshine, to dazzle everyone with my gown and my jewels.

That magical miraculous never-to-be-forgotten day was overcast and heavy with the promise of more rain and perhaps thunder too, if the great black clouds and ominous pressure of the air were any indication. I was still newly back from France and revelling in the joy of an English day once again, the softness of the air, the grass, the very presence of the English countryside. Do I overdo my admiration for the land I had left? It is hard for me not to enthuse even more. I will only say, then, for fear of burdening the reader with too much gushing emotion for England, my England, is this:

It was not France and never would be.

France would never come close to England, even though some coastal areas were pretty enough and similar enough. They carried not the English air and the English way of life.

For me, it was enough – at first – that I was back where I felt I belonged. That day in London proved it. I had all that incredible emotion coursing through me, England was home again, Grenewich was the epitome of all things English, the landscaped gardens, the courtiers, the sense that this was the pinnacle of power and influence, that to be there was the heights of – just about everything. The family, the Boleyns that is, were nearly as excited as me. They had been waiting their chance to prove their ability to take on any responsibility the king decided to hand out. They were in line, they knew that, but they used me as their ace, although I thought of myself as the Joker more often than not. Because, I fell in love the very moment I put one satin slippered foot into the court of King Henry VIII and saw him with mine own eyes. These eyes that had never beheld anyone so golden, so handsome, so striking, so charismatic.

And, I soon realised, so calculating and contrary and demanding too. That made him more of a challenge. I need to make it clear that the reality far outweighed the secret dream, the secret night thoughts that sent me into dizzy spells at the very content which I never revealed to anyone – until now. All I had dreamed of was there threefold. His great height, his great presence, his booming laugh that captivated me, his sharply observing eyes that could also twinkle with amusement and – later – lust. I was speechless, stuttering helplessly when presented to him, unable to be the sophisticated assured woman I wanted to be to capture him. It all fell apart but it didn't seem to matter.

Who would not love him at first sight? And did not all the words of the others come back to me in that instant? Truly I thought the French court had been the very heights of fashion, of elegance, of intelligence and fascinating people. I had been wrong about it all. Very wrong. I knew then that my passing disbelief had been at fault, too. For here was the height of fashion, of elegance, of intelligence and of fascinating people – headed by the king himself.

No one had mentioned his height to me, or if they did, I could not comprehend it. He was a head taller than the men who surrounded him, he towered over them and even more so the women who tried to surround him. He kept them at arm's length, probably deliberately, by occupying himself with his jester, his scribes, his hangers-on and his favourites. It took me a long time to realise why he did this: I worked out that allowing women too close to him meant he could not observe them, who they associated with, who was behind them, as in what family members were ever-present. I wondered often how much he knew about every family who served him and, during my days of imprisonment when there was naught else to do, it came to me that there was nothing he did not know, did not seize upon, did not manipulate to make life go the way he wanted it, not the way the court, the families, the nobles, the courtiers or the advisors wanted it to go. Everything, from dawn to dusk and into the darkness was controlled by Henry himself. None dared go against him. I say this in the sure knowledge that you will think it obvious it was so, for he is known as a tyrant, a savage man with no compassion. Think you now that it was always so? Did not his later years colour the way you see the king now?

Henry was king by the grace of God and the people of England. He ruled by divine right. He had absolute control over everyone and everything. As did every other king the country had ever had, with one difference: Henry knew the power he had and used it. Used it to control everyone's lives, so he could take what he wanted from them: friendship, influence, knowledge, money – it all fell into Henry's hands, manna from heaven which only he trapped and held and never ever let go.

The fact was, few people realised how they were being controlled or even that he had them where he wanted them and those who did had no obvious air that said they resented it in any way.

Henry was a king like no other had been before him, for all their power and prowess and showy lifestyle. He was - and is - like no other who has ruled since that time.

Like Katherine before me in this book, I am diverting because it is my one chance to tell the world how I saw Henry, how much I loved Henry, how much influence he had over me, how much my dreams and ambitions flared when with him. No matter the cost, I wanted to be with him – and no one else. No other man in England could hold my attention for longer than it took to find out who they were and what their position was in Henry's hierarchy. I state this now so you will know, without my having to swear to it on Henry's sacred name – but I have done this and will do it again to prove my innocence – no other man touched me improperly during the time I considered myself to be his and that began on the first day we met.

From that day on, the Boleyn family was back, in court, in favour and with the king obviously looking at me. It was that obvious to me, the family and his many hangers-on. He could hardly stop looking at me, even when I was not within his circle of chattering people. A sideline, I could never understand how he could cope with the non-stop noise around him, voices, dogs, clothes swishing, servants rushing on booted feet here there and all over the place, the clashing of pewter mugs, dishes, flagons, the shouts of those giving orders and in the background, the eternal sound of musicians, for Henry would have them play whether we were dancing or not. It was an overwhelming clatter of noise and yet, within it, he could and did discern who said what, which dog wanted something, which servant had misheard an order and was being berated, which musician was not entirely within the piece of music being played. He would swing round and bellow across the hall or the room or wherever we happened to be that whatever was wrong be put right. Immediately.

It took me many months to acclimatise to this way of living. He seemed to do it naturally.

As he did everything he touched, from sports through politics to people.

He was never subtle when he wanted someone, even when he had a current mistress, he was ever looking for the next one. He had his eye on me. The smiles were for me, the touches; the extra pressure of the hand when we danced…

The advice I had was to hold out for more. Don't leap into bed. Keep him wondering, keep him dangling; keep him away from you. Being head over heels in love as I was, that was the most difficult thing in the world to do.

But the advice was sound for it fitted with the desires I held, that he be mine solely, that I be his queen, his love, his life. That I produce the countless sons he seemed to need to satisfy his need for continuity of the line of Tudors, or do I exaggerate? He made no secret of his desire for a nursery full of children. He would have made a wonderful father and grandfather, he had a way with children; they went to him innocently and with huge wondering smiles. Ever did I see him look at any children brought to court to see the king, something he encouraged, even though later he confessed it set up a longing in him that could not be assuaged as no child - for which read no son - had lived, not one he could claim openly as the next heir to the English throne.

And so I became part of Court. I became part of the higher echelons, for the king had favoured me and so I was sought out, my favours asked, my favours granted where possible. I had my ladies, a minstrel, a secretary, a seamstress, everything I could want, apart from the coronation, the title and acceptance by the English people. That last thing never did happen.

It was troublesome to me for a long time that others looked at me strangely, for I had brought foreign ways back with me, they said, in my style of clothes, my speech, my ways of moving and doing, for I had been long in the French court where everything was different.

Was it then that difference that attracted the King to me? I will not know for he never admitted anything of a deep nature to me during our courtship and slender in years marriage. He asked but one thing of me and that I could not give him – a son. For him the heir to the throne was everything. I knew that and prayed constantly to the Holy Mother to grant his –and my – wish. I wanted it more than I could tell him.

Now let me speak of Katherine, that most patient of women and most loving of Queens.

It was some time before I took proper notice of the slim, pale, quiet woman who was oft by Henry's side. When I first met her, she was wearing what looked like old-fashioned clothes and a strange headdress. She ever had a rosary slipping through her fingers; she was ever accompanied by ladies who surrounded her as if to protect her from the courtiers. I recall making my obeisance to her one day and looking up into a face of utter calm. I thought later that night, when considering my impressions of my early days at court, that I had met someone who had delved into the depths of her very being and knew herself through and through. That she had come to accept the Katherine that lived within her. That she was who she was and the world could go hang if she was going to change for them, to please some folly or frivolity of the court.

I also knew, from the gossip around me, that her life revolved around her husband, although she never referred to him as such, it was always The King, with the capital letters somehow delightfully accentuated by her accent, that they had lived through years of many miscarriages and unformed and monstrous births until the child Mary arrived intact, whole and perfect - but not male. I wondered how anyone could live with that heartbreak and still be calm and serene in the presence of a whole court full of women as bright as spring flowers and every one of them – including me - trying and vying for her husband's attention.

That was something else Katherine had learned to live with, it seemed: her husband's dalliances with other women. She might be wife but he was king and he would have whoever his gaze danced upon, whoever tangled with his desires on that day. Passing frivolous dalliances that meant nothing: a bauble, a token from his vast jewellery chests, did they mean anything when you had been in the king's bed? As long as Katherine was there, none would achieve that higher standing in the land, much as they might aspire to it. And never did Katherine indicate by sulk or frown or tone of voice that she disapproved of this.

Her ladies chattered nonstop, part English, part Spanish, sometimes dropping into Latin. It was a mixture that few could understand and that too was part of her mystique. What was she really thinking?

Henry understood. This monarch allowed nothing to go past him without he understood it fully. He spoke five languages for that reason. It would have been easy to miss something in translation when envoys arrived, so he spoke with them direct. Henry was a huge sponge in a slender golden body at that time; he knew the languages and he knew the other language too, the unspoken one that said when someone lied or attempted to divert the topic or dissimulate the topic. He could and did stop them in their discourse and demand that they begin again 'as he did not understand full well what had been said.' In starting again they would tell it as it really was, not as they thought it should be and I would see a smile begin on the handsome face, the smile that said 'now I know what is truly going on.'

But that was later, when I was queen, when I observed this closely for myself. It was another of Henry's devious tricks and it worked.

Believe me; I have had many a long year to think on all this.

I have asked myself several times, without getting a true answer, why I joined in with those women vying for his attention when he was so clearly married and so clearly fond of the slightly foreign woman he had taken to wife. Her English was good but tinged with that hint of accent that made her exotic and different. Was that the key to their bonding? I never did know. I never did dare to ask. Whilst Henry appeared on surface to allow questions and would answer them, questions of a more personal nature that is, he had a way of making sure you knew when you were crossing an unwritten, undrawn, should I say invisible barrier which, although you could not see it, the thing was there and his eyes would darken and his face go slightly rigid, as if he was about to throw one of his rages, the sort everyone avoided if they could. He never did but you learned soon enough to not ask this question or that: nothing about other women, that was the first one. He was good at keeping most bedchamber secrets. His book only ripples the surface and that only in part. The rest is in his head, his mind and his heart, if any of them ever got that far, if any of us got that far. Does that sound unfair? No, that's the wrong word. I will not ask for it to be erased, for if I said it, I must have thought it for a moment and this is the truth, unvarnished, untouched and unrevised.

I am finding it hard to pin down the emotions Henry generated in me – and possibly his other wives too. I do not and will not know unless they disclose it to this book, this channel and the readers. What I think I want to say is; I felt excluded at times from the inner Henry, the real man behind the golden exterior as he shared nothing of his feelings with me on a deeper level than the: 'I want you, I love you, be my queen, be the mother of my sons' litany which went on for the entire time he fought to free himself from Katherine.

It is true I went to court nursing my secret fantasy that the king would love me, would put aside his queen and make me queen in her place. A girlish childish fantasy that secretly, even more secretly than the fantasy itself, I did not believe would happen. The court was full of beautiful women. Henry attracted them. Who was I but a lately-come to court person who had been in France for my formative years, but could that compete or even compare with someone who was born in the far off state of Aragon and came to England to become a Princess and instead became a widow?

Ah yes, but then she became a queen and I heard often how Henry had been in negotiations to marry her when his brother died and then it was put to one side and then it all somehow got lost until he stood in his father's place, but bigger, taller, stronger and more determined than even that fearsome monarch had been, and rode to Katherine and asked her to marry him.

Romance, I thought, is never dead, is it? For when he courted me it was with these touches of romanticism, of notes and gifts, of soft words and special smiles, of secret assignations as far as any king can have such a thing – he would dismiss his favourites, his hangers-on as I preferred to think of them – send them away and give us precious time together without their trying to eavesdrop on every word which they could then spread about the court to show how much they were in Henry's favour.

Ah, if they did but know how he spoke of them at times… but that is one set of secrets I will keep, for this is about Henry, my love, my life's dream, not about those who surrounded him.

I held him at arm's length and I held on to that tiny flower called Hope, urged on by the family who told me I had the looks, the skills, the personality and the body – if we are to put the matters clearly here and I see no reason why not – to captivate the king and take the family and myself to the dizziest heights of all, elevation to the king's level.

There were many who did not like this, many who eyed the Boleyns with extreme disapproval, who would do anything to block their progress. But that stood for all who ended up at court; all who sought to make their way in the world with the king's beneficence and goodwill. None could sleep easy in their beds or walk with confidence through the court, wherever the king might be, for fear of that knife in the back, both real and metaphysical. There are many ways of getting rid of a rival, not all are obvious… and Henry knew them all.

Let me go back, for again I divert, as Katherine did, for talking about Henry diverts us into many different places and corners of our thoughts, some of which we may not have considered for a goodly number of years. I know I have kept much away from thinking of the great man, for the pain lasted a long time, long, long until I was healed of all that troubled me.

I can now speak freely, for it is healed at last.

What I did know was that Henry noticed me soon after I had gone to court.

It was a small thing at first. He was nothing if not discreet at the start, only later did it become a widely known thing. We caught and held our gaze across the hall where a fire blazed in the great fireplace, spitting sparks and smoke in equal proportions into the crowd that hung around the king, waiting for a word, a command, a hint of what he might want so they could leap into action and fulfil his every bidding.

I was to see this many a day afterwards, whether it be a council meeting of top advisors or his day to be generous to the poor and needy, or walking ahead of the hangers-on to go to his meals or attend a divine service. He ever had the hangers-on and the way he walked sometimes said that he did not wish them to be there, that he was trying to out-walk them so that for a moment or two he could actually be by himself.

You see how easy we divert…

It was a small thing at first. We held our gaze across the smoky spark ridden crowded place and I caught the merest touch of a smile. It was so fleeting I could scarce believe it had been there and it had been for me but my heart and mind, my stomach and legs said yes, it was for me, for in turn my heart beat so hard it hurt, my mind went into turmoil, my stomach roiled and my legs weakened to the point when I could scarce stand.

I knew then I was lost. All the loves I had known, all the men I had flirted with, all the kisses I had stolen were of nothing in the face of this man, the true Golden Prince everyone had talked of and I, disbelieving, thought they embellished and exaggerated his looks and his abilities.

It is difficult to admit, but once again I was so very wrong.

It is here I admit that I was both selfish and self-centred in that life. It will show itself in my part of this book and I am not best pleased with that image of me but there is naught I can do about it. I was that way, I wanted everything and I wanted it immediately.

In that way Henry and I were well matched. He had instant desires and instant gratification – most of the time. Our need to be 'rid' of Katherine so we could marry was not instant and caused many hours of arguing, ranting; demanding. I cannot begin to calculate how many broken nights Cromwell had trying to fulfil his liege lord's demands but the man did the work and did it without complaint, or is it more accurate to say no complaint we knew of. How many minions were berated and abused, deprived of sleep and family life during that long tedious time is anyone's calculation. All I am concerned with in this narrative is the man I loved and the man I eventually married, King Henry VIII, ruler of all he surveyed and he surveyed the known universe night after night. I believe this is when he thought his deep and intricate thoughts, when he was truly alone and could be himself.

It is too easy for me divert but I hope by diverting I reveal yet more of this enigmatic man who seems to attract much attention these hundreds of years after we had both turned to dust on your side of life and learned much about ourselves on our side of life. Henry fascinates and appals and somewhere in between those two extremes is the man himself, the towering colossus that was and is the greatest king England has ever known.

Our marriage was short, but our love was intense at first and I am proud to have been his wife, no matter how limited my time with him. It was enough that I was chosen and for that time I was his.

Whatever is said about us - and much has been said about us, we began our relationship so slowly I feared it would never happen. I was content to be a mistress, whatever the historians say, but my family were not. Therein lies the source of many of the problems of our lives – families, this being whether we lived in ancient primitive England, the Dark Ages, the so-called Tudor period or anywhere else. Families tend to dictate, to intervene, to trouble the living with their many demands and needs, emotional and physical needs.

The pushing began immediately it was clear to the heads of the family that Henry was seriously interested in me. There was money for even more new gowns, shoes, cloaks, for jewellery of all kinds, for anything that would make me more appealing to the king's eyes – and heart.

"It is time he turned away from the Spanish woman," they said, crudely ignoring her status as Queen of England.

"It is time he had an English queen," they said, as if they were deciding for the king himself, rather than the king himself deciding what and who he wanted.

"It is time the king had a queen young enough and strong enough to produce the heirs he needs," they said, overlooking the small fact the king was already married and had been for a goodly number of years.

"It is time for a new young head at the helm," they said, ignoring the fact I could not, in a hundred years, have taken over Henry's role and acted as his regent whilst he went to the Continent. No, that was not for me. Having worked for Katherine, having seen how quiet and outwardly seemingly meek she was, I found I was impressed by her knowledge, her calm resolution and her strength of will which carried her through that time and all her other adversities.

When I was given a place amongst Katherine's ladies I observed her closely, wondering how she had the strength to ride to battle when pregnant, how she felt about the stillborns, how she felt about the many women, so many questions, so many things we could not begin to talk about – any more than we could talk about her husband's increasingly obvious infatuation with me. Henry and I were seen together, the court knew I received gifts and honours, the court talk was of the new honours for the Boleyns and the wonderment was, did I 'buy' them from Henry with my body.

No. I had strict orders, from my uncle and others in the family; give the king nothing until he gives you a crown.

To do that he had to rid himself of Katherine.

My problem was, by this time my love for him had become all encompassing. I knew nothing but the sound of his voice, lived only for the sight of him coming toward me, wanted nothing but to be in the same room as him and breathe the same air. I walked in the grounds after he had promenaded through them, wondering if I placed my feet where his had been. I treasured and kept every flower he sent me, read and re-read every letter he wrote and then, reluctantly, burned them for that was his instruction and I did not disobey a single thing he said – apart from letting him take me to his bed or to mine, until we had something settled between us.

If I had known the cost, would I have pursued my desire for the crown?

The book cannot show that for a long time my channel sat with her hands perfectly still whilst I thought about the question I had just raised and which I had not planned on raising. So I must say it instead.

Having raised it, having committed it to paper, I was forced into an answer which I had not considered.

So, this is the answer I am giving, after contemplation.

The question: if I had known the cost, would I have pursued my desire for the crown?

The answer is: yes.

My channel has given me a chance to change the answer. I have not done so. It is the truth. For the first time in all these years, I have an opportunity to put the truth before the world. If I am to tell the truth about the allegations of being an 'adulterer and traitor' to the king, then I have to tell the truth about every other part of our time together.

To be with Henry fully and completely, I needed to be his queen and consort. Mistress would not do. It would give me a standing in court, yes, a very high ranking indeed but it did not carry the weight and authority of queen. Nothing did. For my family and for myself the crown was the ultimate goal.

And so, for hours, days, weeks, months and endless years, the question of how to dissociate himself from Katherine obsessed my beloved man.

What greater love could a man have for his woman than he change the direction of the religion of the entire country and break away from Rome.

Here I want to ask something that has been on my mind for countless years.

Did Henry break with Rome to marry me out of pure love for me or did Henry break with Rome because he could, because it made him head of the Church of England and gave him even more power, status and notoriety than he already had? After all, it took him very little time to destroy the abbeys and priories and raid their coffers. It was as if that was at the back of his mind and who knows, it might well have been. I knew him, I knew him well but some questions were and are beyond my knowledge. I am only telling of what I know, not of what I suspect when it comes to major issues like the dissolution of so many religious houses.

Henry himself could probably not answer that question truthfully, for it was a tangled one indeed. He wanted freedom from Katherine and was hard put to find a good reason outside of the one biblical reference. That was not enough to set aside a wife of many years and he well knew it. So, in his scheming, did he see the chance to give himself another metaphorical crown, head of the new church for England?

My answer is – yes.

Sometimes I think the years it took to finally make the break from Rome were wasted ones as far as Henry and I were concerned. He spent hours closeted with advisers, biblical scholars, politicians of all kinds, working out the ramifications of every and any direction he chose, for it had massive implications for England. Always we were left in no doubt that England came before anything or anyone else. I was left with my ladies and my pastimes, which for the most part were waiting for him to either summon me or come to me. Only then did the day light up.

I have been asked, in discussions about this book, to describe how each major event changed Henry, for none of us remain untouched by the uncertainties, the problems, the major obstacles of life, do we? We may think we are the same but we should know well that we are not the same when we emerge from the other side of the trauma, drama, whatever it is that has afflicted our lives.

The first major happening of our relationship was the certainty that Henry wanted a divorce. Whether entirely for me or entirely for him, who can say? That is one uncertainty for me, because Henry never spoke freely to me at any time. I knew of his obfuscations well from others, answering but not answering, you think you have it clear and then you dissect what he said and find it was no answer at all, that you are free to interpret it your own way. Which leaves you in a quandary for who can say you have the answer right? Not having it right means risking the wrath of your king. So you don't do anything and hope that's right, too.

Dilemmas. Our lives were full of them.

Henry spent time going over his marriage with Katherine, digging into memories, the good times, the bad times – which most revolved around the miscarriages and stillborns, never about Katherine herself as a wife and Queen Consort, I noticed. I remember thinking she would, no matter how much I thought of my abilities, be a difficult person to replace. I was right. She was. But then, did Henry want someone different, more pert, more overtly sexual, more full of life? But then again, did that not in some ways subvert the role of Queen Consort? Well, try a mixture of both... but then again, if it offended him...

Dilemmas. Our lives were full of them.

I really did not know what he wanted of me.

I knew what he wanted, freedom. But in deference to his queen of so many years, he wanted freedom with dignity for her and himself. That was impossible to obtain without one or other being badly hurt. There was no question that Henry would not be the one to be hurt. He sought a compromise that would give him what he wanted, a degree of dignity and valediction for his views. Whilst all that was going on– and it did occupy an inordinate amount of time, I have to say, he was busy with everything else, including the massive network of informers, if I can call them that to be polite, which told him all that was going on elsewhere in Europe and the farthest parts of England. He felt deprived if he had no knowledge of what was happening in any part of his empire, which he felt extended from the coastline of Wales to the farthest border of Germany and all that fell in between.

I could not compete with that, I doubt any woman could. So I continued to do what I did best – be myself, the exotic one from 'over there', the one who set the trends in fashion in the court, the one who defied all convention and held out from being bedded before I was wedded. It drove the court – and Henry – mad for a long time. It was a game, of sorts, it drove me mad too. How could I be held, kissed, caressed, longed for by the most handsome and powerful man I had ever met and not want to respond fully and completely? I melted in his arms time after time. There is not a woman walking on earth today who could have resisted all that I did at that time. I truly believe this.

How long did I hold out from his advances? Not that long. Despite all admonitions from my family, he was a red-blooded man and I was a red-blooded woman and at that time we seemed head over heels in love with one another to the point and acted as if no one else existed.

I am ashamed to say now I thought nothing of Katherine being dismissed from court, being sent to some castle or other, shamed to say I gave no thought to where she would go and what would happen to her daughter, whether they would even see one another. It meant nothing to me. I could think of nothing but the yearning to be with Henry, to be a full part of his life, to be his forever and he be mine forever.

Such foolish thoughts. I felt in my heart then that I would be the one to give Henry the son, the heir he so wanted, even more than one. I was young and fit and longing for motherhood. I was young and fit and besotted with the king, the golden prince, the athletic, handsome, intelligent, at times caustic Henry who could outplay, out think and outwit the best of them even when half asleep.

The only thing which marred our relationship, apart from the need for the divorce, that is, was that the people of England, London in particular, did not like me. I wanted to be liked. No, I wanted to be loved, adored and fawned over as Katherine had been. She had the touch, the way with the people I somehow did not. I tried, the Lord God knows I tried but it didn't work, it came over false and they knew it. Henry told me to ignore them, but it is hard to do that when you ride out somewhere and have people shouting abuse and rude names at you. Hard to keep riding and pretend they weren't talking about you. Hard to keep riding and pretend you didn't hate the person they wanted in your place, that you were not who they wanted and you wanted to be that one.

Oftimes I would abort the ride and return to the safety of my rooms with my ladies. There I could be myself, be Queen of England, be Henry's great love whilst Henry pursued his Great Matter and heaven alone knows what else. Nothing occupied him totally for long, he was ever concentrating on this new project or that, playing instruments and making music, creating melodies and small ditties to go with them, singing in his pure rich voice songs which only he knew, for only he created them. The rest of us listened in astonishment and wonder at the endless, seemingly endless, list of achievements he could fulfil.

It was slightly daunting to live with but also slightly slighting. Oh, that is a bad sentence but it must stand, for it is correct in every way. How can you be the One Big Love of someone's life, to the point when they want to break with Rome to be your husband forever, when at the same time he is busy with so much else: his astronomy, his music, his writing, his treatises on this theological point or that, his demands for better food from the kitchen, his involved discussions with every envoy that passed through the country. It seemed I was ever waiting for the moments he could spare to be with me.

It was then I wondered how Katherine had handled all this, pregnant as often as she was, with the heartache of not knowing whether she would produce a living child or another dead one to mourn over.

It was then I wondered would I be the same, if I could not produce living children, one after the other, for this demanding king.

The festival of the Twelve Days of Christmas arrived and Henry decreed we were to spend it in true English style, with more greenery than ever before, with more music and more food and definitely more gifts – mostly for him – than ever before.

To make sure it was the finest ever, Henry decreed he would be the Lord of Misrule. This was a complete departure for the festival, usually a servant was appointed and we had riotous games and play but Henry? I knew he was up to something. The unspoken unwritten law was, whatever the Lord said, we had to do.

And so it was he directed some to be animals for the entire festival, not allowed to stand in his presence, others he directed to be female for the entire time, which caused great amusement as he chose the most manly of them to be womanly, those with beards and strong faces - and he directed that I act as wife.

And in that small decision I knew he meant to take me to bed, no matter what.

My family protested, hold on, wait for the crown, hold on and I told them, the King, the Lord of Misrule has spoken and I will obey.

In truth, I burned for him and could not wait for the summons.

I believe he burned for me so much he contrived the entire thing.

And so we bedded. You want detail? I will give you details. He was bigger than I expected, it hurt more than I expected, the rapture was greater than I expected. His body was hard, rippling with muscles, he was extremely capable and passionate and I almost – almost wanted to throw myself from the battlements when he looked down at me when we were done and said, almost calmly, 'well, I'm not entirely sure that was worth the wait. It wasn't that different from the others I've had.'

I said 'almost calmly' with great care. Underneath the seemingly loving but sardonic smile was a hint of what was to come, the cruelty of Henry's devious ever working mind. Why should my body be that different from the others, from Katherine, from my sister, from all the other women he had bedded? We were and are all equipped with the same kind of organs to function as women, are we not? I did my absolute best but I was virgin and had a lot to learn. If he wanted a harlot, he would have to find one. I had my upbringing to battle as well as my need to be the kind of wife he really wanted. If I wasn't, then – love would not matter to Henry. I would be gone. I knew that. Ruthless was just one of the words you could use about him and be totally correct.

And you will ask how I felt at that moment. A knife to my heart could not have done more damage. I swear before Almighty God I stopped breathing for a time, the hurt was so big it took my breath and stopped my heart. My immediate vision was long lonely days, weeks, months and years without him because he did not love me. My second vision was giving up all that the Boleyns had worked for, dizzy heights of power, titles, wealth and recognition. My third was the hint of sadness in Henry's face, for he really thought I would be so very different he would be enraptured for the remainder of his life. And mine.

The truth, the unvarnished ugly truth, was that Henry laid every woman he set eyes on if they were passing fair. Well, if not all of them, most of them. His drive for sex was insatiable. His need for adoration was also insatiable and how better to satisfy both than to hint that he wanted someone to go to his chamber for a short while, as long as it took for a small candle to burn down. He wasted no more time on them than that. They were sent on their way with a kiss and a token, a bauble, a coin and the memory of a session with the great king that set them above others –for a while. I know well that he did this and it was something that I had to live with. It was a long time before I realised Katherine had lived with that, too, along with all the other heartaches she had to bear. No wonder she died so young, or what I thought of as young.

After a while the hurt diminished but it never truly completely went away. It walked with me to the scaffold on the day I died; it helped a little to know that dying would take it away completely. I doubt that Henry had any idea of what he had done, of the pain he had caused, of the lasting damage that it did, making me feel inadequate. It did one thing: it made me work harder in bed than I would have done and maybe that was part of his calculated cynicism. I cannot tell. I truthfully think he spoke the way he felt at that time without considering the consequences. As king he could do as he wished, say what he wished, with no fear that it would ever rebound on him.

I know not what he said to the gentlemen of the bedchamber but they looked at me differently after that. I cannot describe the difference, it was subtle but it was there. Believe me, when it comes to court life, we all notice every nuance of every face, it matters to our standing, it could be the difference between power and nothing, wealth and poverty. The face, the voice, the obeisance, everything had to be right, or you were lost for there was always another family waiting to take over from you.

In fact, Henry is a wild mixture of many things: it's remembering always that what he shows on the outside is often hundreds of miles from what's going on inside and that's where the danger lies.

And the challenge.

I knew it. I lived with it. I loved him enough to risk all and be his wife – if only for a time. I think I knew from that first time it would not be a long marriage. Just that hint of knowing I was not quite what he wanted and hoped I would be.

The problem is – with Henry you never really know what he wants. I was different from Katherine in every possible way and it was not enough.

Let me go back again.

That Twelve Days of Christmas was wonderful. We had the most amazing time, his devious mind had concocted so many strange and different things for us to do, treasure hunts for us to go on, beautiful prizes when we got there, such charades, such balls, such music and the food! I cannot believe the cooks could make such a variety of meats, sweetmeats, sweet cakes and fruits for us and keep the supply coming throughout the time.

Whilst I held a burning hurt in me, a hurt so painful I wondered I could even smile some mornings, such was the effect of his words, to bed with him, to walk with him, to sit with him at table and feed him the choicest titbits, to be fawned over by the courtiers and treated with servile respect by the servants, almost made up for it. I smiled constantly until my face ached, I danced until I wore out my slippers and had to rest my swollen feet, I chased the treasure hunt clues until I won at least half the tokens – and later found that was exactly what Henry wanted me to do. I loved – and hated – every day. Loved for it was colour and fun and Henry, hated because I felt I could not do enough to make myself different enough to secure his love for ever. My dream had come true but it came with thorns. Huge, piercing thorns.

I need to divert again. I now understand why Katherine did it so often. I have something I need to say. My channel has been waiting a goodly part of a week for me to get my thoughts gathered into some kind of coherent order so I can present them to you, the reader. It should answer the perpetual and eternal question, why did it end so suddenly.

It didn't.

In truth, the great love affair, or should that be The Great Love Affair, began to fail from the first time we bedded. That which was adored, desired, clamoured for, as happens so many, many times, did not live up to expectations. That I have made clear and it is the truth. From that follows a course of thought that cannot be argued with: Henry had committed the entire government to finding a way for him to have a divorce to marry me. Now, in all conscience, how could he go to them and say 'it wasn't what I hoped and dreamed it would be, in fact it was a bit of a let-down, so could you forget the breaking away from Rome issue and let's keep things as they are?' You see how impossible it was. You see how saving face was everything. You also see that I was an excuse to break away from Rome, whether Henry fully accepted that or not. He may not have done, he may have truly believed he did it out of love for me but I know him better than he knows himself. His book is a good insight into the man but it is an insight by the man himself, coloured to make him look good, phrased so you will be in awe of his majesty, which we all were. Truthfully! So, my belief is there was a duality of thought going on that he may not have fully appreciated. I was the catalyst for the break from Rome but I was not the sole reason for it.

Having achieved that, having become the supreme head of the church here in England, Henry could afford to relax his stance a little, let people think we were the truly loving devoted couple he had portrayed as his reason for the break. I was pregnant, showing the world his virility, I was still attractive in his eyes, he was still the golden prince, if a little older and a little less flexible than he was, we could still be the king and queen of England to the wonderment of the people. Who still did not like me, no matter what I did.

But the rot had set in and as Henry ever did what Henry wanted, I found him less and less in my bed and more and more in others' beds. Or rather, they in his.

And I realise now that I wanted relief for my body too, just as Katherine did, for Henry was and is a Big Man in that respect and it can be somewhat – difficult after a while.

My pregnancy pleased him. A genuine pleasure, the look on his face when I told him was worth all the agony of walking on glass around him, ready to fall through at any moment, for the glass was fractured in several places. All seemed to go well, he discussed a few matters of state with me but I knew, from conversations overheard and from Henry himself that he did not confide in me the way he did with Katherine. She was able to be regent; I could never have done that. Did he not trust me enough? Was the bond between us not strong enough? And yet, while we waited for the divorce, or whatever would free him from his first queen, I believed we would be as one when we married.

We weren't.

My one fear was losing Henry's love. More than anything, I needed that because of my overwhelming love for him. The thought of living without him was terrifying. The thought of being cast out was terrifying. I believed our wedding would tie a tight knot that I hoped would keep him close to me.

It was nothing like that. To me it felt hollow. Empty. A ceremony without heart. Even as he spoke his vows, Henry looked around as if casting his net for the next queen, or the next bed mate. This was the truth of Henry the man inextricably linked with Henry the king. Henry the man loved women, an infinite variety of them. Henry the king could have the women he loved, an infinite variety of them, by simply being the king. The one fed from the other and those of us who loved him stood back and cried silently for there was nothing we could do or say to stop him in his doings.

I know I repeat myself here, but it is something that needs to be understood, for it is within the context of this particular trait of the great king that so many terrible life changing and life ending decisions were made. The longer I shared Henry's life, the more I became aware of the chameleon that was the man inside the doublet and the man whose head bore the crown, except when it came to women. Then he was the same. Insatiable.

Thinking about it over the many long years I have been in spirit – not counting the many long years I'd waited to be queen in the first place, I came to the conclusion that all men would look for and at other women if they could. They all look. They all ogle, even if it is within their secret hearts. They long for what women can give them. They think every woman is different, will bring something magical to the marital bed or even the unmarital bed.

I know well that is where it went wrong with Henry and me.

Henry continued to be Henry, all powerful, all dominating; all engrossed in the life he had created, which in turn circled around and through the country he was trying to create. At the same time we had frequently to leave court because of illness, and we were separated quite a few times because of this. Henry's overwhelming fear of illness permeated everything and everything had to be done to ensure he never contracted anything. Even a cold he saw as a death in itself.

That first jousting accident told Henry he was no longer the athletic capable jouster he had been and it put him in a rage for weeks. All of us in court kept out of his way, none could cajole him into better temper, not even Charles Brandon. Henry believed that by staying away from illness he would retain his fit and capable body, he would be able to take on all comers and win, he would be the supreme head of England in every way. He refused to accept that every day aged him a little more, weakened the muscles a little more; took a tiny bit of his stamina from him. He denied it and pushed himself even harder. It's just my thoughts but the second jousting accident was a direct result of his inability to see himself as someone growing older. He believed he was the same youthful person he had been when he married Katherine all those many years back. For a supreme egotist as he was – and is – ageing is not a consideration. Unfortunately it led him to being reckless and there were tumbles from horses when hunting and the occasional time he did not win a wrestling match, which again threw him into a ferocious temper which lasted for days.

Nothing anyone said could compensate for his losing, no matter what he had been doing. It was a personal jibe, a reason to resent every day which made him older. But he grew in stature as well as physically during those days, his reputation spread across Europe and to every corner of England too. It was just a tragedy for the rest of us that he could not see this. His mirror – the one he carried in his mind – showed him a fit, golden, handsome man, not the one with new lines in his face and a thickening girth, a slight inability to get up from a chair or a bed without difficulty, or needing a helping hand to mount a hunter. His mind saw one thing, his body told him another and because he could not reconcile the two, he snarled and cursed and tried to push us away when we wanted to help.

Was he liked? Who can tell? Who in their right mind would whisper about the king behind his back when they knew full well he had a massive network of spies and informers everywhere, eager to take his coin and bring him the gossip from inns and markets?

But first, there was the baby to produce for him, the longed for heir, perhaps. I prayed to the Virgin daily that I would be delivered of a boy, for the king all but demanded it, the king needed it; the king had to have his way.

Imagine then my bitter disappointment when the midwife, carefully, said 'a fine girl, your Majesty.' It was nothing to the bitterness I felt when I saw the look on Henry's face when he caught sight of his daughter for the first time. It mattered not that she was a fine child, bonny of face, strong in limb and heart and lungs, a lusty cry when she arrived and a determined way about her to take her milk.

She was not male.

My heart went to her immediately. I never knew motherhood would be like that. I knew I would defend her to the very last, if I had to.

Henry put a brave face on, saying it would be a son next time, adding 'get thee better soon, Anne, so we can start another child.' And walked out of the room without so much as another glance at either his queen or his daughter.

The one thing I see often in your books on our time, our lives, is the fallacy, if Anne had produced a boy, an heir to the throne, her life would have been saved; she would have been secure in her place as queen.

No.

The girl/boy topic is wrong when it is linked with my name.

You need to recognise one major fact here: Henry had made a huge, earth shaking, world changing move in breaking away from Rome. You, in your time, have no concept of how large a factor this was for everyone. England had been ruled by Rome, dominated by Catholicism for more years than anyone could remember and suddenly, it was gone. Broken by the will of one man, their sovereign. How powerful a man is this, they said, who could break the iron grip of Rome on the country's religion, who could ban the priests and demolish the churches, abbeys, monasteries and nunneries, who could sweep up the riches and deposit them in his own coffers?

Such a man would not be content to remain married to a woman who no longer held pride of place in his heart. Such a man considered, and knew, himself to be bigger than any other monarch at any other time in history. Such a man would and could look at others and not simply bed them, but wed them if he so chose.

Here I will whisper to you the name 'Seymour' and see how it resonates with you.

Did I know then for sure I was losing him? For I was abed and bound there until the time I could leave for the chapel. I was abed and could not intervene with any lady in waiting who happened to catch his eye. He was distant with me; he was kind on the surface, cold underneath. His touches were almost automatic, a duty perhaps. *I have a queen I fought for, I needs must be kind to her.* That kind of attitude.

But I thought I was winning his affections back again when I became pregnant very quickly, almost immediately after I was allowed back into the king's bed.

For a while we were almost back to old times, our deeply loving, exciting ways. For a while. Then the tension set in again, concerns about the child I carried stopped him wanting me.

All too late. I lost the child. I lost another child we had begun, too. My sickness was overwhelming, my heart breaking. I recalled every day how many miscarried children Katherine had birthed and asked my physician whether this was my fault or Henry's, for he could father the babies but they did not go to full term. Exactly as it had been with Katherine. So, was it entirely the fault of us women, or a fault contained within the king somehow? Had I spoken these words aloud to anyone other than my physician, it would have been termed treason.

And he had no answer for me. Oh, I should eat healthy great meals and rest all day and every day and do nothing silly like dancing or riding or even walking further than the end of the Great Hall and back again. He said nothing about Katherine's endless miscarriages and I knew then he had as much idea about our lack of healthy children as the horses we rode.

Then I became pregnant again. All was going well, very little sickness, very little aversion to foods; I had a healthy colour and energy and strength – until the day of the joust.

I know not what others say about my miscarriage. I care not what others say about my miscarriage, for it is not for them to know until I utter the words which describe what happened.

I have spoken of my overwhelming fear of losing Henry's love. I have said, and I mean it, I could not live without that love. Now walk with me through that time. That terrible day.

The arena was decorated, as always, with banners proclaiming H and A. It mattered not that the As had been stitched over and in place of the Ks, it was still our initials entwined, combined and I was there, pregnant, glowing, with a brand new gown of blue silk edged with Flemish lace. It cost a fortune and it was magnificent.

Henry had a new suit of armour, he had grown a little larger and needed more room to manoeuvre himself in the joust, or so he said.

It was bright sunshine, the sky so clear you could almost see Heaven. He rode out on his great charger, a startling tall figure in glittering armour, with lance at the ready.

He turned once, looked at me, blew me a kiss and smiled before dropping his visor. My heart was in my mouth, I swear I tasted blood. Had I bitten my lips in my anxiety? And why was I anxious? Henry had not lost a joust in years and yet –

The next moment he was tumbling to the ground and then, most horrifying of all, not moving.

At that point my channel stopped and we sat for a while, contemplating this life changing moment in Henry's life. Not only Henry's, but the rest of us. If we had any idea how much it would change we would have been more than just worried for his health, we would have been worrying for his sanity. For that jousting accident – if it can be called that, for a tumble was the goal of every knight in the joust – changed Henry and changed the course of England. Again.

I was not allowed into Henry's chambers. I know, I know well the point of this book is how us queens saw Henry which means we should not be talking of how we felt about ourselves. But – in my defence – when you see your husband, the king, fall so violently to the ground, to see him so still, that great giant of a man who took on all comers from Thomas More to the Pope, lying on the ground utterly still, with hand-wringing men standing around him, useless, helpless, incapable of rational thought, your first thought is for him – is he all right and your second thought is for yourself – if he dies, will I still be queen?

I have admitted I was selfish. I also say, in my defence, there surely is not a woman reading this who has not at some point seen their world collapsing around them and are screaming inside 'what do I do now!'

I went to my chambers with my ladies, all of us ashen-faced and shaking, silent, not one wanting to voice the dread words *is he alive?*

And there we sat, drinking wine and eating nothing, waiting.

I do swear that two hours we waited, we estimated it to be that long, were more like two months. I could not believe time could so drag itself from one moment to the next, that I could go on breathing, my heart beating too hard for its cage, that my fingers could be still around the rosary I carried out of habit and that I could still open and shut my eyes. I was lost in a state of unbelief and all these things were still going on, so there should be belief that at least I was alive even if Henry wasn't.

But if he wasn't, I didn't want to be.

At last a messenger came with the news that the King had opened his eyes and asked for me.

It was then I broke down into floods of tears and had to be hastily dried, touched with powder and perfume and escorted to his chamber.

Henry looked dreadful. I have no other word to describe it, he looked dreadful. He was white, with huge black rings around his eyes, there was blood dried under his nose and his lips looked bitten and were encrusted with blood as well. There was a limpness about him, a lack of vitality, a lack of – life.

"Methinks this is the last time I will joust," he whispered and I felt a sense of relief at the very moment I felt pain where there should not have been pain. "I will be all right, I just need to…"

His head rolled to one side and I panicked, thinking him dead but the physician took his pulse and said, 'His Majesty sleeps. It is the best thing for him."

I left Henry's chambers, hurried to my rooms and there, God help me, delivered a half formed male child.

Did I realise then my life was over? Very likely, but who admits that to themselves? I clung to the hope that Henry would recover, be his ebullient self, take me to his bed and create a new child for us to share. I clung to hope knowing that was foolish, for Henry had made it very clear in what I thought of as 'bed talk' that we were there to make an heir, not to make a marriage. The lust that consumed us from the beginning had faded, as all lust does, under the pressures of day to day living, of the problems of finding a way to remove the current queen from his life, of the pressures of court life and of diplomacy with many other countries who courted his attentions.

Did I not know that Madame Seymour was said to be eyeing the king for herself? Did I not think in my darkest hour that it would be a sin to be displaced by a pasty-faced milksop who had no charisma, no charm, no dancing ability of which to speak and spoke only the most basic of French and a little Latin? I know, I tested her well and found her lacking.

My dislike was obvious for I could not control it. Jealousy raged through me endlessly and I fought it and it would not submit.

It is only now, considering all things as I have been for these many long years, that I realise what I had done to Katherine, exactly the same as I believed Jane Seymour had done to me. Usurped me in Henry's affections.

Did I believe that losing my son was instrumental in this cooling-off of Henry's affections for me?

Yes.

Did I believe the accident had much to do with it?

Yes. And in that he blamed himself, for it was widely stated that the shock of his accident had brought on my early deliverance. Therefore, he was partly to blame for the loss of his heir and that in turn festered within him as much as the damage to his head festered within him and began the change. The slow, inexorable change from golden prince to oft surly, always demanding, at times unpleasant man who no longer saw a sunrise as something to welcome but a curse as it indicated another day. The sores on his leg began to develop; the pain in his head was more troublesome. He had what we knew were migraines from his first accident; they were aggravated by this second one.

But it was more than that. Much more than that.

I sensed a cold cruelty coming through that was not present before this terrible event. I never saw my husband, my lover, the man I lived for, the only man I lived for, as that much of a cruel man. Mean at times, demanding always, determined, yes, cold, when he had to be and to be a king meant he had to be cold and determined and immovable many times. Cruel, no. Or am I wrong? Going back over his time with me, his words when we first made love, yes, the cruelty was there, but subsumed. Now it was not.

Everything changed. His words, his manner, his attitude generally showed that there had been some kind of inversion, the only word I can find to indicate my feelings. Or is it that the true Henry was revealed; the one buried deep under the courtly master manipulator?

I give you one example. The only one you will need.

Henry came to my chambers where I lay abed, still losing blood from my early deliverance. He came on the arm of one of his companions, for he was still uncertain on his feet from his fall. I recall not which one; I had no eyes for them, only for him. Henry. My love. My heart.

He stared at me for a long time and I held my breath, not wishing to say the wrong thing.

Finally he said: "Is there no woman in this land who can deliver me a healthy living son? Is there no woman strong enough to withstand the sight of my falling and being carried off the field without having fits and hysterics? We shall not try again to bring a child into this world."

And he left.

Henry began to speak to people in a derogatory way about me, saying I had grown tired of him. Never in a million years, should we ever be given the grace to live that long for how many hundreds of years has it been and I love him still and he knows of it. But I knew the charade was beginning to fail. People in court are far too aware of what is going on, of every nuance, of every look, of every word. They watch for body language. We never knew it as such but we knew what we were doing. We knew how we watched, we knew how we moved. They knew and I knew that what I thought – and hoped - was a passing acquaintance with Madame Seymour was far more than that. I heard of his talk of her meekness, of her demure nature, of her quiet devotion, and I knew that the last was false, for had I not heard her with my own ears when she thought I was nowhere around, how she wanted an estate of her own, how she wanted her own household, how she wanted her own children and not to share it with the rest of the country. By 'it' she meant her husband, her children, her entire wardrobe for you cannot move without someone commenting on you. Ever was it thus and it is now for those who walk in your spotlight now suffer the same intrusions into life as we did. In that way, for royalty, nothing has changed.

And so, as I watched the charade breaking down, so I must have subconsciously drawn away slightly but oh my beloved Henry, grow tired of you? Never.

And so it progressed. I began to hear the rumours that I had betrayed him with others, my brother, my friends, anyone. I heard them and disbelieved them and turned them over in my mind, wondering who had begun them and, having begun them, who was feeding them so they went from embers to full roaring flames. I suspected Henry had a big part to play and I also suspected that it was the Seymours who were pushing their milksop daughter before the king to attract his attention. Having found her sitting on his lap one day, I recognised there were two elements at work here; neither was good for my future. I could see my great love being helplessly abandoned, left to drift alone in a hostile world. There is no world more dangerous and hostile to be in than the one of an abandoned queen. Katherine had been dismissed from court with half her entourage and very little comfort. My court was luxurious beyond my wildest dreams. I could not imagine living any other way. But, if Henry chose to dismiss me… in favour of the milksop, I would have nothing with which to fight back. Not that you could fight the king, his word was law.

So, two elements at work. Henry's bitter disappointment at the miscarrying of a son and the unsampled delights – or so I assumed, not having heard to the contrary – of the simpering Jane Seymour. Or did she have hidden depths I for one could not see? And was that because I didn't want to?

I tried to be calm, to wait on Henry, to be the biddable loving wife and queen consort he needed, or so he said. But then I saw the milksop with a locket that only a king could afford. And I saw her snapping it open and shut, open and shut, only when I was around. Something broke in me; I all but attacked her to snatch it from her neck. I did but damage my fingers on the chain. They hurt for hours afterwards and the cuts took a long time to heal. More fool me, thinking there was time for them to heal.

More fool me, thinking there was time for my marriage to heal, too. There are occasions when love blinds you to all that is around and in front of your living eyes. It has taken my spirit eyes to see what I missed then.

Henry was amused by the incident, smiling at me with a faintly patronising air that was until that time unlike him. He asked if I had a problem with my lady in waiting, Mistress Seymour. I said no, of course not, just with her choice of jewellery. He laughed out loud at that, the great booming laugh that I had been missing for months. Then he stopped laughing and looked at me in a horrifyingly cold and calculating way.

"I have spoken with Cromwell to find out if our marriage is valid or not. Methinks this has been a mistake on my part and I am not best pleased about that."

Then I knew it was over. How and when and where and by what method I had no idea – then. All I knew was; Henry was tired of me and ready to move on. His casual bedding sessions were not enough; he needed another queen consort, perhaps one more biddable than I was. Or perhaps one more entertaining than I was. Or more – I have no more words to describe what my liege lord wanted, or I thought he wanted. We were long past the stage when I knew his every thought – but then again, did I truly know? This complex, powerful, manipulative ever scheming man I called both husband and king, did I know him? Did any of us know him? Did Katherine know him after many years of marriage?

I doubt it. I doubt anyone, at the time or now, despite hundreds of books and endless film efforts, have ever come close to understanding and capturing the essence that was and is His Majesty King Henry VIII.

For appearance's sake he ordered me to attend banquets and meetings, to dance with him in the evenings when the minstrels sang and the musicians played and I danced with tears that burned my eyes and I dare not let them fall. It was enough – for me, but not for him, to be with him. I longed for support. I adored my daughter and wanted a son, for me as much as for Henry, I was heartbroken over the miscarriages and the rumours and I could not get near him to talk about anything. I was effectively dismissed and barred from his chambers.

The word fickle comes to mind as much as cruel.

I've also realised this narrative is all over the place but then, I am not reciting my history which is so well known, down to the last steps I took, but about the man who was the cause of it all, Henry, the great king.

I watched him all but gloating over the ransacking of the monasteries and religious houses; saw the indifference with which he met the news of the poor and sick travelling the roads of England, looking for succour and healing and not getting it. Henry only saw the royal coffers filling and, with Thomas More and John Fisher out of the way, as it were; no opponents any more, he began to act more like a tyrant than a benevolent and caring king.

Which makes me wonder whether he ever was a benevolent and caring king.

My feelings now are that Henry, from the moment he was released from his parental imprisonment and found himself King of England, really did mean to have everything he wanted, no matter the cost.

The word ruthless comes to mind, too.

Then we move to the last days.

All my beloved friends, my beloved brother, my innocent musician, were in the Tower. I had no way of knowing what they were going through. All I knew was, they were being tortured and I walked the palace grounds day after day after day crying and crying until my face was a wreck and my heart was totally broken. For I was torn between those I loved and the man I loved and still do. And there was nothing, absolutely nothing, I could do. I could not go to Henry, grab his beard with both hands and say 'leave my friends alone, leave my brother alone, they are innocent of all your deceitful charges. I know what you want. You want her and not me. Just let me go, let them go, let us all disappear and let you have Madame Seymour to yourself and see how she measures up to my abilities.' And the worst part of all was I was totally incapable of doing any of it for Henry would not have stood any kind of intervention. When he gave an order, he expected it to be carried out and there was no way anyone could stop it.

It was then I knew that I did not want to live any more. How could I live loving a man so cruel, so heartless, so unbelievably arrogant that he could just take people and hurt them so much to suit his own ends. It was as if the whole edifice of our love ha\d come crashing down around me and I saw him clearly as the tyrant that he became and yet within it all, my love burned like an everlasting flame and there was nothing I could do about that, either.

One saying is: there is your truth, my truth and the one in the middle. This is very much a part of the nonsensical 'trial' that followed my 'downfall', as it were.

There is another saying which I recall, but have not heard for many a long year:

There are two relationships: the one you think it is and the one it really is.

The 'trial' was of course a joke. What else could it have been? Staged for the sake of the country, of not losing face, of showing that I committed treason – and I would give much to find the person who alleged I was treacherous to the one person I adored beyond all sense and reason – would I find that person in the opposing camp, I ask myself? And to quiet his conscience, if indeed Henry still had one at this time. I began to doubt it, as I doubted so much else, asking myself was his love real or faked because he lusted rather than loved and lust had gone the way of all things when familiarity crept in, asking myself if he truly cared about anyone. He had two daughters and saw neither of them, never asked about them, never wanted to know what they were doing, whether they were like him in any way. If he ever did, it never reached my ears and there were those who made sure I heard every word he said, as if this would benefit me in any way. All it did was make me even more unhappy because I had not heard his voice.

I know, stupid to the end, this Boleyn, clinging to a love that maybe was never there in his eyes and mind. It certainly was in the eyes, ears and minds of the court, we were talked of constantly as The Lovers and many asked why I had fallen so far from grace. And I asked myself, constantly, could they not see Henry for what he was? An egomaniac who saw nothing but his own needs.

The truth is, of course, you never really know someone until you have lived with them. And yes, for a time we can say we lived together, we shared a bed, we shared all meals, all entertainment, shared walks and some talks and you will see the order in which I put that list – it gives an indication of what was really at the root of all this. Some talks. It was truly 'some talks'. 'My dear Anne, you look delightful today. How is the sunshine? Not too hot for your pale skin?' came as easy to him as 'I have arranged a swordsman to execute you, my dear, for I would not subject you to the axe man for fear he would not do the job well.' Either way you can see there was not depth in any of it.

Maybe I clung to false hope, that all we had between us would avoid this disaster, this fiasco of truth and 'investigation', of the ultimate, the death sentence being passed. False hope for in truth Henry was implacable. I thought of nothing but the tremendous times of love we had, how he courted me, how he loved me. I could almost deceive myself into believing he truly broke with Rome for me and me alone, even though part of me shouted the truth every time I walked down that pathway of memories. Those memories that bolstered me through the final days.

The swordsman was a concession I appreciated, it hinted at a vestige of remaining affection.

Even as the court swarmed with gossip of his courtship of Jane Seymour.

I found this passing strange; Henry never courted anyone. Henry took. Yet he was playing the gallant, sending gifts, walking with her with linked arms, was espousing her quiet ways and gentle beauty to all who would listen. My ladies, among others, diverted themselves from my fate by bringing me gossip. They thought it would help. It didn't, it told me what I was losing – what I had already lost. My love was being scorned. My life was worth nothing.

I mourned the men I had lost so horribly through one king's determination to find 'evidence' – it is to be asked again who planted the seeds of treason so that I had to die, not just be put to one side. It is to be asked and I will not repeat the name again, it hurts even now. I know who was in collusion with Henry over this and I knew that Henry would take and take even as he gave the family crumbs from the treasury and that is all they would get. Did I not know this well, knew what the Boleyns did not get, compared with their dreams?

There is little more to add to this part of my story, for I did not see my husband again. I just want to make it clear to all readers, whoever they are, that I was and am innocent of all charges. They were contrived to be rid of me. If 'that' family had not intervened, I would not have been sentenced to death but a king as great as Henry could not allow any hint of treason to pass by without recompense.

I spent my last days praying for my eternal soul and for Henry, that he find true love and happiness somewhere, with someone, to take him into his older years, to care for him and tend him. I prayed for the souls of those I had lost, especially my brother, my sinless brother who did no more than be at court as the other Boleyns had been and do his best to secure some future for himself and those he loved.

I prayed for my ladies, who were devastated at the events and horrified that nothing could be done to overturn the decision. They should have known how implacable Henry was at all times, on everything.

And the last day dawned. I donned black clothes, fitting for the occasion, I thought. I was shriven and I walked out into the sunshine I would never see again, seeing only the face of the man I loved beyond everything.

I walked out to the scaffold with his name on my lips and my love for him in my heart and the certain knowledge that I would not wish to live without his love in return. I would not have borne living knowing he was with someone else. Even as I touched the scaffold I sent a thought to Katherine, acknowledging for the first time the pain she had lived through doing just that.

I said his name as the sword flashed.

The most treasured memories

Above all others, I recall –

The first time I saw him, head and shoulders above the crowd that sought to crush around him. Even then he stood apart, supreme, dominant, the true king.

The first time we danced and I felt the strong pressure of his hand on mine; saw the lips twitch in a secret smile and knew he was mine.

The first time we walked together in the gardens, he and I, all others told to walk 12 paces back and he told me he thought I was the most beautiful thing he had ever seen.

Henry's face when I told him I was pregnant.

These are cherished and will be for eternity.

Expressing Henry in one word: Faithless

Ten questions about Henry:

His favourite colour: gold
His favourite sport: hawking
His favourite animal: his hounds
His favourite interest: his music
His favourite meal: pork in sauces
His favourite sweet: medlars in syrup

His favourite time of year: Autumn, when the colours
were so radiant
His favourite home: Grenewich
His favourite gem: emerald
His favourite musical instrument: lyre

Jane Seymour

Henry's wives, divorced, beheaded, died, divorced, beheaded, survived

Henry's third wife and unwilling Consort (died)

Let me get one thing straight from the start: I didn't want to marry the king. I didn't want to be queen. I didn't want the whole court thing with Henry and myself at the head of it. I didn't want any of it.

Listen to me: I DIDN'T WANT ANY OF IT!

But as always, no one took any notice of what I wanted, it was what the Seymours wanted and always had been. Wealth, power, estates, high ranking at court, all that came before my wishes and desires. I knew one day I would be married off to some aristocrat but I dreamed of a great home with extensive lands where I could be the supreme ruler whilst my husband answered arrays and had other reasons not to be home.

This will make people think I disliked men. I didn't, I just didn't care to have them around too much, constantly interfering with my way of life.

So they gave me to Henry. It could be said he didn't interfere with my way of life at all and that would be right: simply, his life was mine and mine was his and nothing else mattered. Not even my intense loneliness. To become queen meant giving up all that I held dear, my pet dogs, my rooms, my family, in no particular order, just as they came to my mind for me to dictate, for they were to become one step removed from me. Henry promised me pet dogs but could I be sure they would stay with me when we moved from palace to palace, from great halls to gardens and back into our suite of rooms, or rather the ones he allocated for me? I decided not to have any; the responsibility of being queen was enough without complicating life by loving an animal and worrying about it.

The odd thing is, as a child I played at being queen. I would get my nannies or whoever was around to find some length of fabric and pin it to my clothes so I had a train which I learned to swish around me as I walked. I fashioned a crown out of stiff gold coloured material and put that on my head. Everyone laughed at little Jane and her fantasies but I didn't care. My pet dog would bark and bark at me when I was dressed up, as if he didn't care for me playing such a role and in truth, there was much I didn't like about it. I thought all the dressing up to please the court would become a problem in the end – I was right. I thought being polite and friendly to a great mass of people I did not really know would bother me and it did.

What I cannot tell you is how I knew this at such a young age, unless I gathered this from overhearing 'adult' conversations when they thought I was busy with playing out my fantasies. I heard, I absorbed, I understood more than they realised.

It could go one of two ways, either that 'wish upon a star and it will come true' thing but I didn't really expect or want it to come true, or 'be careful what you wish for, you might get it.' I am now asking, did I get a mixture of the two?

For all that, it was a game I could play and grant myself the fantasy for a time. I seriously never dreamed it would really come true.

I had heard of the great king, I had seen him once or twice when he went on one of his Progresses around England, but I could not tell you now what I thought; he was for me just another man, albeit hung with more jewellery and with gold edged robes and a fine, fine horse to ride. But as a child, could I appreciate these things and have them matter to me? I think not. He was just – the king – we curtsied and bowed and did all that we had to do to let him know we were subservient to his every whim. If only I'd known… I could have found a way out – somehow.

Or could I? Was this not my fate, to be chosen by and married to the most notorious king England had ever had?

I came to court as most aristocratic daughters did, to be a lady in waiting to whoever was the ruling person at the time. I served the lovely Katherine until Henry sent her away. It was my first real meeting with this exalted king, whose very image had been promoted to my family as being almost Godlike. I recall clearly being intimidated by him, his booming laugh, his great voice, his great presence. He seemed to see everything and everyone with one glance round a room, you felt you had been noticed, noted and written down somewhere on his own personal checklist. Whether you were in the good or bad column, only he knew and that was part of his ability to strike awe into the hearts and minds of all who sought to serve him. Did I not see this many times during our short marriage? But there I am again leaping ahead.

So, what were my thoughts when I first saw this much vaunted king? I saw a tall, well built, handsome man with blonde hair and beard, with piercing eyes and a mouth that would and could go from narrowed pressure to full on charming smile in the merest blink of an eye. I saw cared for expressive hands accentuating his speech and noted how all his favourites hung on every word. The women did too, the whole court seemed to lean forward not to miss a word, for fear of misinterpreting something he might want – or demand. I saw his aura of power, it seemed to radiate from him, perhaps because of the deference shown by all around him, so much bowing, curtsying, fawning over him, rushing here and there to fetch whatever he wanted. I remember thinking 'he could have walked over and got that himself' but then chided my foolish self: this was the king. Kings did nothing for themselves if they could but get someone else to do it for them. I am talking fetching and carrying here: Henry never asked anyone to take his council meetings or his hunting days, both of which were extremely important to him.

Watching him over the days, weeks, months that I was there, I worked out that Henry loved the council meetings as much as the hunt for one reason: he was in control of both. The meetings were chaired by him, directed by him and the results were those he wanted. The hunt was controlled by him, he decided when to change horses, when to change direction, when to stand back or go forward for the kill. In everything, every single part of life, Henry was supreme head. Everyone deferred to him.

Was that smothering? No. Henry was smothering me when he finally chose me, but before then, it seemed a natural way of life, that we all did everything Henry wanted when Henry wanted it because of the natural law: he was king, we were his servants. Every one of us.

I was there at court, serving the gentle Katherine, learning of the heartache and sadness she carried daily, afraid of incurring the wrath of the king in any way, spending my time keeping out of his way as best I could. I was by then ready to look for a husband for myself, if my manipulative family would let me make a choice, that is. My heart would ache for Katherine, that anyone could suffer so much out of love for the – dare I say this? overbearing king who seemed to demand everything of everyone whilst distributing favours to those he favoured most. I will say it, for this is a book of honesty of how each of us felt about our husband, the king.

Then the shock news came that Katherine had been sent from court and that we were to serve Her. The devil woman. The ultra-critical, ever demanding, sharp talking vixen herself.

I felt as if I had arrived in the king's life somewhere between the ending of his marriage to Katherine and the start of the obsession, for surely it was nothing short of that, with Anne Boleyn.

In my quieter moments, usually on my knees in the chapel, I acknowledged that she was as much a product of her family as I was of mine, but that feeling, that acceptance, only lasted a few seconds. I thought Katherine was wonderful. I thought Anne was a man stealer. It was almost hate at first sight - for both of us. You know how you just sense that someone hates you? I wondered what there was about me to hate, for I was everything she was not, quiet, pale, slender, not particularly pretty (in my own eyes, that is) and having not very much to offer, which is why I dreamed of a man of my own, my house, my estate, my servants, who would honour me because I was lady of the manor, which was about all I thought myself fit for.

Life was very different without Katherine. The quietness had gone, that peaceful atmosphere that others said Henry actually liked as a rest and a change from the dramas and tensions of political life. He might have said that but he seemed to be entranced with the flaunting daunting Anne Boleyn, who was perpetually flashing her figure, her smile and her oh-so-dark eyes in a way that Henry had no chance, no chance at all of staying with the sober ageing Katherine, much as he loved her and I know well he did. He never stopped loving her. All outside stuff was show; look at the big strong powerful all-knowing king who never stops to show emotion.

Wrong. He did and he did often, too. Who knew what went on behind closed doors? The Gentlemen of the Bedchamber thought they knew it all. Believe me;

they knew virtually nothing, for he had them fooled. They knew what he wanted them to know, not what they thought they were discovering and spreading around the court. It was precisely because of that Henry had them all dancing to his tune, marionettes on strings. And not a one of them realised it. Fools.

Bitter, am I? Now tell me, would you not be? I wanted a quiet life in a household where I could direct and organise and be myself. Nothing more. I wanted children, of course I did; does not every woman crave a child at her breast? Does not every woman want to flaunt the swollen stomach which says 'I am fertile, look at me!' But every woman wants that with the man she loves and adores and who loves and adores her in return and who will be there with her forever. Not the possibly fleeting interest of a predatory king. Again you will call me bitter, looking back on a very short marriage and a very short life but – remember this, I have had the same length of time in 'history' to think on it all as the other queens, so what you are getting from me is what you got from them – the truth. Whether Henry likes it or not is immaterial right now, I understand he chose the theme of the book, so, my liege lord, you accept what comes. Is that not right?

The Seymours needed to be seen, to have their presence noted, to be there when the handouts came around: titles, estates, money, all that could be gained by being devoted servants of the great King. The Seymours needed money, they were desperately short, down to the last bushel of gold, so they were, not accepting or even realising that the peasants who worked their land were truly poor, truly starving, truly wanting to better themselves with no way of doing it, unlike their landlord and Lord of the Manor, who had every recourse to better the family name by pushing the unwilling females into court where they might attract attention.

Be careful what you wish for. You just might get it.

And so, dutiful daughter that I was, I went to the palace to work as best I could for the highest ladies in the land. And so I did, and one I loved and one I hated. Towering over all I did and felt and was at that time was the king himself, a massive presence, one that would and could strike terror into the heart of the strongest person just by walking into the room. It was that ability I spoke of, his sweeping glance of everyone and everything in there and assessing it instantly. If something displeased him, it was mentioned immediately, roared sometimes and everyone cowered for fear of being on the receiving end of that blast of royal disapproval. I recall shaking head to foot when it happened, I never thought such a phenomenon could be real but it was. I felt it. I lived it.

The strange thing was, to me anyway, that Madame Boleyn believed Henry had eyes only for her when he walked in, that he sought her out in the crowd –and there always was a crowd, ladies, favourites, jesters, hangers-on everywhere – but I never felt this was so. Not that I ever said such a thing to anyone at any time. I knew better than that. My feeling was that the king first checked every single person in the room and then looked for Madame Boleyn. Oh but she would not have liked that being the way of it. But that was the way of it. Treachery was ever on Henry's mind, there were few people he truly trusted. I think he inherited this paranoia from the other kings – he came from a long line of kings who gained power because they deposed another and he was well aware of it.

How did I know Madame Boleyn felt that way? She told us, often. Henry looks for me first, she said over and over and over, as if we didn't believe her the first, second or third time. Mayhap we didn't, in her eyes, or did she need to repeat it because she didn't believe it herself?

From the beginning I didn't like being there. I hated the eyes of the other women on me, knowing I could not compete with their beauty, their courtly skills, their fashionable clothes and elegant way of talking, walking and dancing. I did my best but my skills were different from theirs, I had an upbringing of housewifely duties, of sewing and embroidery, of caring and attending to meals and ordering the supplies needed, the running of a household rather than the life of someone who would be queen. I felt totally inadequate most of the time, waking every morning with a sick feeling in my stomach that I had another day to get through, wondering if I would get through without doing something foolish to annoy the king or Madame Boleyn or anyone else, come to that. And I was desperately lonely. I made no friends among the other ladies; they chattered like the birds squawking over the best nesting place and were often cruel beyond belief against one another. I stayed out of it - and so I stayed lonely, if unhurt.

I began each day with fervent prayers to the Virgin Mary to take care of me, to guide my hands so that they would not drop things, to guide my thoughts and words, so they did not offend in some way. So many worries and cares to beset me and the king, always the king, over riding them all with his demands, his imperious manner, his overt interest in women. We all saw the way he looked at women and I knew, from their endless chatter, they and I wondered if he would cast his eye over us and what we would do if he did.

I watched the Boleyn family flaunting themselves around the king and wondered how long it would be before everyone saw through the façade she had created, the loving queen, the desperate-to-have-your-son queen who was at the very same moment flirting with every man who caught her eye - and there were many who contrived to do just that. She did it because she could, not because she was serious about any of them. It was her nature.

And I hated her. With every part of my being, I hated that woman. My heart ached for the displaced quiet faithful totally loving Katherine, taken from her sunny country to come here where the walls were always cold and the sun didn't always appear. Sent from her sunny country to be married to the Prince of Wales and then left a widow – we knew the sad tale and we commiserated with her in our own home. We were not of a standing to send letters to the queen and when she became the put-aside queen, we had even less chance to tell her how we felt.

So I ended up divided. Deeply divided. I wanted the Boleyns to trip and fall, to disgrace themselves so they would disappear from court and my life and I would never have to see that woman again. But it seemed that the only way this would happen was if Henry took a fancy to someone else and contrived to rid himself of the French devil.

He did.

He looked at me.

And I spent the next year or more in tears and closet hysteria.

I dared not let anyone see my tears, I dared not let anyone know of my hysteria, for it would have been reported to the king immediately and who knew what that would do to Henry's ego and Henry's plans? So I cried alone in the privy and had hysterics in the privacy of my bed, under the coverlets, where none could hear my cries or see me shake. By morning I would be under control again, with the Virgin's help, ready to take on my role once again, that of Consort-in-Waiting and later, Queen-Consort for real.

If I paint a word picture of me at that time, you will see why there was one thing I asked myself many times, what did Henry see in me? I asked my ladies, why me?

There were so many other women in court prettier than me, livelier than me, more enticing than me, surely.

But for me, I was reasonably well read, understood most of what the cleric said at services, understood half of what Henry told me about astronomy and diplomatic ventures and how to deal with envoys. I had Latin and a little French knowledge but was better at stitching and planning a household, of ordering fine foods and matching them with the right wines. That I could do. That I didn't have to do, he had someone to do that for him. He had a Fool to make him laugh although I did not see much laughter going on, no matter how much the Fool cavorted and jested with His Grace.

I was – a mouse compared with his other wives.

The mirror told me I had a reasonably pretty face, but whether I had a good strong personality to go with it no one said, or if they did, they were using words to flatter and both Henry and I hated flatterers, we preferred the truth even if we didn't like it. My body was passable, I had breasts Henry found adequate to hold, he liked my flatness and my roundness, he said. He spoke of my hair, indeterminate brown as it was, with a few natural curls but nothing like Hers.

So I have to say, truthfully, I don't know why he chose me and why I was the one he was buried with. But I am right glad I was; it vindicates me in the sight of those who – even now – put me down as a nobody; a pale insignificant person. I have heard the historians speak so of me and that, if nothing else, makes me stop being a pale insignificant person and turns me into someone who wishes to fight back.

A sudden thought, was it that which appealed to Henry, perhaps?

For all my time with him, for all his quiet walks with me and the drowsy evenings when the musicians no longer entertained him and he dismissed them and half his entourage too, for all he talked of this and that and some other diplomatic crisis that had to be averted and he was the one to do it – of course – I knew him not. And so I could never understand why he chose me.

Much of this came from being in awe of him, of his greatness, his overwhelming personality, his aura of undiluted power. It came from fear, too, that I would fail him when he had chosen me above others. I did not want to fail. I did not want to end up discarded or executed, I wanted to be a dutiful loving wife even if it was not my choosing and at times I hated the attention and the fuss and the demands made on me.

And the loneliness. Let me not forget the loneliness. It was all pervasive and nearly as devastating as the constant tension and fear. I hated that, too.

Loving wife? Definitely. The one thing Henry knew without anyone even having to throw hints in his direction was when someone faked their love and affection for him. Thus it was he knew well that Katherine would have gone to the ends of the earth for him, that the French Woman was totally besotted with him – which made his 'treason' accusations the more cruel – that some of the women he bedded fell for him heavily and mourned his 'one time only' activities with him. And he knew that although I was reluctant at the start, I did fall in love with Henry the Man. My task was to make sure Henry the King felt the same way.

Even as I was divided, so was he. Henry loved the magnificence of majesty, the court, the jewels, the richness of his life, his many courtiers, counsellors, councillors, minions by the hundred, the great show he put on when hawking, hunting or jousting, he loved it all. He relished the attention of those from Europe, who came to gawk and went back to relate tales of the great powerful king who did so much and went on huge expensive Progresses around the country, showing himself to his people whilst keeping more than a thumb on the pulse of England as far as every coin that dropped into his coffers was concerned.

Henry also, at times, longed for the quietness of our walks together, and I recall he walked often with both Katherine and Her, for the gardens were a balm to his oft troubled besieged mind, and with me, the quietness of our evenings, as I said, when musicians were dismissed and his favourites were thrown out and we did nothing but exchange small talk that meant nothing and meant everything. For it was then he would sometimes fall asleep, and a look of utter peace would be melded onto his face and the cares and worries of kingship would slide away into the dark hours until he roused himself and mock-admonished me for letting him sleep and thus waste our precious time together. Little did he know how astonishing it was for me that he could sleep thus when others found it hard to get him to sleep. I heard talk of his nocturnal life, his study of stars and planets, of the aches he had in his head which kept him awake and so everyone else had to be awake too. With me he was relaxed enough to sleep and for me that was everything. For in that time, which was precious to me in every way, I could indulge my thoughts and picture us as man and wife in that stately home I had long envisioned as being mine to run as I wished, without interference from the man in my life. Foolish vision, foolish dream.

And so I say to you, I know not really why Henry chose me, but with me he found a large element of peace and that, to him, was everything. If I did nothing else for him, I did that and with that I am well content.

But I needs must go back to when this all began.

I first heard it from my father, who came to my chamber where I was sat stitching and told me the king had spoken in admiring terms of my quietness, my calmness and my charming ways.

My father rarely came to my chamber; we usually met at the table for meals so this told me how serious this statement was. I immediately knew what this meant and my reaction was to burst into tears, the first of many, much to the astonishment of everyone in the room. My father thought I would be delighted, my servants thought I was being foolishly hysterical and I should be happy and rushing to my closet to find beautiful clothes with which to entice him. My mother, who had followed my father into my presence, no doubt excited to see how I would react, ignored my protests; she thought I would get over it and come round to the thought I might one day be Queen.

No one asked if I wanted it, no one heard the silent scream that I didn't want it, then or ever.

No one.

Especially the king.

It was after it had been mentioned that I realised they were right, that when he was at court, not engaged on some council business or other, he would seek me out, would send me favours, comfits and small items of jewellery. The locket with his picture in it was one of these items. It so infuriated That Woman she tore it from my neck. Word was her fingers bled. Good, I thought, if you only knew what it had done to my skin! But more than that, it was what it did for her reputation. Already there was talk that she was not the highly held wife she had once been, that her conversations were not suitable for a wife although good for a mistress and of course the most crushing fact of all, no son and heir.

Should I confess now, in a Kiss and Tell book, that I walked around opening and shutting the locket just to see what she would do? All right, take it as fact. Miss Compliant occasionally rebelled. In this instance it showed That woman up for what she was, jealous beyond sense.

I gloated over all that went on under the nose of the haughty about-to-be-deposed Anne Boleyn. I knew she was heading for a fall, knew that the occasions when she found Henry and I together cut through her like a bone knife. I did not, for one moment, let her know I hated the new relationship, that inside I rejected it, even felt repelled by it. I wanted Henry the man but not Henry the king. I wanted a home and family, not a court and more hangers-on than anyone was entitled to have. I wanted a husband, not a philanderer and if Henry could turn from sweet Katherine to flamboyant Anne and to plain little uninteresting me, there was no hope I could hold him loyal to the marriage bed, should we ever get that far. Loyal husband? I think not.

A part of me rejoiced in the possibility of a Boleyn downfall, a part I told my confessor about for I knew it to be a mortal sin that I should feel that way.

He walked a fine line, poor man. He wanted the Seymours to triumph for he thought the king's marriage illegal anyway, but to say anything against the Boleyns was treason and so he hesitated to censor me for my thinking. Eventually we left it that I had confessed and he had heard and so it was done.

The rest was between God and myself and God knows well, from my fervent often rabid prayers, that I did not want this joining of man and woman, that every part of me rebelled against the thought of it, that all my mind was given to wondering if there was a path I could walk to get me out of it.

There was not. The king was supreme and the king had made it clear he wanted me.

So came the dilemma. I could make myself ill very easily by simply imagining myself at the king's side. It made me feel physically sick and on a few occasions I was sick, much to the consternation of my physician, my ladies and my family. Weight fell from me; my clothes had to be altered so I could still look presentable when the king called, as he did, often. I could make myself die by continuing to be ill, not eat, waste away to nothing; it almost seemed like a good thing to do.

My family were pushing hard for the one person who could rescue the Seymours from certain poverty, they said, losing status, they said and who was I to disbelieve a father, uncles, cousins who all wanted a share of the royal munificence? The problem was, I knew in my secret heart it was greed on their part and I was no more than a pawn in their nasty game. Women were dispensable items, we were there to be bartered, used, sold even and there was nothing we could do about it. Only obey.

Did I allow myself to die, or did I allow myself to be sold to the king for the price of titles, land and money?

I tried the title 'queen consort' on my lips. It burned me.

I spent all my waking hours worrying and fretting and feeling ill, devastated at the fate life had handed to me and from which I could not escape. I had terrible headaches, constant awareness of nausea, broken sleep, an inherent weakness that made me hold tight to Henry's arm at times, for fear of falling. He liked it; he thought I clung to him because I wanted to.

A dream came one night; a vivid frightening dream that truly invaded my night's rest. I dreamed that I was in court with Anne Boleyn. She was wearing black slashed with scarlet and someone had painted her face with black and scarlet lines, as if she had been carved open in some way. She pushed through the crowd to stand before me, hands held wide apart, eyes blazing with fury and hatred, as if she would attack me. But then she waved her hands at her face.

"This is what happens to those who consort with the king!" The words were a scream and everyone fell back a few steps, uncertain of their safety. She seemed on the edge of insanity. "Lie with him at your peril, Madame Seymour!"

And in that moment she swirled her massive skirts and stormed away from me, disappearing through a wall. Her brother George and several others also walked through the wall and left the rest of us staring at the empty spaces where they had been.

I burst into hysterical tears and ran from the room but the voices followed, "Queen Jane, Queen Jane, Queen Jane!" And over it all I heard Henry's great booming voice: "Come to me, Jane, I need you!"

And I ran and ran until I could run no more. I did not know where I was in the dream, some far away palace where I had never been. I ran into the hall but could go no further. An angel stood guard at one of the doors, stopping me going in. He spoke in the softest tone imaginable, whispering to me: "your destiny is set, my dear child, there is no way out. We suggest you accept for the sake of the king's sanity." I bowed to the angel, turned and walked all the way back.

To the king.

The nightmare bothered me so much I did not eat for three days. It was not my intention to starve myself to death, I just could not eat. I kept recalling the sheer viciousness and hatred in Anne Boleyn's face and eyes as she confronted me and showed me, in that moment, all that I feared. That being with the king would be the death of me.

But then I wondered, did that matter? It was, after all, a pathway out. As long as the Seymours were not disgraced by my passing, did it matter?

Henry sent messengers to our home, asking where I was, what ailed me, what could he send to make me better? His physicians attended but I sent them away. What could I say to them? I had a dream about the

Queen and it had upset me? It would not be a wise or sensible thing to do, so I didn't do it.

My problem was simple. I was one of the ladies who attended the Queen. The Queen did not like me. She never had. Was she one of the far-seeing ones and knew I was being groomed to take her place? It was extremely obvious by this time. Or did she just dislike me for no reason? Or, I must think this in my head to be truthful, did she dislike me because she knew well I hated her, every part of her, the elegant slender perfect body, for even after the pregnancies she was slender, she was beautiful, men wanted her. I hated the hair, so rich, so silk-like; so perfect. I hated the face, such fine cheekbones, such slanting come-to-me eyes and he did and he should not have.

At what point in that tumultuous marriage did love die? You want the truth? You get the truth. It was when they were married. Before they married she was the unattainable, the flirt; the exciting ever dancing ever sexual ever not-quite-available dream. When the dream was captured, disrobed, bedded – what then? What then when the king comes from the bedchamber and mutters to his Gentlemen of the Bedchamber that one ---- is very much like another in the end. Or so I was told by the husband of the cousin of one of my ladies. And so I believe. It is the way I would see it, Henry kept dangling for so long for something anyone could give him. And did, he did not stay celibate whilst waiting for his One True Love. So why would he think her body would be so different?

And so I lived my days waiting for this capricious king to cast his eyes elsewhere and thrust the Boleyns from his life. I knew he would do it. I just never thought it would be with me. When the truth came out, it was a shock and I doubt I – or the court - ever truly recovered from it. So many beautiful, rich, highly placed women to choose from, all falling over themselves to get into his good graces and his bed. He took them – and discarded them. He kept on coming back to me.

And I found I began to admire Henry the man far more than Henry the king and that I could, in some way, separate the two.

It became serious very fast. The attitude of everyone around me changed so quickly I could scarce realise it at first. It went from courtesy to deference and a sense of anticipation in no time at all. The king came often to see me, when he could, for he had much to do in the parliament building and the state office and had Cromwell and others pulling on him all the time to sign this, read that, meet this representative of this other country or that. Attend this banquet, go on this visit; take part in this joust or tennis or hunt just to keep his courtiers happy and at his side and in his service. In between all that he tried to keep his Queen content and visit me. I wondered when he slept and when he did whether he dreamed of me or of the many things he had done and seen since the last time I had seen him. I never asked. It was not for me to question the king. If he talked to me of it I would have been pleased but instead he spent time praising my looks, my abilities, such as they were, my quiet pleasant nature and how different it was from the French she-devil, although he never said that, he always said 'my Queen.' But it was said with finality, with determination and with defiance at times.

The day came when we walked in the gardens together, his favourite pastime, admiring the flowers, the smoothness of the lawns, the shade of the great trees; the glowing redness of the bricks of the buildings. On this particularly beautiful day he said: 'you will be my Queen one day, Jane. I trust you will be happy with me.'

I curtsied, took his arm, smiled and said 'but of course, Your Majesty.'

He frowned and I stumbled on the gravel of the path. It was never a good thing to see our king frowning, it meant royal displeasure.

'Jane, would it pain you so much to use my name?'

It was said with hurt and damaged pride, it was thrown as a challenge. It was my test and I had not to fail it. Family fortunes depended on my responses at all times. It would seem the king's happiness depended on it, too.

'Henry.' I said it with a smile and saw the frown lift and sheer joy flood his face and realised something in that moment, something that shocked me to my satin slippers. He loved me – in his own way, he loved me. The king loved me.

'Henry, I will be honoured and delighted to be your Queen.'

The words were easy to say in the light of that revelation. Only later I realised I had committed myself to a lie and a life I did not want. But oh, in that moment, the joy on his face compensated for it – for a while.

It was about then that the living nightmare really began. Everyone walked a fine line in court during normal times, the everyday life, for we were all watching one another and suspecting one another but once the king showed a special interest in someone, that intensified to a level that was smothering, suffocating, unbearable. In addition to the headaches and everything else, I found I was shaking a lot, weeping without apparent cause, suffering from upset stomachs and all that entailed with rushing to a private place to deal with it. Henry's physician bothered me with herbal tonics and foul smelling 'cures' which I threw away. I knew what the cause was: fear. Fear of doing the wrong thing, as I almost did in the garden that day. How easy it was to offend when you didn't know someone very well, when you were innocent of the deeper currents of court life, when you were the object of everyone's attention. I walked in fear, ate in fear, slept in fear – when I slept at all. Life was one long round of worry that something would go wrong. The Seymour family would never speak to me again if I lost them this God-sent chance to be powerful barons in the land, Henry would never get over choosing wrongly, where would I end up being banished to if it all fell on its face? And so I walked and talked and chose my words with infinite care and at no time did anyone see the real me inside, the one tearing out her hair, clawing at her face to destroy her looks, biting her nails and slamming her fists into the prayer desk until they were bloodied and broken, tearing her entire wardrobe into shreds so she could not get dressed for yet another dinner by the side of the man she loved/hated at the same time.

Outwardly I was calm, smiling; happy to be at the king's side as often as he wanted me to be. Outwardly I was Miss Compliant. That's how I thought of myself. Two people. Jane Seymour, who wanted to scream and shout and hysterically throw herself off the nearest keep or any other high place and Miss Compliant, wanting to be the King's consort. Yes, when I arrived at the channel's home I shouted that they butchered me. They did. Yes, I wanted out of life but I wanted out of life on my terms, not theirs! I would have found a way if it had been possible, anything rather than have the king put me to one side and then quietly send me out of court and into the wastelands of wherever. I didn't want to be lonely and old and ill like Katherine was, they said. I didn't want to be scorned. No one would want that.

I didn't want to be executed. It would bring condemnation onto Henry; he had already disposed of a queen that way. It wasn't a good thing.

I didn't want to be the king's consort either.

Miss Compliant and Jane Seymour were locked in battle every day and most of the night.

Whilst they bought fought, they both realised one thing – the life was devastatingly lonely, for who could either of my personas turn to for advice and help? Who would listen to what might be construed treason? No one. So I had no one to confide in and no one to advise me and no one to comfort me.

I walked alone. Both sides of me.

The Seymours, my entire family if we are to be accurate, were ecstatic. I was showered with gifts, bolts of fine cloth, lace, tapestries, embroidery wools and needles, fine parchments and quills – in fact, if you think on it, I had just about everything a woman could wish – apart from peace of mind. No one offered me that. Not even Henry.

No one saw my anguish. They saw riches, power, prestige, estates, compliant me. Not rebellious me, who wanted to snatch the bridle of a horse, any horse, and ride for the country where I could hide. But who would hide me? Who would risk the king's wrath by giving me sanctuary?

I could not talk to my confessor, he erred on the side of caution in all things, advising me to do my duty; my chosen duty was the unspoken words. I had not chosen this, Henry chose me.

My husband-to-be talked long of his life with me at his side, of the coronation he would stage for me, of the great wedding we would have and how good an influence I would be for him, my calmness, my quiet ways, he said, would benefit him. This I doubted, for his temper was legendary and no woman could stand up to that. If the French Whore failed at controlling it, how could I begin to do that? People ran when his temper began to build, when he went red in the face, when those huge hands curled into fists and things were likely to be smashed into a thousand pieces if he got hold of them.

But I smiled, rubbed his arm, touched his face, wrapped a curl around my finger and said 'of course, Henry, we will be so happy together you will wonder how you managed without me.' Which brought a smile and a caress and a lifting of the thunder that sometimes overcame his face.

I asked for an easement of the confines of the Princess Mary, which prompted an argument but there was an easing of the court toward her. It was good, it was something to be proud of in a time when I was not proud, although my family felt I should be and argued with me about it. I told them then as I have said here; it was not what I wanted. It was done under duress. The nightmare haunted me throughout my remaining days.

My unhappy days. And they just got worse as time went on. It was harder to keep up the pretence that this was what I wanted, that I was the happiest person in the kingdom because the king had chosen me to be his queen consort.

It was obvious to all, including me who had worked hard at trying to pretend it wasn't happening, that the whole situation with Henry was serious and the situation with That Woman was also getting serious. The one thing Henry could not do was divorce another wife so soon after Katherine, or even at all, in truth. He and I did not talk of it; it was not something he felt concerned me. He was too busy being the charming courteous husband-to-be, showering the family with honours and me with gifts, which I dared not give away although I longed to. Some of them were so far from my tastes that they might have been for someone in Europe, some remote princess somewhere more suited to be consort to the greatest king Europe and England had ever known than I could ever be. Miss Compliant was also Miss Inadequate at this time; it made the whole thing worse. I suffered endless violent headaches whilst Henry seemed to grow even more in stature as time went on. I saw him physically growing upwards, rather than outwards, in that he seemed taller, more confident, more sure of himself than he had been for a goodly time. I wondered how much the Boleyn woman had undermined his confidence in himself. Did he doubt his ability to make decisions about people, after being so wrong about her? I wondered but dared not ask. It was not something anyone could do… well, Brandon could, if anyone else tried it they would be out immediately, but I didn't see him asking either. In fact, during the last few months of the Great Love Affair, even Brandon's ebullient self seemed subdued, which was very unlike him.

The one fervent hope of the Seymours, in particular, was that this did not drag on. We had been through the misery of finding reasons to divorce Katherine, finding reasons to break from Rome, now it was finding reasons to rid himself of another wife. The first was a long drawn out affair, the second was even longer. I cried myself to sleep during long lonely empty nights, wishing it was all over, that I was married to the king, that the speculation and attention would die down and let me live in some kind of peace, but had the terrible suspicion that would mean That Woman's death, how else would he rid himself of her? I was not nasty enough to wish that on anyone.

Apart from Henry seeming to grow taller as time went on, as he distanced himself from his queen and turned more to me, I found him more introspective. Sometimes he could not be coaxed out of a black mood, as if the weight of the entire world, not just England, rested on those huge shoulders of his. It was these moods which worried me more than any other for then he was unpredictable and I was not experienced enough to know how to handle his unpredictability, which ranged from rages to overwhelming solicitousness which I found smothering.

In the end, the Boleyn saga ended as it had begun, dramatically. From the moment she burst onto the court scene, she had dominated the court and the king. At the end, she dominated the court and the king, although by then her domination was reduced to who he believed and how much it was necessary to convict her of treason so that she could be beheaded and the marriage ended.

Ask me if I believed all the stories. I tell you I will not answer. There are stories and then there are stories and none can believe the truth or the lies in any of them. I do believe that the lovers, for they were portrayed as such for some time, became non-lovers when the first child was not the boy he craved, not the heir to the throne. Her miscarriage was a natural one; she blamed it on his accident. A good excuse for her but it rankled with Henry for it cast aspersions: if you had not failed at the joust I would have carried the child to the end. And so the drifting apart began, or rather, the rift was there and widening by the day.

I knew she flirted outrageously, this I saw over and over, but whether she committed any acts of adultery I cannot say. Even as one of her ladies, I could not say for I never saw any of it myself. Incest, no, that was definitely not right, for her brother was a righteous person in every way. He obeyed all the laws of court, spoken and unspoken, at all times. The poor little musician, ever did he seem little to me, for some reason, again, who can say? My opinion is he was innocent but my words were not sought and my opinions not asked for. The king had spoken without speaking, he wanted her gone and he may well have started the rumours himself to get her gone without saying anything to me. And why should he? I was no more than his next in line. He only discussed with me how happy he would be with me at his side. Court matters, European policy, church policy, governmental problems, none of this entered our conversations.

Excluded? Definitely.

Treated like a walking talking doll/plaything? Definitely.

Bitter? Definitely. By this time I was a total wreck and he didn't see it. But then, did Henry ever see what was in front of him if it did not suit him?

Let me consider that for a moment.

Henry wanted Katherine from the moment she arrived in England but was unable to have her, the documents binding her to his brother were just that, binding. Her becoming a widow conveniently allowed him to have her for his own. But, a long marriage puts a strain on people and when the extravagant creature arrived in court, he lusted for her and her family, like mine, connived and contrived to get what they wanted – the crown of England for their chosen one who was put before the king like the biggest lure ever. And he fell for it. Then, when she proved not capable of giving him what he needed – I hesitate to say wanted, it was an obsessional need – and the marriage folded in front of his eyes, he wanted a replacement. That replacement was me and the fact I was against it in my heart and mind was incidental to everyone, especially him, but then I doubt he ever realised I didn't want it. I did not, for a moment, allow him to think I was anything but head over heels in love with him - as king. He would never have understood that if he had been just a knight, an earl or a duke and we had our estates and our friends and our life, I would have been content. Not happy, for he was not my choice but content. In this life, in the glare of court, it was torture.

I watched him torment himself over signing her death certificate and then taking the quill and signing it with firm steady strokes. Later he said, in a quiet moment, 'it is done and right glad I am too.'

And he ordered yellow clothing for himself and for me.

And ordered a swordsman for her.

We were betrothed the day after her head left her body.

He put on a show of 'I don't care' but he did and I resented that, for it was a falsity I had to cope with. He walked with me, bright in our yellow, like canaries out of a cage relishing our freedom but his brow held the lines of worry and sadness and his eyes did not lie to me. He could not lie to me. He regretted it even as he rejoiced in our freedom to become man and wife. King and Consort.

Regretted taking the life of someone so vibrant, so enticing; so enchanting that she stole his heart, mind - and some would say sense too – for what? Because he wanted another woman, another love, another life, or because he wanted an heir more than all of that put together? The problem was, always, you could not guarantee the sex of your baby. You took what nature gave you and made the most of it. But Henry was obsessed with an heir, a son to carry on the Tudor name. Was he not the eighth Henry to wear the English crown? Surely there had to be a ninth somewhere…

We did not have a grand wedding as he had promised. I wished it not for I was not marrying the man of my dreams, I was marrying a king and I had in my heart and mind the snarling angry face of his former queen in its startling black and scarlet, for the nightmare never left me. But for all that, I wore cloth of gold and he wore scarlet and gold and our ceremonial was befitting of royalty and I had ladies in glorious clothes to accompany me.

Henry seemed content and we spent much time together, time which I thought precious and held it to be so. It made a cushion which I could hold against the Boleyn presence in my mind, I could muffle it for a while but it always wormed its way through. It never left me. That Woman left a lasting legacy in the court and in our lives. Her vibrancy had been such that her death was like the sun going out and bringing in a period of utter darkness. The nightmare haunted me to the day I died and even now it occurs, drops into my mind like an unwanted insect would land on you at a picnic or the wrong moment during a solemn ceremony. Those who say we are totally healed when we return home are only half right. That which is very deep seated, the venom from her to me and my hatred of her are two examples, will take many centuries to eradicate. Writing this for you is helping toward that goal, and for that I am eternally grateful. It should be said now, before I go any further, that I want Henry to know that at the end I loved him both as king and man. He is that powerful, that charismatic, that mesmerising, when you walk, talk, make love and live with him. All of you who dismiss him as tyrant and ogre and other such terms see only what you want to see. I lived it.

The Boleyns did not attend court, which helped, but the Seymours did and I was astonished at how many there were when it came to the giving of honours and titles. I accepted that which Henry gave me with reluctance for I had all I needed in the way of money and attendants but he showered me with gifts. Ever was he generous with his new wife.

It was never my intention originally to speak of our private bed time together, but this is a book of truth and revelations, things no one else could tell the world about our liege lord. It is good that we tell these things, for there are those who need to know that the image of the man is the whole man. That nothing is exaggerated, not the portraits or the scripts written at the time. I hesitated before committing myself to say these things but say them I will, for I see the others have, especially That Woman. I will not be outdone.

And so… when Henry first laid with me, nothing happened for he was far bigger than I expected and I much smaller than he anticipated and we could not fit together. The two of us, naked, nervous – at least I was – uncertain of each other, for walking and talking is not a substitute for – excuse me – wedding and bedding. I realised immediately that my new husband was huge in his equipment and he realised immediately that his new wife was extremely small, that the dresses, large as they were, concealed a very slender body indeed and a very small place for him to go.

We laughed – oddly, together - and I was relieved, for I expected disappointment and even temper, for then, as I have said, his temper was beginning to show, the façade of good nature, the golden prince, the man who got his way through manipulation, diplomacy and sheer power, was cracking and the true man was revealing himself. Beneath that diplomatic image was a man of iron. That man was determined always to have his own way, no matter what or who stood in the way as an obstacle. He proved that with his break from Rome, surely the biggest event any monarch has ever managed to do, or wanted to do, in the entire English history. And then condemning his queen to death and walking away from the entire situation…

And so, I anticipated a touch of the king's temper but instead we laughed and his laugh ever echoed around the rooms where we were.

"Tis good and strange and exciting for me to find someone where I do not fit," he told me. "Worry not, my tiny songbird, next time I will bring the remedy."

And for the rest of the time we were together, he held me close to what was a well muscled body, full of virility and need, which I knew enough to satisfy so he did not leave me in that state, with enough strength and consideration for me to be unhappy that we did not fit together. He was satisfied, I was not. How ironic is that?

He kept his promise; came with some sweet smelling viscous oil that left a hint of lavender and rosemary and other herbs I could not identify. It smelled of summer and felt like spring. And so we coated him and he slid easily and gently and with the utmost consideration into me and in that moment we were one. I knew then that my feelings were right: I loved Henry the man but not Henry the king. Had we been husband and wife in some vast estate somewhere in England without the pressures of court and courtiers and councillors and scribes and others pulling on him all the time, our days would have been sunshine and flowers, humming working bees and the sound of birds, which he delighted in. There would have been problems, of course, arrays at times, calls to Court, all the usual things aristocrats have to deal with but nothing on the level of business Henry carried out sometimes way into the evenings, when he should have been resting. And so that first joining was heaven, my feelings opened and enveloped him as my much loved husband, and hell, for I wished so much it could have been on different terms.

Yes, I repeat myself about the estates and a separate home, yes I know I should have been overwhelmingly grateful to be chosen but – to be Queen Consort requires something more than just being – there were diplomatic difficulties to overcome and Henry to understand on a much deeper level than anyone would think, for to know him was to help him and not provoke one of his blazing temper sessions. I was afeared of them for ever did I walk that fine line, that one that cracked my mind into pieces in the end.

Our times in bed were precious to me. During those times he was Henry the husband, the gentle lover, the caring man who sought affection and an heir in that order, I believe, although he would deny it if asked.

He was courteous and considerate and unfailingly loyal in that he never spoke of any other woman, all his attention was on me and what I could give him in return. All of me, for I had no reason not to do anything else. When he left me I would be exhausted, longing for sleep and he would be energetically looking for the next task, the next session of star gazing, the next pile of papers to sign.

We gave each other satisfaction, if I am to believe all that he said to me during those times and although I had seeds of doubt, the fact he asked to be buried next to me proves that there was a tremendous bond between us and that pleases me more than I can say, for I know I had nowhere near as much to offer as the other queens. I was not royal, I was not foreign and exotic. I was, as he often said, his English Flower.

I will just say that the Boleyn face oft came between us although I am not sure he realised it. Once he murmured her name when holding me and I bit my lip hard to stop myself retaliating. He never mentioned Katherine in my presence but he did to others, to his Gentlemen of the Bedchamber, for example, I was told he spoke of her from time to time, of her gentleness and her dignity and her quiet acceptance, comparing her with the Boleyn woman, comparing her unfavourably in that the Boleyn woman did not measure up to his first wife and then I knew, even though I had always suspected, that he loved Katherine more than any of us and I believed he always would. Why else would he speak of her in such loving terms? Did he seek to calm his conscience for the Boleyn woman? I know not and I would not speak of it with him for it was not a wise thing to do, any more than I could have spoken of the nightmare to him. He would have called it witchcraft and demanded that someone remove it from me, I am sure of that.

I knew of this for courtiers do like to talk and talk sweeps through a court as a storm sweeps through land and takes with it all that it will and deposits it elsewhere. Rumours abound and to get the truth out of them you need to use a toothpick and disinter it and use that as your basis for another rumour which was coming on the heels of the first. My ladies talked much of what they heard and where they heard it. I let them talk and took my own toothpick to the stories, dissecting and prying for the truth within them and allowing only that to fill my mind. All else I dismissed as impractical, stupid or just not worth the effort of remembering.

And none of it was spoken of to Henry, for he did not overly care for me to talk to him of court tattle when he had enough of his own to share. And yet, talk was the lifeblood of court, for what else do the highly colourful highly paid power-hungry courtiers have to do with their days? It was talk which ultimately brought down the Boleyns and talk which told me that my husband still favoured his first wife and Queen and that the Boleyn woman held a small part of his affections still even though he said I was his ideal queen and consort and he wished he had known no other. Of such flattering comments I made little, for I knew Henry well by then. He loved so to talk, to praise; to receive flattery and praise in return and more so, for he lived by them. He had been given all he wanted throughout his life and so could not get enough of all that he wanted – adulation more than anything. It was truly a bold and courageous if not outrageous move to break from the Church of Rome and commit England to another course in her religious history, it provoked outcry and upset and much discussion around the court that went on endlessly. No matter what any thought, what Henry wanted, Henry had and none could or should or would gainsay him his wants.

What then of these 'drowsy evenings' of which I spoke? Henry would come, surrounded by his entourage, which he would dismiss, most being sent from the room, the others banned to the far end so we could be together. We would sit on a couch side by side, before us a table loaded with fruits, comfits and ales and wine for his delight. My ladies would be at the far end of the room too, where they would be flirting outrageously with the men.

Henry would talk to me, sometimes at me when he needed to say something and dispose of it, but I noticed time and again that although his attention was on me, he never missed a single thing going on between the men and ladies in my room. It was as if there was a part of him there in the centre of the group, overhearing all that went on. I realised after a while he was watching their actions, which spoke to him louder than any words. It also became very clear to me that Henry knew at any moment every single thing that was going on around him and he was manipulating it to his advantage in some way or another. His power terrified me. His abilities overwhelmed me. His knowledge was far superior to anyone else's in the room and none of them knew it. How many fell from favour because they did not recognise that? How many tried to outwit him and failed and fell? Countless. New faces every day and every day someone still tried to be cleverer than his monarch.

Fools. Every one of them.

My family tried to coax me to ask for this and that but I refused. They were not going to use me as a puppet to get things from Henry, because that was not how I wanted our marriage to be. It was not my choice but having had the choice made for me, I determined to make the best of it and be better than anyone expected. I had much to overcome and worked hard at it.

And Henry knew it.

In our quiet times together Henry spoke not of diplomatic matters to me, he left that to those whose place it was to know these things and write of them and deal with it. With me he spoke more of his plans for England, for my coronation and then eventually why I would not have one, for the plague had visited London yet again and he was afeared of illness, especially the plague. The death of his brother Arthur had bred a fear of illness in him and he avoided it all the time. I recall a time when the Boleyn woman had the sweating sickness, that illness which took his brother, and she had to stay away from court and from him until her physicians declared her fully recovered.

It mattered not to me that there was no great state coronation. I am not one for such huge exhibitions of wealth and power. I was content with my role, Queen Consort to the mighty King of England. I would have been more nervous than I already was if I had to go through that elaborate ceremony without a hitch.

My problem was, even as I loved this man who had become my husband, my heart ached for the true love I felt was somewhere out there in the rest of England and I would no longer have the chance, the opportunity to meet him and to know him and to give him the love I had tightly bound inside me. I never let it go, this love, never gave it to anyone else. I reserved it for the one I wanted to love but knew I never would. It was my barrier, my sanctuary, my need to have something that was between me and the court that was Henry VIII's domain and never mine. I had a secret, one I held tight close to me, a secret longing for something that could never be, not now I had been given to the mightiest man in the known world. What person would take me on, if God forbid I was left a widow? None, for I had been the possession of the mighty king and who would be able to fill his shoes, his place in my life?

We made love often. I say 'made love' for that is what it was. There was no sense of being possessed at those times, it was all the rest of the time I felt like a possession, a china doll being paraded around the court on the arm of the mighty man or left in my rooms with my ladies to stitch and embroider and be 'useful' whilst I waited for that happening which we both wanted so much, the missing flux one month and the next to confirm the pregnancy he needed.

We made love for there was love between us, incredible tenderness, amazing softness, a completely different side and aspect to the man who was ever changing, ever himself and yet revealing new things all the time. I never spoke of this to anyone, I never spoke of it until now when the words want to spill onto the brightness of the screen and I can see what I am saying instantly translated into modern English through a modern channel with deep links to the past. Both of us. I find this exciting and liberating at the same time. I am being released from all that has held me back. But enough for now – it is Henry we are speaking of, the centre of our lives.

In that deep passionate love making and tenderness I conceived his child.

And I said to the Lord God that if He let me survive the ordeal of childbirth, that I would allow all the love within me to wrap around our child and let him know he was loved, for as the son of the king all would be ready to use him, not love him. I asked the Virgin Mary the same thing, she who gave birth to a son and found that many were ready to use him and not love him. Did I not know this well from my reading? My prayers were more fervent than ever, even as Henry boasted to the known world that he had another child to come, one that would be the son he so wanted. His mind was made up. I had another fear to add to the ones already there, for if I produced another girl, what would he do? Where would I be after the unfortunate birth? Both I and my child? You see how fears beset me the whole time, I could not escape them. I could not take the joy from Henry for he was growing bigger in stature all the time, this new pregnancy sealing the happiness he seemed to find with me.

My pregnancy went well, I swelled up enough that all could see and be praising of my fecundity and of Henry's great tender affection toward me. I shut myself away from all whenever I could so that I could rest and be tended and sleep when I needed so that the child could grow strong and I could bear the child without problems.

And as I did this, as I rested and slept and dreamed my dreams, I knew that my happiness in being with child would have been greater and more fulfilling had it been with a man of my choice, not the one thrust upon me as husband, despite that man being the king of England and of many domains. The king of all, the head of the new Church of England and how proud he was of his new status! It was mentioned to every diplomat who came to court, to every visitor, to all the courtiers as if they did not know of his new position. His treatise had been printed and given to all, validation of his stance to divorce England from the Papacy and create its own church. For Henry it was not just a divorce from Katherine so he could marry Anne Boleyn, he had by then been tired of the bonds which held England to the Roman Church anyway and he was delighted to have been given a chance, a perfect God-sent opportunity, to make the break. He did not know that was what he desired until the proposition was put before him. This much he did talk with me in our hours of wandering the gardens and eating fruits and sweetmeats together on benches set for us to rest on as we walked. It was as much for me as for him, for if he had been busy with hunting or jousting or sports of some kind all day, he needed to rest. He could not accept each day aged him a little. He needed to prove himself all the time.

When we sat, all were forbidden to encroach on the space around us so his gentlemen huddled in clusters, as bright as the flowers themselves, eyeing us with suspicion for fear that we might be discussing them and their downfall at court, just as the Boleyns were being quietly dropped from the courtly society.

My ladies clustered together, also as bright as flowers, and giggled and gossiped and looked at Henry's gentlemen and giggled some more which added to their paranoia. I did nothing to stop this: it was good that they had a sample of what I was enduring.

You can ask again, bitter? Definitely.

In that time, that wonderful time of pregnancy and closeness with Henry I grew to accept and be more than passing fond of my husband. There were great depths to him; his knowledge was substantial on every subject you could think of. He understood the heavens, the movements of the stars and planets, he understood deep philosophy, he spoke in the language of the visitors to the English court; he argued in Latin with those from Rome and confounded them with his arguments.

In that companionable state I was loathe to leave his side and go into my confinement. I did not wish to be shut away from the world for the world had just begun to look passing fair to me in every way. I wanted to watch the season change from Summer to Autumn, to watch the fair colours fading and the new bright ones come to celebrate the coming of Winter, to watch the leaves change and drop and carpet the grounds of our homes. I wanted - but society forbade this and I went to my chambers with my ladies. nurses and a physician to attend to my every need.

Do you wish the details of my confinement and birth? But of course. Everyone does for none were allowed in at that time to tell the world. I swelled up so large the physician for a time thought I had more than one child in my womb. God forefend that it be so but it would have resolved the problems for Henry had they both been males, would it not? But no, there was only the heartbeat which I felt for myself and the movement which I endured for myself of one child eager to be free of the confines of my body.

It was not the place for a man, in the birthing chamber, I know not who was more ill at ease, the midwives, or so they called themselves, or the man himself but Henry ordered him there and ordered me to have him there for another verdict, another knowledgeable person at the royal birth. Such was the longing he had for a child that would endure, the son that he craved. How did he know, I wonder, that this was his longed for son? I know not, I only know he was confident of his heir from the moment I told him I was bearing his child.

The last days of September dragged themselves through the world turning, somehow, utter boredom made them seem like a year on, not a few weeks. It was hard to walk, difficult to rest, sleep was impossible and I longed for Henry's arms and caresses. I heard tell that he was busy with court matters, with telling everyone who would listen that his son and heir was about to be born. I wished, oh how I wished he was right. We stitched and embroidered, we created scented oils; we did everything we could to pass the time and still it moved on leaden feet.

October arrived and I knew the time was close. For a while all movement stopped, the child still, waiting its time to make its entry into this favoured world, for there was nothing this child could need or ask for that would not have been instantly given or procured somehow. I grew weary of the same faces, of not being able to walk properly, of not appreciating meals or mead for it all tasted of ashes and dust, no matter what it was.

When everything began, I cared not who was in the chamber with me, only that they would end the torment. Everyone went into action, fussing me and ordering me to do this and that. I ignored all of it. I needed to walk, to pace the floor, to ease the pain and they wanted me to be still.

This went on for a day and some of a night, during which the child kicked and fought, turned so that I knew not which way it was, then it went still and seemed to drop so I could scarce walk the floor of the confinement chamber. I burned with fever most of that time, they bathed me with cold water and salts and herbs were burned in the room to help me to breathe for I fought and fought for my breath time and again. It got that I could scarce move for the size of my stomach and I was afeared I would die before the child came. Part of me could not have cared if I had, the other part of me wanted to know the child was the longed for son before I passed on.

I knew; somewhere deep in my heart, that the nightmare was right and lying with the King would be the death of me. If I could but produce the heir he so wanted, I felt my time would not have been wasted at all. I did not wish for Henry to have wasted his affections on me in having no result, no heir.

When the labour began fully I thought I would die. Again. I thought it so often it was a merciful release when it actually happened and I could at last be myself, albeit not in my body any more.

The pain was immense. First came the torrent of water, the reason for the swelling. It gushed forth, tinged with red and frightened the midwives and physician standing by. The child, for all his willingness to leave me, did not seemingly want to leave when the time came. Waves of pain shuddered through me, leaving my throat raw with screaming and all my nails were broken from grasping so tightly the birthing rope which I had asked for. It went on and it went on. Hours turned into days and nights, I know not how long it was but it was a long, long time.

And then, when I thought I could not endure another stab of pain, my son began to come into the world. And became stuck. I could feel him, feel the pressure tearing at my insides, feel flesh giving way as he thrust against me.

I heard the voices, the arguments, *pull at the child, no, it will damage his head, then cut her, release the child, cut, don't cut, what if, pull, dare not, the King said —*

Then a noxious potion was poured into my mouth, to help the pain, they said, and even as they poured so they cut and I screamed enough for all of them to cover their ears. They cut me in that most tender of places and the pain was more than any human could stand, surely.

And he slid from my body. I heard the voices: *'A boy! A healthy boy! God be praised!'*

The fever flared within me. I was burning; every part of me was burning.

They handed me a tiny child to hold, all blood covered and crying loudly. He looked ugly, he looked inhuman but he was alive, he was lusty, he was – mine. This tiny body I held in my arms was the boy child my husband needed. This was our son. In that moment I would have given Henry everything he asked, knowing I had given him everything he asked.

It was only when I gave him over to the midwives and nurses to wash and tend to him and the runner had gone to tell my husband the king of his newborn son, that I realised I was still in immense and all consuming pain. That there was a flow that the physician and others were desperately trying to stem and I knew that my life blood was pouring out of me.

Somehow they stopped it, somehow they bandaged up the massive cuts which they said were the child tearing his way out of my body but which I knew was caused by their knives for the child was struggling to leave me and needed assistance. That assistance was given – by cutting me open to let him come out.

When Henry came, bearing gifts and bright smiles, his joy was obvious and overwhelming but equally his shock at seeing me so pale and lifeless was also overwhelming. He told me to get well soon, that our son, to be named Edward, was to be christened and that I was not to worry about anything ever again.

Never was a truer word spoken. I began to decline from that moment on, the moment my husband the king left my chamber and the helpless people standing around watching me die.

I lasted twelve days.

I think on this each Christmastide, when the courts at that time celebrated the Twelve Days of Christmas with foolery and food, with gifts and gaiety.

For each of the twelve days I survived I received a gift from Henry and he visited when he could, bringing his undying love and worry that I would not survive. I think he knew as well as I that I was not going to be his queen for many more days.

I was haunted during those days, haunted as no person has surely been. That Woman stood at the end of the bed and taunted me. 'Did I not say so?' was her constant refrain. I knew she was unreal, no one else saw her, the nurses walked through her; Henry ignored her. But she was real to me if no one else. I knew she had been right all along, that I should have heeded the warning of the nightmare but then, the angel told me I had to go back, that it was my destiny.

I saw long dead family members come and visit and commiserate with me, I saw tiny malformed babies which I knew were Katherine's offspring and I wondered if she knew they had survived into the other realm, the one I was sliding toward at a steady rate.

I saw Henry's father who smiled a death's head smile at me and beckoned even as he turned and walked away.

And I watched Henry go from elation of his son to deep despair as I deteriorated. I saw the joy fade from his face, saw his great shoulders slump, saw the weight he carried. I heard his booming voice before he reached me and I knew the effort he made to come, for he hated with a violent all pervasive hatred anything that was to do with sickness of any kind. It was truly abhorrent to him and yet he braved the sickroom that was my dying place over and over again. He came to croon over his son, to hold him, to give me his thanks, heartfelt thanks, for giving him the heir he so longed for.

If I did nothing else for this great king, I gave him a son to show to the world that he could produce an heir after all.

It could not last, the fever burned me day and night and the flesh I had left fell from my bones as if I had the cancer. At last it was done and before Henry could reach me one last time, I was gone.

I watched the court go into deep mourning when I finally died, racked with fever and pain. I know what killed me but none recognised it or if they did, they said naught about it to anyone outside my chamber. They cut me too much to let the child be born, they were not surgeons; they were physicians and nurses. Did they have orders from Henry that the child came before me? I will never know these things. I do know that Henry sorrowed deeply over my death which surprised me. I knew he loved me but not the depths of that love.

I think it right to say that Henry VIII was a man who loved deeply when he found the right person to love. I know he arranged a fair and beautiful funeral for me, as if in compensation for the coronation I never had. I know too he asked to be buried next to me.

I know too my son did not survive into old age as I hoped, but I did all I could, I gave my all to the man I did not want to marry, not want to lie with, not want to be with, but in the end found I could love him after all.

I know too that was not a nightmare I had about the Boleyn woman, but a prophesy. I would wish sometimes I had been given the strength walk away from the wishes of my family, leave court and allow Henry to fasten his affections, attentions and desires on another woman. But then, my son would not have been born and given him so much happiness. But then again, another woman might have given him a whole tribe of boys. I cannot say what is right and what isn't any more. I only know what happened was sad beyond belief. I was only 29 when I died, leaving Henry young enough to have fathered more children if he had found the right queen.

Could I go down in history as the one he loved most? I think not. I think the burial alongside me was a thank you for his son more than his love for me, although I would like to think it were so. Even now vanity can touch us, it would seem.

Let me go back to the start now and reiterate: I did not wish that it were so. I did not wish it in any way. But having no choice in the matter, the king having spoken, I did follow strictly the words of my motto 'bound to obey and serve.'

In that I find relief and easement for my mind.

The most treasured memories

The first time I saw him, head and shoulders above everyone, watching everyone, assessing them. I was in awe of him and thrilled to be there.

Walking in the gardens together, he so large to my slenderness, feeling protected.

Nights together, as long as he could give me before his other interests called, the tenderness, the joy he showed.

Henry's face when he held his son. It cannot be described.

His loving kindness when I was dying, to venture into the sickroom and be with me.

Some things can never be forgotten.

Expressing Henry in one word: Smothering

Ten questions about Henry:

His favourite colour: blue
His favourite sport: hawking
His favourite animal: hawks
His favourite interest: astronomy
His favourite meal: pork with apple sauce
His favourite sweet: medlars in syrup
His favourite time of year: Autumn
His favourite home: Grenewich
His favourite gem: emerald
His favourite musical instrument: lyre

Anne of Cleves

Henry's wives, divorced, beheaded, died, divorced, beheaded, survived

Henry's fourth queen put aside (divorced)

So thrilled I am to be asked to contribute to this book. I am the 'overlooked' queen in many ways and yet… and yet… Henry confided in me occasionally, treated me like a close friend; was welcome in my homes. But in a book on the queens of this great king by other writers, my pages are very slender indeed. Then comes the invitation to be part of this book and a chance to be equal with the others – a great thrill indeed.

Where do I begin?

I lived a quiet if rich and comfortable life at home. I had, of course, heard of the great king of England, one who stood head and shoulders above all others, one who conquered every problem, every obstacle that came his way. I heard of his break from Rome to marry his One True Love, or so the story went. I did not know whether it was true or not, but oh, for someone who sought to love and who could not just go and find love where she wished, such a story was beautiful to the heart and to the mind. I thought often of the sacrifice he made to win his love, to confront and overcome the power of the Vatican and to appoint himself head of the church of his country. I admired him long before I met him.

In truth, and there is no place in this book for anything other than truth, I never thought to meet him, let alone be his queen. Such things were beyond my dreams, never entered my mind. In normal life such things do not happen, do they? Not to one such as I, a woman no one had heard of in the English court.

Then I heard how he tired of his One True Love and she was beheaded. I mourned her for I believed she loved him and I believed he loved her but oh the stories which came through letters, envoys and messengers sent from other regions, to make sure we knew what the king of England was doing, were mixed.

We all feared him, in a way. He was so powerful, so overwhelming; so rich beyond our wildest dreams that we knew he could do anything he wanted – and would, too, should the desire take him.

And then we heard of his new love, the quiet beautiful Jane who bore him a son and who died in doing so.

Ah, what heartbreak is there in that? We all knew of the burning passion of the king for a son and heir to carry on the Tudor dynasty, for surely that is what it was. Am I not right?

From the moment she was laid in her grave we - those of us in our small ineffectual court far from England – wondered who he would marry next. We were intrigued, we were interested, we had little else to gossip about and so we gossiped about the great king who was said to be a giant among men, of handsome visage, of slender well-muscled body, a man who excelled at everything from hunting to jousts and sports of all kinds, one who knew hawks better than the raptors knew themselves, one who outrode all others, one who – was simply the most excellent of men in every way, knowledgeable, intelligent, caring – could we believe otherwise? We had no way of knowing the stories be right or not. When you are starved of interesting facts, fiction will do just as well. Or so I found when the days seemed long and no marriage seemed to be forthcoming for me, so I could have my own home and my own domain and my own children.

You must imagine then the excitement when news came there were negotiations going on for me to meet and possibly marry this king. I cannot begin to tell you how it affected me, the sleepless nights, the worrying days – to be chosen and then turned down before it happened would be devastating to me – the panic that I would not be good enough a consort, that he would not find me attractive enough in every way to make a success of the marriage… imagine then how I felt when artists came to draw my portrait for him! Terrified. I knew I was not pretty, did not have the beauty of the Spanish queen, for she was dark and exotic in her foreign way and he loved her for many years and then the beautiful Anne Boleyn who had her own foreign ways brought from the Continent into the English court and I… I had my German background and little education in the ways of pleasing a man, whether he be peasant or king. I was sick to my stomach with worry and excited at the same time. What if it happened? What then?

How then did I think of and imagine Henry? As a masterful all-knowing king, who had a kingdom to rule and needed a consort at his side.

How then did I really think of myself? I did not see I was the right person for I lived a quiet life and had little interest in the wider world and to work alongside Henry would mean knowledge of the wider world.

But who was I to question the King's judgment in these matters? If I was chosen, I would not say no. No one would. No one would dare to say no to the great king.

I was truly in a state of absolute panic and delight at the same time when he said 'yes' to me.

Then the doubts came in like a storm all over again. I was not pretty, I was not lively, I did not dance well, I did not converse easily, I knew little to nothing about politics – and then my final worry, the big final worry was that if this did not work out, what would happen to me? Would I find myself exiled to some distant place or some charges be brought to end my life?

The delight turned to tears, floods of them. My family besought me to cease such things or I would wreck what looks I had left and then what would Henry think of me?

I tried to stop crying but I could do nothing about the lack of sleep which robbed me of energy and enthusiasm for anything, even marriage to a king.

It was about then I realised how long Henry had been without a queen. Nearly two years. Nearly two years of endless negotiations, of sending artists to paint pictures and convey them back to him, all this took so long, travel being so difficult from country to country. It did occur to me, one lonely night when sleep defied me yet again and I tried to envision myself in another country, speaking another language, with other ladies to attend me and a king as my husband –all this seemed beyond being, it could not be, it was too fantastic, like a fairy tale all of its own – I wondered why I had seen no portrait of my husband-to-be and wondered if he had aged much or at all during that time of waiting. What had grief and mourning done to him, if anything, what had time without a queen done to change his personality, if it had? What new advisors did he have who may not have agreed with his choice and would turn against me when I arrived in England?

I longed for a portrait for myself but did not dare ask, I had no right to ask and so I had no idea of the way he looked at that time. I tell you this because it is important, it is the key to why – as my channel puts it to me – it all went horribly wrong from the start. When I look at it through her logical eyes, it all makes sense.

Back then, all those many years ago, when I was so excited and so worried and panicking inside about my future, all I could think of was the man I was told about, the Golden Prince, he who conquered Europe and Rome and was ready to take on the rest of the world by himself, the king who did not need an army to succeed but who had one at his command anyway. The king who lived in absolute luxury, who had palaces he journeyed to all the time, his many favourites, the great stately homes he visited when on one of his Progresses around the country – all these things I longed to see, to share in. I wondered how many beautiful dresses I would have so I would look the way he wanted a queen, his queen, to look. I wondered what jewels he would give me. I wondered how much he would share with me of his day to day council meetings. I wondered and I had no answers, for there was no person who knew the answers to give me. I had to wait and the waiting was difficult. I think I was more than half in love with Henry before I even left Cleves.

The journey was endless, the weather endless in its badness. I longed for calm, for rest, but we pushed on day after day until we reached the coast and there we stayed, to await the weather changing so we could cross to the strange new land – for me – of England and the strange new man awaiting me – Henry VIII, king of the new land. At this time I felt sick to my stomach, not from travelling, although that wearied me more than I thought possible but from worry.

My escort, my attendants, sought to teach me card games; they told me my husband to be loved to play. I could not comprehend the marks on the cards; they made no sense to me. I tried to learn to dance but the music, although charming, meant nothing to me. I could not lose myself in the rhythms. I was too stiff, too ungiving. I began to despair of being the queen Henry would want, despair of being the ideal replacement for the queen he lost so tragically in childbirth.

I also had to consider the son he now had, would the child accept me; could I accept the child? Would I be able to bear the sons he needed and wanted?

So many questions, so many answers lacking. I asked them, no one answered. In the long empty dark nights I prayed for help and had no answers. Surely God had not forsaken me, surely He had guided the king's advisers when they finally drew up the papers for us to be married, why then did He not help me with this time of indecision and desperate loneliness, for who was there to comfort me in my time of worry? My husband-to-be had his country to rule and his advisers had to be there with him.

I asked myself if the advisers were there with me, would they give me the answers I sought, the truth, or would they give me answers that they thought I would like to hear, that I would fit well into the king's life, that he would like me, that he would grow to love me and we would have many children together… of such things are empty fantasies made and I did not want that, I wanted truth and none were there to give it to me.

And so the thoughts went around and around and so the nights grew longer and the days more empty and worrisome until we were on board that ship and finally setting sail for England. Where all questions would be answered and all doubts settled and all would be good.

At least, that was my prayer, one that I spoke over and over until I grew mad with myself for keeping on.

At last there was England, the great soaring cliffs, the raging waves, the grey clouds everyone told me would be there. It mattered not; there would be sunshine when I became Henry's queen, when I brought sunshine into his life. Poor dear man, left a widower and no one to console him, unless he sought solace in the arms of willing women in his court, but then they were not permanent, were they? I wanted to be permanent.

When then did this change come about? I went from doubts to certainty and back to doubts through needing answers and then back to certainty and wondered whether every bride-to-be, I understand that to be the right term, yes? goes through the same torments as I. Not all brides had the difficulties I faced, though, not knowing English, not knowing the man I was to marry, not knowing the English court and the English ways and whether I would be attractive enough to capture the king's interest and attention…

So I say I was certain but in truth the doubts clustered around that certainty and spoiled it, over and over. I walked and talked and sat and was quiet and at prayer with the same sickness of the stomach I had from the moment this marriage was proposed and I agreed to it. As if there was a choice, as if I had courtiers and husbands-to-be awaiting me on every corner and in every room of Cleves!

Be aware, those who read this, that being so sick to the stomach is a bad thing. I lost weight, it fell from me, no matter how much I tried to consume, heavy thick stews, thick breads, meats; nothing worked. I was not physically sick but the churning of the nerves in the stomach prevailed upon whatever turned food into fat not to work. I grew thin and my flesh sagged. I worried about that too, I may not be appealing to my new husband.

So, as the great cliffs of England came into sight, so my nerves almost broke. I almost demanded to be returned to France and thence to home, away from all that sickened me. Away from all my worries, my fears and my loneliness. I have not mentioned this so far, but being away from my home, from all that is familiar, all that is comforting, to be conveyed to a coast that is so far from all I know, to be kept there until the weather permitted a sailing made it even worse. I longed for home, for familiarity, for comfort and there was none to be found. The tears were bitter indeed at times.

But arriving in England, being welcomed by dignitaries, saluted and waved to by English people who had been forewarned of my arrival, I found myself beginning to look forward to my new life. I liked the villages and towns we passed through, the stone and thatch made them look cosy, is that the right word? I still struggle at times. Inviting is one word I wanted to use for them. The doorways were small, the windows sparkled in the sun, they looked as if you could disappear inside and shut the door against the wind and rain and never be worried about a thing. Foolish me, of course the peasants had many worries, landlords, droughts, storms and disease but I am giving you impressions, not facts. They are cold and uninviting, do you not think?

The towns impressed me, their huge gates, their flat roads, their many stalls where food and other items could be bought, I thought this a good country and longed to tell everyone I am happy I am going to be your Queen. Even the results – unfortunate as they were – of eating some meat which was not as good as it should have been did not dissuade me from thinking all was good. My ladies travelling with me were not so prepared to be forgiving, they ranted against those who did not cook the meat sufficiently, for they too suffered from the same unfortunate malady. I told them, it is something you have to live with. This is not a time of plenty; I saw under-nourished cattle which did not show the silken hides of those I had left behind in my native land.

And finally we came to the palace where I would meet with my future husband. My nerves were fluttering like drunken butterflies for ages, to the point when I did not need rancid undercooked meat to upset my stomach and cause yet more unfortunate problems for me.

***

At last, free of travelling, free of ships and weather and muddied roads and many, many obstacles, I found myself in a lovely building where I waited impatiently and anxiously for my new husband.

Here is the truth of that time, with my feelings and I know Henry's too, for we talked about this in later times when we were together.

The window looked onto a huge courtyard where bull-baiting was going on. I disliked the sport but was fascinated by the movements of the men and the way the bull treated them, how it responded to them when I suddenly realised there were five hooded cloaked men in the room. They took me by surprise but remembering manners were strict at court, I made obeisance to them. Then one approached me with a token I did not immediately perceive as coming from the king. This person tried to kiss me and I pulled away, for I was bidden to His Majesty and none other. There were shouts and a scream from the courtyard so I turned hastily to the window to see what had happened. When I looked back, in that moment all five had gone and I wondered if I had imagined them. There was nothing in the room to say there had been people there at all and I believed I was overtired and anxious and inventing things.

Then the door opened and His Majesty was there. I was shocked at his appearance; no portrait had shown his great weight and girth, the difficulty he had walking because of his heaviness, the shortness of breath that came with this huge weight. A portrait could only show me his face and then I realised, with even more shock, that the person who had approached me with the token was His Majesty and I had rejected him.

Now what was I to do? Admit I knew who it was or pretend innocence and make him think I awaited him only? An instant decision for he was standing waiting. I

161

made obeisance to him and said I was delighted to be in his company at last, for it had been an arduous journey but now we were well met all that was of no consequence and he was as handsome and majestic as his portrait showed.

I could see by the smile and the look that the words were well received but my heart had turned to ice. I was going to say stone but that would have been false. I grew to love this huge arrogant demanding authoritative and kingly man over time so 'stone' would be wrong. But ice, yes, it turned to ice for the love I carried had been crushed under the weight of the huge man who approached me.

We sat for some time talking of inconsequential things, of my journey, of the court I had left behind, of the court I would find here in England, of the bad weather which had rendered the roads all but impassable… it was friendly but lacking in the attraction I hoped to find, Henry to me and, I was very well aware, me to Henry. He looked at me with a total lack of what I can only call fancy, he did not find me attractive; he was not drawn to me in that way. I in turn found it difficult to equate the huge man who sat with such difficulty because his legs were so large and his belly so big, with the stalwart figure painted by Hans Holbein, who had made him look like a king. To me he did not look like a king, but he acted like one. He was imperious, he was arrogant, he was demanding and his courtiers ran to do his every bidding, no matter how small, how trivial.

I feared for the future of our marriage. I could not see that we would be a loving and comfortable and companionable couple and that saddened me. For even though I did not find myself drawn to him, I knew I could like him very much and that liking would be enough for me to be a good Queen Consort for him.

When we had sat for a time, I sensed his impatience and knew our meeting was drawing to a close. I hoped to see him again that evening but he did not appear. Only later did I hear of his ranting to Cromwell of my looks and my inability to be what he wanted and Cromwell's inability to answer his king. Both of us had relied on portraits and they do not disclose the whole person, do they?

You want my thoughts on the person I saw, above that already given, I am sure of that.

I could see amidst the rolls of flesh that once there had been a handsome man, but he had allowed his inactivity, which I knew well of, to feed his body and not exercise it and so he had grown massively large. That repelled me in many ways. It showed an indulgence and lack of willpower to control his eating and make himself get some form of exercise.

I could sense under his friendly informal talk with me that he was not excited by me in any way and I wondered if my bitter disappointment showed in any way. I tried not to let it, but it hurt deeply and I wondered how I would not cry myself to sleep that night. Eventually I did just that.

I found his mind to be sharp, full of intuition and knowledge and wondered if we spent time together how much I could learn from him and whether I had anything to offer in return, other than the history and geography of Cleves, which might not be of any interest to him. I had no skills to match his, this master of all sports, playing or judging, this composer of music, this expert on astronomy and many alchemic subjects. This expert on all things religious, books, papers from the Vatican, I heard of the hours he spent studying and knew I could not even begin to bring anything to the marriage that he would need.

I wondered if there would be a marriage.

I watched this lumbering bear of a man struggle to his feet with the age of a stick and call for assistance to leave the room. I watched and wondered if I could cope with that body in a bed, knowing I had no experience of men or real knowledge of what they wanted of a woman, let alone one as experienced as this king. The worst thing was; there was no one to ask. What shame would there be in asking what happened in a marriage bed and how to cope with it! Much, much shame. I see now your historians take all that was written at the time I lived and pick over it like old women at the well drawing water and chattering their gossip gathered up during the day. Every word I was supposed to have said, every word my king was supposed to have said, translated to vellum by – those who had a bias, a reason to like or dislike the king or even me. So, can their words be trusted? I think not but who am I but a lonely spirit seeking to get her words before the world so the world can know how I felt back then, when life was different and kings were supreme and none dare broach any subject for fear of losing their life?

At that point I was consumed with utter despair, intense loneliness and a burning desire to pack everything and return to Cleves immediately. Only pride stopped me.

That pride turned my thoughts. I stared into a tiny bronze mirror, saw my face, saw it was not a beauty, oh I had heard the words my king had said about me and they hurt, they hurt more than the loneliness and despair, if I am to tell you the truth and why not? I am but a woman, I was but a woman and would anyone not be hurt by such comments? I knew him for a cruel man, something told me of this but that level of cruelty was beyond my comprehension.

I am using words here that I did not really know I knew, if you understand that. should I use any wrongly, I beg forgiveness from the reader. I am doing my best. I did learn a lot of English during my years in your country, and have learned more since being in the Realms and watching this channel develop her skills, hoping but never being sure in my heart that I would be given this chance.

Let me return to my thoughts. I looked at my face, knew myself not to be beautiful but thought I might be considered passing fair and did this great king really only seek looks and not companionship, not conversation, not sharing of kingly duties and diplomatic problems? I knew nothing of his way of running the country, for no one had enlightened me on this point. Nor should they, it was for the king to share with me when he was ready or thought I was ready.

I thought I was good enough to be his queen. I did not know then what I learned later, that he was already looking for a way to break the contract of marriage.

Would I have been returned to Cleves in shame and ignominy?

We were married, I think because Henry had no way of getting out of the arrangement without considerable loss of face and, knowing this proud - dare I say arrogant - man, that would not do, he would not live with that. So we had a private ceremony, joyless, I would say colourless but Henry was never dull in dress. He was resplendent in his multitude of jewels and fine clothes, his feathered hat, his decorated boots –I think he wore boots; it could have been jewelled shoes of some kind. I wore dark red, I thought it appropriate. I took no comfort from the service, which I hardly understood. The signs, yes, the movements, yes, the words went over me. The Latin spoken in England had a different intonation, a different accent, than that I was used to and it meant nothing to me. I just knew I was married and was a real queen.

It meant nothing.

After so many weeks, months even of imagining this moment, of seeing myself by Henry's side, seeing myself as his helpmeet, I knew the truth – it was empty and there would be no true marriage for me.

The celebrations went on for some time. In the intricate celebrations, the dances, the music, the songs, none of which I understood but could allow it to go over me and into me, I could, for a time, forget where I was, until I saw the bland face my new husband turned on me, saw the curious faces of the courtiers and gentlemen who surrounded him, watched how they watched me, my every move, my every look and knew that I would have to guard myself well.

I realise that this so far has been about me and not about Henry, but I knew nothing of him at that point. I knew only of his reputation and the way he was with me – indifferent, which leaves me very little to speak of. My knowing of this great man came later, when we spent time together and talked freely, or as freely as he ever did speak with anyone. I do swear that man contained more secrets than any archive of the Vatican. He absorbed information and stored it in some compartment of his mind, there to hold it until he needed it or he thought he might need it at some time. I have never known anyone with such a capacity to absorb and retain and re-circulate information as His Majesty did. It was impressive and that is putting it very mildly indeed. There was no topic on which he could not speak at length and with authority and never, for a moment, with boredom in his voice or in the faces of those who listened. There was no topic on which he did not wish to learn more, explore further, read about, understand and practice and make part of his everyday life.

This is one reason why I for one cannot speak at length about the two of us together, for he was ever busy with this or that, with a diplomat or envoy, with books or astronomy or alchemy or parliament matters – he never missed a single word spoken around him in relation to parliament. He confounded many a member at times by reciting back to them the very words they uttered during a meeting. This I saw for myself on my visits later on to whichever great home he was occupying at any time. Ever busy. His hands were never still. He wrote, he played his harp and composed short pieces of melody which were enchanting to the ear.

Then there were the sports, oh the endless sports at which he excelled. Yes, the other queens have spoken of this and I will too, for the sports in which he could no longer take part gave way to others that he could. He could still ride, he could still hunt, he could still go hawking, among many other interests. Bowls could still be played, and none gave him quarter despite his disability to walk very far or very quickly, and still he outplayed them all. The smile of victory was as ready and as genuine as any I had ever seen.

I have not said to my channel that I am procrastinating but I know I am. This morn we were writing without music. I have asked for and received the background of tranquil medieval music, much of it composed by the king himself.

For we must now step beyond the bedroom door; we have stood in the hall too long and discussed the weather, the abilities, the reactions, now we must make the effort to move inside and discuss that which matters, that which is at the heart of this part of a Kiss and Tell book, the part which will throw history out of the window. My channel is used to this, it comes as no surprise to her that there are yet more secrets to be revealed.

The king came to me in a silken robe, with silk slippers on his not inconsiderable feet and a mass of gold rings on his fingers. His courtiers came with him but he dismissed them at the door and locked it behind them. He walked over to me, as stately as ever, as if he were in a great hall about to receive some envoy or visiting duke or earl, stately despite his bedwear. He wore that as casually and as elegantly as he did his heavily embroidered and jewelled day clothes.

"So we are truly alone, Anne." I cringed a little, thinking what a very coarse statement it was, or do I mean bland? Or do I mean uncaring? I did not know at that moment how I viewed his words, I was grateful he had come, but afraid of what would happen. I was unsure of myself and my abilities as a woman, even less sure of myself as Queen. I had no one to guide me on this, the courtiers spent their time being so polite it put my teeth on edge and I longed to slap them and say 'treat me like an equal, not an idiot!' Henry never spoke to me that way. With him it was always straight talking, which I preferred. But this night, our first together, I really did not know what he wanted, what he meant, what I was supposed to do. Oh for some guidance from another experienced woman!

"Truly we are, sire." What else could I say? I could not say I yearned for him, for that was as far from the truth as I was from my homeland.

"What think you of me?"

Then was I truly flustered and tongue-tied. In the name of Heaven, what did I say to that?

"You are a fine figure of a man, Sire," was all I could manage.

He looked impatient for a moment. Then the look passed and I saw resignation on his face instead.

Think you I disremember all this? The night is engraved in my memory as clearly as the moment we were married in the sight of God and the witnesses, the words we spoke echo in my mind even now. I have had many a long year in which to recall every word, every movement, every expression, even the texture of the air in the bedchamber: heavy, sultry, loaded with anticipation on his part, fear and uncertainty on mine.

Not a good combination no matter how you looked at it…

And before you ask, yes, he told me later how he anticipated a night in my bed, despite the fact my face did not accord with his desires for a queen.

'Ah, dear Anne, ever the diplomat, aren't you?" He sat on the bed then, and it tipped slightly in his direction because of his weight. He pulled himself up and looked at me.

"Methinks I offended you with my comment on your looks, Madam."

Now I really was in a quandary, what did I say to that?

The truth, was my first thought. I agreed. Henry hated waffle and admired straight talking.

"You did indeed, sire, but I remain here and I remain cheerful and pleased to be your wife and consort."

I recall the dark look which crossed his face at that moment and in that moment I knew I was afeared of this man. The man I had crossed the sea to come and be wedded to had put fear into my heart and mind and I knew too that I was not the only person to see this and wondered in my then troubled heart how many had seen that look and not lived to tell another about it.

Some questions do not need to be answered.

"So, as we are straight talking…" he shifted then on the edge of the bed and I realised he was disrobing and about to get into the bed with me. I was consumed with rigid terror for I had no idea what to do.

The huge mountain of a man/king threw the covers back, lowered his large body into the bed, pulled the covers back over himself and turned to me, with difficulty, for his weight was creating what felt like waves in the feather mattress on which we lay.

Let me start from the very beginning. I was wearing a nightgown of pure Flemish lace and silk, the better to make me look half attractive to him. He admired the gown, as well he should for it cost a goodly amount of money. He asked me to remove it and I did. Then he held the candle high so he could look at me. He touched my breasts, my stomach, my thighs and sighed.

"What think you of me, my new queen?"

"That you are a fine figure of a man, Sire."

I repeated it because that is what I thought he wanted to hear. I thought that was plain enough talking but he knew, ask me not how I knew this, that I was flattering rather than being truthful.

He gave a short barking laugh and I knew it was the wrong answer. Again. That he tolerated it the first time but not the second.

"Anne, for the sake of our marriage – such as it is – will you not be honest with me? What think you of me, my new queen?"

I took a deep breath, put my thoughts together as best I could, for the fear made me think strange thoughts, and answered him.

"I find you a large and somewhat heavy man, Sire, one who would not appeal to a woman without your fine clothes and jewels, but clothes do not make a man, any more than a crown makes a king. It is the man inside that matters and there I find a true king, one who rules by being himself, rather than being a puppet for the crown."

A hint of a smile. I had pleased my new husband but I knew, deep down inside, if we were to stay married, that would probably be the last time I would find the courage to say these things to him.

His response was to explore me even more, his hands were everywhere, or so it seemed. I recall thinking how smooth they were, how free of anything that would cause discomfort.

And still he made no move to embrace me, to begin the process of what I understood this whole marital thing to be about. So in return I began to explore and found what I dreaded; an indifference. I pulled away then and saw another smile, a more cynical one this time.

"Well, my queen, we have come to a pretty pass here, have we not?"

"Indeed, sire."

"You agree we find ourselves with desire missing from both of us?"

Could I answer this and not be insulting? But then, the king was wrong. "I have desire for you, sire, but I find it not reciprocated so may I suggest we spend this night in sleep instead? It has been a tiring day and I am sure sleep would be welcome."

This brought a genuine laugh, the first I had heard since we met. I welcomed it and I think Henry did, too.

"Tis a good thought, my queen, a good thought. We must then consider what we will do about this difficult situation."

"That, my liege lord, I will leave entirely in your hands." Submissive but firm, I thought. Henry said nothing else, just punched the pillow very hard and laid his large head on it. He seemed to be asleep in a very short time, while I laid awake all night, wondering how we could resolve this, rehearsing my speech of regret to my family when I returned to Cleves, no doubt to find some aged useless Count somewhere who needed a wife for nothing more than appearance's sake. By the time dawn touched the windows and the Gentlemen of the Bedchamber were there with silken robes, bowls of warm water to bathe his legs and give support and help for Henry to walk, my mind was in total chaos, my eyes hurt and my head ached abominably.

"I will speak with you later," he said, in a mild, friendly tone and I knew somehow he would make it right for me, one way or another.

Before the door closed on Henry and his courtiers, I heard him bellow for Cromwell. Henry wasted no time, not even the time given in going from one bedchamber to another, for he had to return to his own place for the day's clothes to be fitted to that large body.

Alone, I explored my feelings, instead of panicking about the future.

How did it feel to be rejected by a king known for his penchant for women?

Hurtful beyond bearing and yet – truth? You seek truth; that I know. Truth, then, I felt a tinge of relief.

Explore that feeling.

The court was bigger than I expected, even given the reputation of this amazingly powerful king. There were people everywhere all the time. Everyone, from his favourites, his courtiers down to the lowliest messenger boys, surrounded him. I had no experience of anything like that; it would have been a tremendous trial for me to keep my demeanour at a level he would appreciate, if not actually demand of me.

That many people meant that many names to learn - and their rank too. I was not used to this and would find it extremely difficult and complicated. Only those who had grown up in and around this great king could cope with the complexities of his court, his entourage, his life.

Relieved it was not for me?

Yes.

Tired? More tired than I had been in my entire life. I had spent the night hours worrying at the problem from all sides, nibbling at it like a mouse with food. I could see no way out. Henry did not desire me, therefore he could not bed me; therefore I could not be impregnated. I was but twenty five years of age, I could have borne him children. My body was regular, healthy, primed for child bearing, even though I was perhaps a little past my most fertile time. Still there were years ahead for procreation. If only.

I laid awake beside the sleeping mountain of the king, for lying down or standing he was of considerable bulk. I dared not move during the night hours, for fear of disturbing him, he seemed to sleep so deeply, himself hardly moving, only occasionally throwing an arm out and then withdrawing it under the coverlets again, for the night was chill.

I practised my words to my family when I finally reached my home again, knowing I would not say them, knowing that when I got there, my resolve would snap asunder and I would do nothing but cry. Tears flowed even as I thought this in the coldest deepest pits of the darkness. I longed to reach out, to touch, to hold, to find comfort at least in his arms for the fears which savaged me were sharp indeed and my heart was an empty pit of loneliness and despair, mixed with the deepest regrets that nothing had happened which I expected to happen, nothing had flared between us when we met. We were strangers greeting one another across a room, no more. Sharing this bed this night we were strangers, no more.

I was consoled and comforted by his words as he left.

My ladies came to dress and tend to me, trying to disguise my tear marks and sleepless night marks. It was not an easy job.

We confined ourselves to our allocated rooms for the day, not venturing out until summoned to feast at the table with the king later in the day. There again we were nothing but strangers.

I thought everything was considered closed, but the messenger boy approached me shyly and in stammering German said the king would visit me in my bedchamber again that night. I must have looked surprised for I saw Henry gesture to me and blow me a small secret kiss.

Was it that he had changed his mind about my looks, my body, or was there some other motive? I had learned already that he never did anything that did not further his reign, his interests, his well being.

One of my ladies nudged me discreetly and indicated the people further down the table, considerably further down the table. There sat a pretty girl with a mass of curls spilling from her stylised headdress and breasts spilling from her elaborate gown. She was staring at Henry with a look of total adoration.

But so young, I thought, so very young! Surely someone so young, so pretty would not be idolising this mountainous king, would she? Was it his aura of power which drew her, or the hope of a trinket of value if she showed her devotion to him?

In my musings I almost missed Henry speaking to me and hastily drew my attention back to the man to whom I was married. But I could not deny the sharpness of the jealousy that stabbed me through and through at the thought of all that youth adoring the man to whom I was married.

Youth I could not compete with.

Later I asked my ladies to find out who she was and they came back to me with the information. She was Kathryn Howard; her family were rich and powerful and held great estates and prestige in the land. And she was young, no more than about eighteen or nineteen years of age, ripe for plucking, I thought, but never said anything to my ladies. I trusted them, but only so far. In this land of contrary thinking, of difficult relationships, I dared not let anyone know my thoughts. For surely there was no relationship more difficult or contrary than the strange marriage in which I found myself.

I was treated by some as Queen Consort, by others as a visiting dignitary, and yet others managed to avoid calling me anything by clever wording or by simply not speaking to me at all. I was never comfortable whilst with Henry and those around him were never comfortable with me. They had heard Henry's comments and took them to heart. I was almost a non-Queen, if that were possible. At that particular time, a good many people were not speaking to me. It left me time to think, and in thinking, to give myself all sorts of worries.

After our meal, which I struggled with as I did not know what I was eating and that bothered me, the musicians struck up a lively tune and Henry beckoned to me to dance. For such a big man with such obviously painful legs, I had seen his face at times when he tried to walk, he danced remarkably well. It was as if he was determined not to let anything stop him being what he was, the supreme king. He still rode and hunted, hawked, attended endless meetings and danced with me as light as any courtier ever did. When the music ended I told him this and he seemed to become a little happier. He did not dance again, but sat in a huge chair and watched the rest of us cavorting. I had no choice but to sit by his side and watch the dancers and listen to my husband telling me who was who in his court. I wondered a good deal at this, for surely if we were not to continue as man and wife, and I had some other role to play, why did I need to know who these people were?

It was only later I realised how clever he was, for I needed to know these people who were a part of my life for the rest of my life, or at least a good many of them were, the ones responsible for my allowance, my homes, my small court. Because of Henry's thoughtfulness I was able to greet all of them correctly from the start. This put us on a better level with one another. Unlike Henry's other queens, I had a different part to play in his life. But we will get to that later. Before then…

As he had promised, Henry came to my bedchamber that night. He was wearing a different silken robe, one that was heavily embroidered with astrological signs. I commented on it and within the week a smaller version of it was delivered to my rooms. It was incredible. He never missed a comment anyone made, or anything anyone did. Ever. Us Queens saw this side of him,

Cromwell and others who were close to him saw it and the majority of the court did not. It is a given fact, judging by the books I have seen, that no historian has seen this side of him, or if they have, it has not been mentioned. It is as if they want to do no more than continue to promote the image of the tyrant king, killing all who crossed his path if they should as much as look at him the wrong way. I lay this on the novelists too, those who give themselves licence to draw what inferences they wish from the events written down, without looking beyond them to the person himself.

But I divert. I say that but the diversion was meant to be made, I had to make the statement. Too many people do not understand this great king, too many people are quick to make of him only what they know from your TV and films, and of course the novelists who dramatise everything and you are supposed to take it all as entertainment but in fact some take it as fact. It is this which has made us spirits anxious to give our stories to the world ourselves, so you can read the truth. Not as we see it, but the truth. If four of us already are saying the same thing, and possibly the other two will also say it, can you deny it is the truth?

I think not.

And Henry came to my bedchamber that night. He came with a different demeanour, more enthusiastic, more friendly, more at ease than he had been the night before or even during the meals we had taken together. He was more the king who had asked me to dance and had performed like the fittest courtier in his court. I was able to relax in his company for the first time. Not completely, I could not allow myself to do that, there were still many potholes in our journey toward getting to know one another. His German was good, better than my English and between us we made a good conversation.

And then he cast himself upon the bed, the robe fell open and to my complete surprise, the 'indifference' had turned to 'interest.'

And with sign language, for he did not dare commit himself to any words for fear of being overheard, I knew that without him saying a thing about it, he wished me to climb onto him and lower myself onto that 'interest.'

I had heard of this way of copulating but never having thought it through, why should I have done? I did not know what to expect. He was large, larger than I anticipated, for the 'indifference' had given me a false idea of his capabilities. He had foreseen this and took a small bottle of beautifully scented oil from a small bag attached to the girdle of his robe. Its perfume filled my bedchamber and eased my passage onto him.

To my surprise it was a pleasant experience. Everything touched, everything responded and I saw a smile of intense satisfaction cross Henry's face, before he resumed his usual bland expression the one which hid so much of his feelings.

To my surprise there was no pain, no blood. Henry explained that some women who ride lose their virginity and do not realise it. So there was no trace of what we had done when the women came to change the bedding in the morning and Henry could continue with his specially concocted story that he had no interest in me, that he had found me uninviting.

He left me shortly after that to pursue his study of the stars, for the moon was particularly dark that night and the stars shone clear in the blackness. None of them equalled the stars which had exploded in me in that moment of fulfilment.

We had exchanged no words. No one had overheard a thing. No one knew anything but what they were told, that Henry had tried again to consummate his marriage and again found himself incapable of doing so. That he would try one more night and then he would have to surrender himself to the fact that the marriage was not for him.

And so, none knew that the whole thing was repeated the next night and if any noticed the trace of scented oil in my room, I was to say we used it to try and arouse His Majesty but it did not work.

And after that third night, when no words were spoken, Henry handed me a small piece of vellum on which he had written:

My Queen.

Whilst I cannot profess to have found you to my liking, I wish to say you have given me pleasure I did not expect. From now on I will say the marriage is over, we will have an annulment and then can you live in richness and style in a home I will grant you in perpetuity here in England. I ask only for your discretion and silence.

Henricus Rex.

I destroyed it, shredding it into threads and crumbs and dropping them into the midden. The note said far more than the few words he offered, far more than the piece of vellum could contain or the time he had available to write to me.

I knew that Henry could not bed with a woman and not possess her. It was not in his nature. I knew that he did not care to have me for his Queen and, having lived in his court for a short time, I knew I would not be happy there, not ever. It was too busy, too secretive, too complicated and too emotionally fraught for one such as I. I was grateful for the chance to bow out of the marriage gracefully, without being returned home as a failed wife and Queen. Such a shame would not be good for my family or for me. This way we could make a show of an annulment on the grounds of His Majesty not finding me attractive enough for him and, knowing his reputation, this would stand well with his people.

For 'show', I think is how you say it, Henry came to my chamber some nights, got into bed, slept, got up and went his way. We never spoke. We never touched. We might as well have been in different rooms for all the notice he took of me. And how did I know this was all show, all to bolster the annulment? I know not, I just did. I took no pleasure in those nights, for knowing all was dead and there would be no loving or giving between us, I saw him as not just the great king, but a gross mountain of a man who had difficulty in rising from the bed ere morning came. I was sure to be covered to my nose when his gentlemen came to help him rise. I knew too that this was part of the show. It said 'look, I slept with this queen of mine' and nothing happened. It became a way of life but I was right glad when it ended.

I knew that Henry had a sneaking admiration for the way I had handled myself during the awkward time when he realised I had overheard his damaging and hurtful words. His gift to me, of a future home in England, was compensation enough for that. I would have money to live on; I would have status and security. Could any ex-Queen ask for more? The others three Queens had met a tragic end; I would at least be living and living in luxury at that.

I knew that Henry had caught the adoring glances of the provocative Kathryn Howard and I longed to warn her of his proclivities but decided against it. She would find out herself, the hard way. If she were fool enough to allow her family to cajole her into being in Henry's heart, arms and bed, then she had to take the consequences of that decision.

I had but one problem to resolve: I had tasted the joys of the bedchamber and wanted to do so again. I dared not invite a man into the home Henry would give me. There had to be another way.

There was, but it was some time before I could do anything about it.

So you know now that the annulment was false. Invalid. I was a true queen to Henry, a true wife, but Henry wanted me not.

And so my channel asks the big question, the one I sought to avoid but knew really in the heart I could not do so. For what is written is only half the story. And less than half the story, if I were to be truthful with myself.

My channel asks, Anne, how did you *really* feel about these things? How did you feel when Henry said those things? How did you feel when you were rejected? How did you feel about being used in the bedchamber in that way, and then dismissed with a curt note?

She is right to ask but – I wished to avoid to talk about these things.

But – what is my section of this incredible book if not the truth about all things, not just what happened but how I felt when it happened and how did I think Henry felt when it happened? I can only give glimpses of my husband's thoughts, for he concealed them well behind a face that had learned not to give anything away. Not a single thought could anyone read – unless he was in a temper and then the world, the whole world, knew it and the whole world ran from him until he was calm again.

I can tell you that when he had one of his bad heads and they were bad, believe me when I say that, no one wanted to go near him. His physician was the only person who could approach him at that time. My lord Brandon told me, in a rare moment of confidentiality, for he spoke little to me at any time, that the bad heads started after the jousting accident which laid him unconscious for so long. From that time on these bad heads would come upon him very suddenly. He would brush at his eyes as if he could not see clearly, his face would change, distort slightly, one eye would be half closed, the left one, and he would hold that side of his face and begin to walk to his chamber. Someone would shout for the physician, others would nudge one another and clear a path for Henry to walk, carefully, often with a courtier by his side but not touching him, for at these times he could not bear to be touched.

And we would not see him for some time, the rest of the day or night, whenever the attack began.

How did I feel when I knew of the words Henry spoke about me? As if every dream I had ever cherished had been smashed before my eyes. As if my heart was taken out of me and cut into pieces. It was a physical pain, not an emotional one. I know not, even now, if he intended me to hear it or not. There was a streak of cruelty running through the great king, this I knew without being told and, having seen the testimony of the other three queens; I know it to be true, for they experienced this cruelty during their lives, too. The other Anne was hurt so badly by Henry it is a wonder to me even now that she maintained her love for him.

In some ways I was fortunate, for at that time I was not truly in love with him. I was in love with the image Holbein painted, with the reputation that came with it, with the dream that sustained me through my journeying and difficult crossing, that I would be Queen of England. That it would be given to me as a right after all the papers had been signed and the agreement made with my family and myself that I would marry this great – and oft married – king and be his contented fourth Queen Consort. And it was all swept away with one comment. I doubt even after all these years that Henry would admit to intending me to hear the words. I doubt he would give me the courtesy of the truth. You only have to see how little space I took up in his book; it was as if he leapt from Jane Seymour and her son to the flesh of the provocative Kathryn Howard. And I ask myself, can I blame him for that? I was older, plainer, that I knew but thought I would be acceptable and accepted – and I was not.

I faced a blackness and bleakness that threatened to devour me. For some days I could barely eat but had to try because not to eat when the king is present is not considered good manners. I had a position to uphold, regardless of whether it was satisfactory or not. But the food sat within me, unwanted, undigested, causing pain and difficulties in turn. I was utterly bereft of hope, of any hint of happiness, of friendship for all had heard of the outburst and did not know how to treat me. My ladies were reticent, afraid of saying something out of place. I could not say to them 'tell me of your thoughts; do not hide your words from me!' for that would have embarrassed them and confused them and that would never have done any good for any of us.

And those nights.

Yes, I found pleasure, eventually and fleeting as it was. But the terror that gripped me, the knowledge that before he found my bed he found me wanting in every way did not inspire me or draw me to him. How could it? How could anyone commit themselves to a lifetime with someone who felt that way? I was a core of ice by then; the terror had transmuted itself into ice and black ice at that.

When he left my bedchamber the second night I knew the true meaning of 'used.'

These many years distant from that time have not dimmed my memory of the pain one bit. Not one tiny bit. I can and have and no doubt will – cried - cry many tears, many, many tears, over the memory alone. I bid you now, try and calculate how many tears I shed at the time it all happened, at the moment my bedroom door closed behind that impenetrable back, turned so coldly toward me after I had given pleasure. Turned so coldly and my knowing, oh how deeply I knew it too, that one day would come when it would be the last time we shared a bed. And so it was. From then on I slept alone, and did so until the day I laid – alone – in my coffin.

Ah, this night the music I bid my channel to play is deeply emotional, very, very sad and this is not the one which is titled as sad, heaven forbid she finds that to play, for this is difficult enough. But then, I ask, would it be possible to write of these acid bitter memories if the music were uplifting? Very likely not. I know I failed as a wife and queen, failed as a woman, failed as a lover – I need no music to remind me of this. I know I failed but I ask, what fault lies at my door? Henry chose me, Henry agreed to marry me, Henry took me to wife and then set me aside with what the world thought was his repugnance at my body. Now I tell the world that it was not entirely that… I suspect but cannot say for a surety that when he met me, I was not instantly smitten by overwhelming love and gratitude for being chosen. It did not help that I did not recognise him, it did not help that his first glance at me was not a favourable one and whilst that is not good English, I think you will know well what I am trying to say. For it was not his first impression but his first glance which brought the disappointment, and so I did not find favour from that first glimpse. That first glance. That moment when eyes meet across the room and it is favoured that people fall in love. Or so it is said that happened when he met Anne Boleyn for the first time. Mayhap it was. I cannot say.

What I can say is simply this, I did not find favour in the great King's eyes and mind but I did, and I swear on the most holy of all books set before me, that I gave the great King pleasure on at least two nights.

And I declare that our marriage was consummated and that the annulment was a lie.

I have waited these many hundreds of years to tell the truth. For I am tired beyond belief of being the 'forgotten' queen, the one about which 'not much is known' as it says on the screen. I know, I have seen it. How does that make me feel? As if I am nothing.

Nothing. And yet I am there in the history books as the fourth queen of the great King Henry VIII. I am there, I am part of history and yet history dismisses me as nothing. And so, given the chance I have here to speak of my husband, and so I thought of him for the years left to me on this earth you walk – and still do, in truth and this book is about truth, is it not?- I have to tell you that we consummated our marriage on two nights in succession. And then he rose from my bed and walked away and never returned. And the negotiations to annul the marriage started the very next day. I saw Henry and Cromwell in deep discussion and, though neither of them as much as glanced at me as I walked past with my ladies, they knew I was there and they knew I knew they spoke of me. It was in the tension they showed, the way they stood, the way they talked. I had not known Henry more than a few weeks and already I knew this about him… that he allowed nothing to get in the way of what he wanted.

And what he wanted was Kathryn Howard.

I could see it in all he did and how he looked when she was around and surprisingly, or not, she was around a lot. Were the dresses tugged a little lower around the bust, were the dances deliberately fast to show ankles, were the curls tossed a little too much at times? Were the smiles real or false, as false as the adoration she turned on this ageing overweight ever chronically out of mood king? Or was all that entirely in my jealous head? For I could not compete with youth, no one can when they move past that stage and age of being bursting with life, sexuality and fertility. The problem is… as far as I could see… Henry did not believe he was past the prime of his life. I could, just, cope with the sores on his legs, provided they were bandaged with herbs and salves before he came to me and even then the smell was at times more than I could stand – and he knew it. I saw the look on his face, the disdain, the thought unspoken, 'I am king. Why can you not tolerate that which is my body? So it is rotting, are we not all rotting away from the inside?' and so I did tolerate it as best I could, learning to control my expressions even as he controlled his. He rarely gave anything away and when he did, you knew you were either honoured or in danger of your life.

And so we entered a strange phase of our lives. I was 'invited' to eat at the king's table, my place being close to Henry, my ladies further down the table. We would talk, lightly, almost casually, of his latest compositions, of the proximity of this planet or star, of the finer ingredients of something for his sores, for no subject apart from the obvious ones which would offend was not touched upon at some time. I learned a lot... and grew increasingly aware and conscious of the vast gulf between us. This king, this husband, for he was such until the annulment went through, had a mind so far ranging there was no one in the court who could keep pace with him. He could and would discuss philosophy with this one, herbs with another, astronomy with another, religious tracts and text with a clergyman he had invited, music with one of his talented musicians but no one person could satisfy him in discussions and as there was no other person like him in England, I am prepared to say in Europe either, he had to surround himself with various persons to have discussions on all the interests he pursued daily, within his singular mind.

I could not come within any distance of this mind which seemed to me to fly above the palace roof and into the heavens, so in depth were his discussions and his reasoning.

And so once again I find myself defending him against the slander and libel that historians have written about him.

'That brute of a man' one Professor wrote, dismissing in that one sentence the greatest king England ever had or ever will. For he saw nothing, but nothing of the mind of the man and he could not, it seemed, allow that the five hundred or so years between then and now have changed your thinking to a state when you cannot seem to comprehend the majesty of His Majesty, you cannot understand or begin to even think like those of us who surrounded the king. For us he was virtually the equivalent of God on earth.

Too dramatic, you think? I think not. I know how we felt, I know how we acted, you cannot and you are unable to comprehend it for your minds are conditioned by the many years between us.

And I lived in a sort of limbo. I was Queen, the court accepted me as such, I was Queen Consort to His Majesty King Henry VIII but he had set me to one side and in many ways I had no status, no reason to be there, apart from the fact he had yet to sort out the many problems consequent upon attempting to obtain an annulment. I had to state several times what happened in my bedchamber, which I did with a face as still as Henry's, knowing I was lying and yet not lying, for he only referred to the first night when truthfully nothing happened between us. He persisted in the fiction, the myth that he found me wanting in many ways. I dispute this even now, for why then did he return for two nights of what was to me illicit pleasure, for I was not to speak of it?

And here I wish to divert slightly for a moment. I told my channel about this last night and whilst she did not ask me to put it in the book, I knew I must.

Before this book was commissioned, and there is no other way to put it, Henry visited his queens, one after the other, and told them of his idea for a book which would give his Katherine, his reincarnated first wife, a boost to help her with her channelled work. He also said it would give the historians much to mull over, for this had to be the truth and nothing more or less than the truth, no matter what contradictions it might make to the 'acknowledged' facts about our lives. Oh, the channel typed lies there, not lives. That is where this book is different from any others on the six wives of Henry VIII, for they are not written from what we know to be primary sources, us. From each of us you will have truth. Simple truth. This is what happened, this is the way he was; this is the way he is now, to some degree. I am pleased I learned enough English to be able to write this coherently for you!

Then Henry visited the channel and suggested a book in which the Queens got to talk about Henry. It was done in such a way that it was almost as if she had thought of it herself but she knew well she had not. So it was obvious the idea had come from Henry and at first she thought it was because of his ego, which truthfully was – and is - as large as the empire he ruled, that he was looking for compliments, for love statements, for anything to boost his spirits, if I may use that word for a spirit. It was not so. This was to be the truth, this is to be the truth, for so many lies – we come back to that word and we know well it was the right one – have been written about all of us over the years since the time we walked the earth plane and mingled with you on your side of life. Lies because every historian and novelist thinks they have *the* answer to the great conundrums: why did Henry have Anne Boleyn executed, why did Henry put me to one side, why did Henry… they think on this with their own closed minds and spill the result onto pages that a publisher deems fit to be seen by the world.

We realise one of the problems is a lack of mediums and channels who will not instantly say 'oh, this is all my imagination' when one of us approaches them. This one does not.

And so we come with our truths, ready to share them with you. We trust you will listen, read; take note. We are not some far distant long dead people, we live on. And we resent the lies told about us.

This is enough of a diversion for now. We must move on. The question is being asked:

Which Henry is the real one? Which Henry is the man I married?

Were there more than one 'Henry's in the court? Yes there were. There was the Henry who was all solicitude and caring and smothering to some degree, the one who made you feel as if you were the only person in the known world and he was talking to you at that moment. In that brief time you could almost forget how powerful he was, what control he exerted, what schemes he had set in motion and what knowledge he had acquired, mostly about you. That was one thing few people knew. He kept a dossier on vellum and in his head of every person, he knew their contacts, their background, their flaws, their hidden agendas and produced the information when he needed to. Some people got through their lives without ever being made aware of what Henry knew about them. They were the fortunate ones. Others crossed an invisible line and found that Henry knew them very well indeed. Some were fortunate to escape with their properties and wealth intact, others were fortunate to escape with their lives.

And what would cause these drastic events to happen, you are asking. I answer with one word.

Treason.

It was the one thing Henry would not and could not tolerate under any circumstances.

Should any of us be surprised at that? All kings and high ranking people in the Plantagenet, Tudor and Stuart periods lived with a dagger under the pillow, in a manner of speaking. Ask yourself how many unexplained deaths there were, how many people simply disappeared. Ask yourself about the executions, of which there were many. No monarch was secure in their position. No favourite of the court was secure in their position. No advisor to the monarch of the time was secure in their position. None questioned this; it was the way of life.

Ask yourself if it is different in your time. How many have been turned out of office for an offence against the nation, for which read the government, for which read the head of state? How many dictators have there been in the years between our time and yours?

I wish you to cease calling this king a tyrant. He is no more a tyrant than many who have walked the earth plane since, yet some act as if he was the greatest of them all.

I cannot answer with surety which Henry was the one I married, for he showed one face to me and another to those gathered around him. I knew him as considerate, caring, fully aware of the position in which he placed me by asking for an annulment, fully aware of the delicacy with which he had to word any documents to go to my family for he did not wish the dowry, such as it was, to be returned and I along with it. He offered me a home and I was grateful for that. He made an allowance for me so I could live and I was grateful for that, too. I did not sense there was any bad feeling between us and so I accepted the situation with good grace.

For I knew one thing for certainty, I did not love this man as I did when the portraits arrived and the excitement which had filled me at the time had long since dissipated. The reality was so very different from the dream. But then, how many have woken on the morning after a wedding and asked themselves what they had done?

I had a dream of the great king, the one who ruled most of Europe with his knowledge and personality, taking me under his wing, teaching me the protocol of his court and sharing his great knowledge with me, teaching me the secrets of the bedchamber, of my presenting him with child after child.

It all failed in the moment our eyes met across the room and I, foolishly, turned back to the window to see what commotion was going on outside. In that moment the marriage was doomed - before it had even begun.

The next question, I see it hovering like an autumn mist before my eyes before it is asked, is:

Was I sorry?

In many ways, yes, for my dream shattered like ice as the winter temperatures let it revert to water. I liked the dream, I liked the idea of being Queen of England, I liked the thought of being important, venerated… does this make me sound empty, a mere sounding bell? Does it make me seem vain, grasping, sycophantic? Would you have not been the same, when sent a portrait painted by one of the greatest portrait painters of our time – by which I mean yours and mine, by the way, you have many clever artists but none equal Holbein for the lifelike portraits he produced, you must agree I have a valid point there.

I divert and must cease to do that: you want the words, the history, the truth but in truth the history is in the background to the two people out at the front of the stage. The truth is in the backdrop painted by artists, the portrait of the great king, the portrait of the willing-to-be-queen woman who sought no more than to be loved. Oh, jewels, land, clothes, more land, big houses, they are nice to have but love transcends all that, which is mutable where love is immutable.

And so we played our parts, Henry as the greatest king England has ever had, myself as the queen who was rejected before she had a chance to prove herself to the greatest king England has ever had, because of her looks. I wish you now to discard the fact he said he touched my breasts, my belly and found me wanting for I have told you how he did in fact find himself wanting and could not resist sampling before putting me to one side, transported out of his life with a piece of vellum which, had I not followed his instructions, if I had but kept it shut up in a box or folded into a book and kept safe and could produce it and show it to you now… well, then the channel would indeed have riches for the rest of her life and the historians would have the proof of her/my words, where now they can dismiss it all as fantasy if they wish.

I know it's the truth for this entire book is the truth. And I ask you, seriously, to consider this. Henry bedded countless women. Do you *really* believe he shared a bed with me and nothing happened?

I lived a half life for some months while negotiations went on, seemingly endlessly. No one asked me for my opinion on the settlement, no one asked if the monies granted were sufficient for my needs and whether the home I was given, Hever Castle, suited me. There were other homes, too, I visited them often, keeping large wardrobes of clothes in each so I could dress well, for I never knew if my former husband would care to visit, or some other courtier would come and report back to Henry how I looked.

Being put to one side, as I was, made me feel inadequate for a long time but with Henry giving me precedence over the ladies of the court, giving me titles that made it seem that he had chosen me as a friend rather than a wife, allowing me my own entourage of ladies and guards, what was there for me to resent? Oh I made all the right sounds when the men came to tell me of his decision, what else could I do? The truth then would have resulted in… a diplomatic crisis. As it was, our unfortunate marriage was the end of Thomas Cromwell. I never thought I would be directly responsible for someone's death and I know well that Henry regretted it the moment it was done but as with every execution, no matter how powerful the king, he cannot bring the dead back to life. And so I walked the fine line of being a forgiving queen and a good friend and companion and bolstering Henry's massive ego which had taken a serious battering over this whole business.

And still his eyes sought and found the plump pigeon that he had in mind for his next wife. That I knew well and that I deplored, for I had my doubts about her. I saw her casting the same adoring looks on any and every handsome man who passed by, no matter who they were. But there was my dilemma, as a good sister, honoured sister or any other fancy name my king put on me, I could not share my doubts with him for he would have taken them as jealousy and pique and he may well have been right. Can I say, at this distance of years, that my feelings were entirely free of jealousy and malice? In truth, no. So I kept silent knowing that if she displeased him, wronged him – which I expected her to do, she was too young, he was too old and infirm and probably repugnant to a young woman without experience… but then again… did she retain her virginity? I doubted that, too – he would find a way to put her to one side, too. He was not above any trick that would give him or rid him of a woman he did not want.

And I, for one, did not blame him for this for, as I have said at length in my section of this book, he was our supreme ruler and we obeyed his every word, as we were bound to do, by convention, by law and by our place in his country under his rule.

And so our lives continued, I had a place in his court; he had a place in my life, for my life was bound up with his goodwill, his continued patience with me; his ability to tolerate me in his life. I knew nothing of what he did with his nights after that last one, I never asked for it was not something I needed to know. But you need to know how I satisfied that new sensation that he aroused in me.

The problem was a simple one. I had been awoken in that regard. I could not take a lover, any man would be at risk from Henry's wrath if it ever came out and in a court like that here in England, nothing was truly secret, unless Henry bid that it be so. None dared go against him, and if he spoke, it was as if the words had come on a rainbow from the Heavens themselves.

And so I turned to that which was secret but which was not denied me, love with a woman.

And now secrets are truly revealed, are they not? I found love in the arms of a woman, one of my ladies, bound to secrecy with me and from the others. It was easily done; no one took notice of a woman flitting from room to room, for who would think of this? Who would question the services I might require? None seemed observant enough to notice it was the same person every time, but there again, why should they? My lover was part of my household, they who were busy packing for me to move from Henry's court to that of my own making in Hever Castle. And it was not lost on me that I was moving to the home of a former queen. It seemed right in some ways. She was rejected in the worst possible way —or was she? She had six years of love, total love it seems, from the stories which came our way, stories of the Great Love which went wrong in the end. She had that at least, I had no love, just Henry using me for his satisfaction and I had to settle for that.

Was it enough? Who can say? Without love between us, the answer could well be yes. But then again, I hoped for so much more when I came away from all I held dear to something and someone who did not really want me.

Well, not in the way I hoped. And yet there was a strange satisfaction in being a friend and confidant in some respects to this great king, to be accepted by him on any level after being so cruelly thrown to one side was reward enough for me.

I can almost hear the women of your time shouting at me that I should have claimed more, demanded more, been less subservient and more assertive, but you cannot get into my mind for you women have not lived in my time and if you have, your memories are buried deep. Not all of you understand past lives, not all of you can venture into your past as the channel does, she knows well who she was and is, but for many of you it is a new concept. Accept that it was not right for me to do anything but accept His Majesty's largesse and be grateful for it, grateful beyond words for not being returned unwanted to my homeland. I have said this before and I reiterate it so you understand. We were not capable of doing anything else. And I really did not wish to be returned to my homeland unwanted, unloved, unmarried.

Would you?

And so the channel asks... what did you think of the queens who followed you, Anne?

And I say, well, I knew it would take Henry no time at all to get involved with the plump pigeon, despite all the reservations of everyone around him. Not that anyone dared suggest that he should not marry her but look somewhere else, somewhere more – certain of loyalty and consideration. That was obvious to all but not to Henry, who only saw youth, slender ankles, bouncing breasts, curls and come-hither eyes. He saw not the scheming family behind the beauty set before him, did not realise, as we all did, that she was a man-trap, a snare into which he blindly walked.

And what would he have said had any of us dared approach him? Imagine the conversation.

'Your Majesty, the girl on which you have set your heart and mind is frivolous in nature and much given to fluttering her eyelids at young men in your court. Her heart is not entirely yours.'

The indecision was always: Should you wish to destroy your life, your family and yourself, go to his Majesty and say it. If you wish to preserve that which you have, let the king make a fool of himself over a silly young girl who has no mind of her own, only that set in her by the Howard family, no doubt directed by Norfolk himself, that she would bring much wealth to herself and the family were she to be chosen as the next Queen.

Oh yes, just ignore his huge girth, his bloated face, his suppurating ulcers and chronically disturbed bowels, they are by-products of his terrible eating habits and surely, for the sake of the family, you will have no trouble coping with that…

Once the annulment had been made 'legal' and accepted by the court and the parliament, I could stand back from any jealousy and resentment and look on in wonder as a man of mature years began to make a total fool of himself over a woman scarcely more than a girl in her head. I knew this for her talk was ever of her latest gown, slippers, mantle, the flowers which bloomed outside her window, the antics of her puppy, the colour of her newest pony and what her tutor had said to her about her attempts at playing the harp. I never did know why she chose such an instrument… or perhaps at this distance in time, I do. A harp is an elegant and beautiful instrument and those who perform with it look elegant and beautiful as they pluck the strings. Methinks my

Lady Howard was trying to make herself more than she really was. And yes, there is still a sharpness and a need to fire barbs at the plump pigeon for I might have had a better time with my one time husband had he not been all but drooling over her exposed flesh and imagination of what lie beneath the satins and silks, lace and gold threads.

In truth, it was almost a relief to leave the impassioned king to his new love and travel to Hever Castle to start a new life, one where none would criticise me for indulging in English ale and the occasional gamble, for such chances to add to my generous allowance were a temptation I could not resist.

Of course I heard the court gossip, nothing ever escaped those of us who were not part of it; we were part of it by proxy and so I heard how Henry had married his pigeon, had delighted in having her around, had seemed like a newly renewed man. It was not very long after that before the rumours began, that she had been using the back stairs of the palaces and homes to cavort with a young man, one she professed to love to her dying day. I doubt she ever thought that day would come so soon; I doubt she believed for one moment that Henry would find out, as if –

As if anyone would keep anything from such a king, who knew every movement and every heart and probably knew from the very first time she made an excuse and, flipping up her skirts, ran up the stairs and into the arms of Thomas Culpepper, her one true love.

I could not find it in my heart to express sorrow for her execution, for Henry's said to be broken heart, for they should both have known better – and didn't.

Not once did I ever hear him utter a word about the matter in my presence, for he would have known well what I would say, what any woman would say, and avoided it by avoiding it.

And so he took Katherine Parr to wife. More companion and nursemaid than wife and by that time I doubt Henry needed or wanted more than that. For the first time I saw him content with his new Queen and for the first time I could relax in his company when he met with me at court. I liked his new Queen, a calm steady woman who understood men and their fractious needs. I was settled in my heart and mind that Henry had found – at last – a replacement for the wife he loved most but never admitted, his first Katherine. Had not the lust of the man edging past his prime coincided with the arrival of the exotic Anne Boleyn, history might have been very different indeed.

And then I think further and say, then I would not have been enticed to leave my home and become the king's fourth Queen and given a chance to live out my life in your fair country, with money and homes, companions and lovers to fill my days and ease my nights. Life has a way of rewarding some of us whilst stealing the breath and blood from others. Always someone will benefit from what another has lost but I will admit my heart ached for the gentle Katherine who lost so much after having so much.

I was – and am – grateful for the life I had and even more grateful for the chance to give my words to this in-depth book on the man we called husband.

My channel, my thanks go to you. May this book bring you success.

Treasured Memories

His gentle smile to me when we were wed, despite knowing he did not want me he was considerate and charming and smiled just at me.
The time he came to my bed with need, for then he had a different air about him and a sense of excitement and as it never happened again, it is a memory to cling to.

The time he told me the great homes I would have and how much my allowance would be. He was so much the munificent king at that moment I was in complete awe of him and wondered how I could ever have been married to him, even for so short a time.

And the wonderful memories of being a valued visitor to his homes, where we would walk and talk and we would be friends, rather than lovers and in many ways that suited both of us very well.

Expressing Henry in one word: Selfish

Ten questions about Henry:

His favourite colour: blue
His favourite sport: bowls
His favourite animal: hawks
His favourite interest: alchemy
His favourite meal: pork with apple sauce
His favourite sweet: medlars in syrup
His favourite time of year: Autumn
His favourite home: Grenewich
His favourite gem: emerald
His favourite musical instrument: lyre

Kathryn Howard

*Henry's wives: divorced, beheaded, died, divorced,
beheaded, survived*

Henry's fifth queen, young and unwilling (beheaded)

And so we begin.

If anyone – and I do mean anyone – thinks that the great hulk of a man who cast his covetous eyes on me and expected me to love him to the exclusion of all others was someone worth loving, I beg of you, think you again. I say now, I say it clear across the centuries that divide us, death came as a relief. I would as lief have died at the beginning but not dying then granted me the time in my Thomas' arms, to hear the sound of his voice which asked and not ordered, to feel the strength of his body, which was clean and smelled good, which was slender and comely in every way. My regret – and it is a very big one, trust my word on this, would you? is that he had to be tortured before he could be released. I doubt not he pleaded for death, even as I longed for it but dared not say it for fear of making things worse for everyone.

And so we begin at the beginning.

The Howards had watched with greedy eyes the falling down of the woman from Cleves, the Queen Anne who I grew to like in the short time she was in court and it was my privilege to serve her. I found her to be courtly, nervous; anxious to do the right thing, not to displease His Majesty even when it was made clear to all that she had displeased him by simply being. Even as the courtiers laughed behind her back and sometimes not so discreetly, I had every sympathy with her, for I was in the same predicament, looking to do the right thing all the time. Ever was I afraid of making a mistake, of incurring the wrath of the great King, even as I knew his lust-filled eyes sought me no matter where I went in the room, the hall, the gardens, anywhere he was. And I could not be anywhere he was not for it was his wish I be there. The King's wishes were ever obeyed.

I know from reading Anne's testimony, for it is such, is it not? that she was afeared at all times and this I know well, too.

The Howards had watched closely all that went on with the King, as all did, but they were particularly in need of a boost. All had overspent; all the families had debts and bills to meet and could not meet them, the Howards more than most, so it came about that all were jostling for a position that allowed one of their family members to become prominent in the court hierarchy and if one could be aimed at the ultimate position of Queen, well, that would be the true shining star, would it not? And so they came with honey in their mouths to coat the lies I was fed as truths, to persuade, cajole and even demand that I attract the King's attention and get into his arms, his bed and his life, so I could reap the benefits in the way of status, jewels and gold. And if that reads to you like a list written on vellum and presented to a clerk, then that is precisely how it seemed to me. The really dreadful thing, God give me strength to speak of it, was the thought of the bed. All else I imagined and believed I could cope with. Was I not mature enough to be Queen?

No, but none advised me otherwise. My mirror, inadequate as it was, told me I was fair of face where Queen Anne was not, that I was curved of body where Queen Anne was not. Others had told me my voice was sweet to their ears, that my conversation was interesting, that – need I go on?

The Howards worked hard to persuade me that it was in my interests, not theirs, that I give my heart and mind to the great King.

That I leave Thomas Culpepper behind in the family home where he had rooms, to forget he was my love and my heart and my mind and my soul.

From this distance of time, I have to ask myself who truly loved me. Mannox used me, as did Dereham, but did Thomas use me or did Thomas love me?

Memory says he did for his face, his demeanour, his entire attitude changed so much when he found that the King's eyes had rested upon me, for he knew well what that meant. Heart says he probably did, truth says he was infatuated. Life says whichever one it was, it served him ill and for that I have an eternity of regrets for I loved him dearly and deeply and until the King sought me out, I planned to spend my life with him.

And so we move on.

I state so blithely 'the king's eyes had rested upon me'. In a court of bright shining women, beautiful accomplished women, how then did he choose me?

The Howards schooled me well. Each day when he was at Grenewich, the King would walk – or should I say progress – the entire length of the corridor, looking at those who bowed and curtsied to him as he went. He would choose one here and another there to accompany him, to make small talk, to entertain him for a while. There was much competition at these times. You who live lives so very different from ours may find this hard, but I would ask you for a moment to think on something I have seen on your screen. There is a presentation of some kind, a statuette is given, am I right? and do the people chosen to be at the presentation event not walk upon a red carpet and do not the people of the land crowd close to see their favourite one, to ask for their name on a piece of paper, to have a photograph taken with them, to say for a moment they had 'met' the one they favour. Am I right?

I wish you to translate that to the King's promenade along the corridor each day, looking at those clustered around, making a line for him to walk, each longing for notice to be taken of them for that notice could lead to a favoured position in court, for riches, for titles, for all that others take for granted, those who were already favourites of the great King.

And so, the Howards planned and schemed and schooled me into what they wanted.

I had me a new gown, one of frills and flounces, of the sweetest blue you can imagine. I had black satin slippers, I had blue bows tied into my hair which was in bunches of dark, dark curls. I was to wear this gown, which was revealing already before I was instructed to tug at the bodice and expose yet more of myself. I was to wait for the king to come alongside me and then, with a flick of my skirts, drop into a deep curtsy and then say something like 'excuse me, Your Majesty' and turn and skip away, twitching my skirts so my ankles were revealed.

It was a risk. It was a huge calculated risk. No one, but no one, left the corridor until the king had passed them by. I could have been banned from Grenewich; the Howards could have incurred the royal wrath.

The day was bright, the day they chose, so very bright, or was it my imagination and nerves which made it so? The corridor was flooded with sunlight. Everyone looked beautiful, even the men. I saw the King coming, saw how the sunlight picked out the great jewels on his doublet, saw the silver head of the stick he used to walk with, saw how tired he looked as if he wished to be anywhere but there. For a moment my heart went out to him and so it made it easier for me to carry out the Howard plan, for I felt a deep pity and wondered if I could be the one to ease his suffering.

Foolish child that I was.

I hastily tugged at my bodice, much to the amusement and carnal interest of the courtier stood alongside me, swept into a deep curtsy when he reached me, uttered some words I now disremember, smiled at him with my most dazzling of smiles and flicked my skirts to leave his presence.

I heard the shocked expressions of the gathered courtiers and women, heard the King's booming laugh and then heard him ask 'who was that charming girl?' as I ran from the king's presence.

It had worked.

The King had seen me many a time and many, for I was lady in waiting to his fourth Queen, but then, so were many others and I was not sure, neither were the Howards generally, that he had 'seen' me as me: they believed as I did I was one of the many. Heaven forefend that should be so, but the court was full of people of all ages, of all colours, of all abilities for the King liked to surround himself with people of intelligence. For all that he dismissed Queen Anne's looks and body shape, he liked to talk with her of her homeland, one he had not visited. He asked many questions about the people, their customs; their ways for ever did he seek to extend his knowledge. It never came into my mind that he would one day want to share his life with me, me who has little knowledge of the world outside my home, Queen Anne's rooms and the court itself. I walked in the gardens but knew not a single flower by name. And it seemed not to matter, for who would look at me among the many who thronged to the court?

And then I saw that his eyes were on me at times at table and then the Howards put the idea in my head to entice the King to look at me a little closer.

God forgive me for agreeing to do this, for it worked. And I, having that which they wanted, found I did not want it at all. For having it meant I had to give up all that I had, including my freedom.

And so we look afresh at my life then.

Queen Anne's legal work was done, she was officially free of the King, the ties of marriage were severed and I saw no difference in her demeanour at that time. It was as if she was what you would call a mannequin, a stuffed doll that had no emotion in it. My belief is that she was grateful for all she had and that it mattered not she was no longer Queen. She had not had a coronation, she had no real status in court, she was – there and he walked with her and talked with her and went to her bed at the beginning, slept and left again, or so we were told. I see now that was not entirely correct but close enough. I now ask myself why am I not shocked that she considered herself used. Because we were used to the King's ways, taking what he wanted and discarding the rest?

We all knew that Cromwell's days were numbered over the whole marriage fiasco, knew it and split into the parties who welcomed it, for he had too much power and those who did not want it, knowing that the King was about to make a second mistake and remove someone from their life and his who was of great benefit to him.

Never was anyone able to talk sensibly to King Henry VIII and they never would. For the king knew best what the king wanted at any moment in his life and there were none who could gainsay that, no matter how learned they were or clever with words.

So I am there, young in years but not in my head, for those who walk the court ways and play the court games are older than their years. There is no other way to describe it. Being on the defensive all the time is tiring, watching every word, every glance, every dance and who you dance with, how you eat, what you eat, how you dress, what you dress in, and yes, there is a difference, for silk is not satin and cotton is not silk and there are those who can recognise a cheap gown from across a crowded room and are sure to comment on it to those around them. And thus you are scorned as a cheap person. It is vital that you wear the right clothes, say the right things, act the right way every single waking moment, for fear of someone commenting adversely on you and it being blown up to something virtually criminal before the whole court.

It is tiring. It is wearing. It is ageing and thus we are older than the years would reveal. 'So young' they say when they report my execution. Ah, but in those years I had I had lived more than twice yours. Groomed from first step to making those steps the right ones into a future life ages you.

For the rest of me, I could not sing, I could not compose. I played the harp badly, the lute passing well and could dance. I could talk on trivial matters but had no understanding of the wider world for none had introduced me to it.

So then, you ask, what did I bring to the King?

Youth. Innocence. Ability to make him feel like the golden prince again, even as I fought my revulsion for this bulk of a man with the ulcers which stank like old middens long neglected.

In his bedtime talk, and I am free to talk of this to you, for this is the secret heart of this amazing book, he spoke of Katherine, his true love, of Anne, his violent lust/love that died when she did not produce his son and he wondered aloud why that should be so.

I asked him, in a bold moment of post-nuptial pleasure – for him – what should be so, the love that died or the lack of the son. 'Both,' he told me. 'I lusted for her beyond comprehension, ached for her through the long years of divorce, longed for the sons that would surely come from such a young, lithe body and found... first that the body was not that different from all I had sampled and taken and cast aside and second that the body did not and seemingly could not produce the son I needed. Disappointment is a great quencher of desire.'

And then he reached for me again and I struggled to surmount the bulk that was his belly and ride the desire that awaited me and wondered how long he would live. The Howards had told me I could, if I wished, induce a heart stoppage for the king and all would be over and done. The jewels, the houses, the horses and all given to me would be mine to keep forever.

But having got to know this great, difficult, interesting, fascinating, repulsive man, for he was all faces and all things to me at times, I could not have caused a heart stoppage, could not have been responsible for depriving England of this king who knew so much and did so much and would go on doing so much. Ah, you ask, what did he do and I say, you need to study the papers of his government, see what laws he put in place, what changes he made, what small changes that made a big difference down the years. So many people only see the wives, the eating, the jousting, the hunting; they see not the intellect, the music, the writing, the learning. If you try to tell them of these things, they deny any existed. And yet, his knowledge of the stars is well known, his music is recorded even as today, his legacy is all there in the works he did and the works he undid with his reformation. And for that there are both good and bad arguments. A controversial king, a challenging king, and I say, as others have, not one person in your time has come close to capturing the essence of Henry Tudor in their overall view of him. Not one single person, for all their learning and fancy degrees from this university or that. For none have looked beyond the image they hold before them. Not one single person.

And I, reluctant as I was to involve myself in someone so old, so repulsive in many ways, was captured and entranced by his talk and his knowledge.

Love never entered into it but respect did and I take that as a great step into the understanding I had.

And while we speak of such things, let none say I was a foolish young girl who knew not what she did. I knew well and it was calculated and worked for and the Howards benefited for a while. What I did not think on at the time and should have done was my longing for the young love that was being denied me. And when it was given to me – I will tell you later of this – I found it had lost its savour but not its love.

I promise to speak of these things for you have to know all to understand the man, the king, the all-powerful, all-encompassing, all-great Henry VIII. He was not only great in girth but in personality, in powerful presence, in intellect and intelligence and, I have to say, cunning and craft of handling people, too. Oh, you historians who see nothing, what have you missed these many centuries, which it has taken six separate and yet cohesive queens to point out to you? Are you not ashamed of your preconceived ideas of this great man now you have read this far?

In truth, I say you are not ashamed, you will deny all that is written here, you will not see the logic we set before you, all of us, Katherine, Anne, Jane, Anne, Kathryn and Katherine. We knew him, we loved him, some of us; we spent time with him. You did not. You see nothing but what you want to see and what you want to see is false, as false as the words your politicians feed to you these days and which you cast aside and yet you cannot see you need to cast aside all that you think you know of Henry Tudor and learn from what you should see as the primary source – the queens.

I also want to say, without fear of censure for even if a Howard dared to enter the rooms of my channel without her bidding it, there is nothing but nothing they can do now, I had no true thought that the jewels, the houses, the horses and all given to me would remain mine if the king died, for there were too many Howards waiting to dip their sullied fingers into the money pot I would have. In moments of spite, and I admit to having them still, I am glad it ended as it did for they came away with empty sullied fingers. I carry the name but not the commitment to the family.

And Henry and I talked often.

Henry called me his Rose Without a Thorn, often with the large letters, not easy to say such things with large letters but there was little my king could not do, if we discard: the inability to walk well, to curb the appetite, to control the problems of the stomach, to stop dismissing people from his employ and his life as casually as he threw aside the bones of the meat he consumed each day. But these are small things in the great king's life and reign, after all. For him, that is. For those of us bidden to tend to his every need they were very large things indeed. He could not reach well to cleanse himself in any way; his attendants had to do that. He could not dress himself, he could not bandage his legs or force his feet into soft slippers without help and he could not rouse himself without someone young and nubile in his bed or hers.

We talked, he asked me many questions about my home life, about the Howards; oh I knew well he was spying in his own way, by being open about it, but I told him all he needed to know for there was no reason not to. What I didn't tell him he would have found out anyway, he had enough people to do that. He had a magnificent spy ring, that I knew, we all knew, but who they were – no, that was another matter entirely.

We talked of Queen Anne. Having put her to one side, quietly, gently and with no ceremony at all, he wanted to know all I knew about her, what I thought of her, which made me wonder if he had a little regret or two at not being able to create any feeling with her or for her. Why else ask me so much?

He talked to me; I say this advisedly, of court matters, wanting me to be involved, wanting me to understand my duties as queen and I listened and I tried not to let him know I didn't understand all that he said, for it involved people I did not know, situations which I did not know and problems I could not begin to understand.

But then I realised he did know and it didn't matter, for I was someone to talk to or at, someone who was a captive audience and I would sit or walk with him, ignoring the pains in my body which demanded I get to the privy in a hurry or I take in some food or liquid also in a hurry. No one did anything that Henry did not authorise if they were with him. And so it was I had to wait until he needed the privy or food or ale or mulled wine or whatever took his fancy at that time.

And if it took his fancy to give me another great home, another jewel, another bag of gold coins, who was I to argue? And even though they were not there, not before our marriage or after, I knew the Howards were smiling at me, smiling with the greed in their eyes and the honey lies in their mouths.

And inside my whole body ached with longing for my Thomas and I had no way of knowing if inside his whole body ached with longing for me, for I did not want to risk notes or messages. Not then, anyway. Then it was new, it was thrilling, it was – euphoric, for everyone deferred to me where few had before. What girl, woman, person, could resist that? Power.

So where did I divert? Oh, with Anne Boleyn, the Great Love, the Lovers as they were known. It went wrong so fast it was a shock to those of us who lived on the periphery of the court, listening to the stories and the lies, and which were which, we asked ourselves? I see now that the story was a mixture of the two things.

Then we knew of Jane Seymour, the quiet one we all said, who seemed to make Henry happy with her quiet ways and gentleness and of course an immediate pregnancy.

Then we knew of her death, which scared me to the point of not sleeping. Was it so easy to die of giving birth to a child for the king? Surely he had the very best of surgeons, nurses, midwives and others? But Jane had died; his quiet gentle queen had died.

But he had a son. Henry had an heir and who were we, mere Howards, to criticise the help and assistance his queen had?

But oh, I wondered, what if that were me... and I cried into my pillow for nights. Cried for the quiet subservient Jane and for the possibility that I would go the same way. Never to see my child grow up.

And I wondered how Henry coped with it.

And then there was Queen Anne, the gentle one, the loving one, the caring one he put to one side without really finding out how gentle, loving and caring she could be. Those of us who served her knew this and I felt the hugest regret and heartache that of all her ladies, Henry should choose me. No, change that, I felt the hugest regret and heartache that of all the ladies in the court, Henry should choose a lady in waiting of his current queen, which only added to her sorrow at being put to one side. And she did, trust me that is, she cried and asked what she had done wrong, apart from being willing to come to a strange country and be queen to a strange – dominant, powerful, all knowing, all seeing – king and find that the king did not find her attractive and immediately sought a way to dissolve the agreement and the marriage.

I could not begin to understand how she felt but I saw the results, the loss of weight, the dark ringed eyes, the sorrowful air she carried as a cloud around her shoulders, until the benevolent Henry finally accorded her the properties she could live in and the allowance she could live on. Then she knew she was able to stay in England. From that moment on she worked twice as hard at learning English as she had done before.

And I must go back to our relationship.

For we did not become a married couple instantly. Henry, ever the courtier, courted me with gifts of jewels, fine horses, gold and silver and the Howards, those of the family who were around constantly, watching every move and trying to direct the ones that did not seem to go well, were very pleased. Henry and I rode out at times, sedately, with a retinue of course, and we would talk across the divide to one another. Oh but that divide was wide and deep and impassable at times, for he would talk of things of which I had no understanding. What I did like was the evenings when he would play whatever he had composed during the day; his mastery of the lyre was something that had to be heard to be believed. The lilting melodies were always well received and although it would be easy, and in some instances truthful to say he was applauded because he was the king, I have to say that he was a wonderful composer of short lyrical pieces. They were enchanting and we told him so, in truth and not flattery.

I liked it when he read to me from one or other of his books - he had a huge library of them and had read them all – or talked to me of his astronomy. To me the stars were there to adorn the darkness but for him they held mystery and interest and he would watch them and chart their movements. At times like that I would listen to his voice more than the words, for his voice was deep and rich and golden, as golden as I imagine he once was, when young.

When he was the Golden Prince and not the ageing overweight man I saw when I looked at him again.

And compared him with my beautiful Thomas, whom I had been forbidden to see, of course.

At that time.

Sometimes it was hard to believe it was me, Kathryn Howard, who was to marry the king of England. Sometimes, when the ladies came to help me, a task I did for some time for the gentle Queen Anne, it was as if we were all part of a masquerade, a mummer's play, that someone would burst in and push me back into the lady in waiting mode again. It was difficult to really comprehend it was going to happen, that he had chosen me, above all the other butterfly bright women who thronged the court, looking for positions, for favours, for notice and adoration. I just looked at that and thought, not necessarily in that order, either.

Sometimes I thought about the age difference and wondered if it mattered.

Sometimes I thought of his child and wondered how I would feel holding an heir to the throne.

Sometimes I told myself to grow up, that it was all a dream and the morning had yet to come.

And sometimes the reality smacked me in the mouth and I knew I would not make a good queen. Because, my longing for Thomas was more than my longing for the position of Queen of England. I never wanted to be Queen of England, but I had wanted Thomas forever, or so it seemed.

It is at moments like this, when the channel sits patiently waiting for the next words, when the intense emotional music she plays at times like this, that I look at the words on the screen and am surprised at what is coming from me. Surprised even that I can remember so much, but then, there is no time where we are and it is all as if it were yesterday. I know this book is supposed to be about the way we felt and perceived Henry, but I also know, as one of the other queens said, if we did not include how we felt, it would not all make sense. I think she said that, not that it matters; there is my interpretation of the situation. You need the balance, you need to know how I felt so I can describe how I related to Henry, King of England.

The family told me I had never looked prettier, that I glowed more with every passing day. I disbelieved them then and I disbelieve them now. The strain of being queen in waiting was telling on me in many ways. My seamstress was ever altering and adapting my clothes which hung on me, shapeless and unalluring. That would not do for Henry.

He missed nothing. He missed nothing in that he watched everyone, what they ate, what they did not eat, how much they drank, who they talked with, who they did not talk with. He told me that he did this to keep in mind who had disagreed with who, for they could not bring themselves to speak even in the king's presence. I wondered then how many knew how closely they were being watched. I have noticed that the queens, Henry's chosen ladies, did know, had been aware and that was a very revealing aspect of the women he chose. It also makes me feel better about myself. We were not mere mice, following the cat to the trap, we all had our individual strengths and intellect and to know I was not and am not alone there makes a big difference to me now.

This book is helping in so many ways. There are those of us who are now released from years of storing secrets, thoughts and impressions; there are those of us who have been desperate to tell the world their side of the Henry/Whoever story, because of the way historians have taken the basic facts and twisted them to suit their own interpretation of events. There are those of us who have read what the others have written and taken solace from it, knowing they were and are not alone in the way they felt about this great king, about the way they perceived him. They and I have taken comfort from the fact they have contributed to what is an overall impression of a complex, difficult, incredibly intelligent and often misunderstood man. Those who dismiss him as tyrant, brute, and other expressions which do not fit the man any of us knew and were wedded to, are completely in the wrong. They read the words of other historians rather than, as has been pointed out, going back to the primary sources – us. The Queens. Henry's Queens. The women he chose to be his wife and consort. Henry never was a fool, I say that knowing that he became obsessed with my plumpness and youth, but I say to you now –

No. Let me hold that for the moment. I have said enough about the book and I needs must move on. Tonight the music is deeply emotional, moving; full of vitality and rhythm. That is how I was at that time.

The Kathryn I was then.

The person I was then was part child/part woman. No one had allowed me to grow up, or educated me to be the elegant worldly-wise wife of a courtier or aristocrat. I am sure the Howards had one in mind for me, they were busy enough working to arrange advantageous marriages, I knew that. But what did they expect me to be? I asked questions but had no answers. I asked how to choose good servants and was ignored. I asked if I could choose my maids and nurse and was ignored. I wondered whether they planned for me to be child-like and be given in marriage to some older man who would appreciate my youth. There had to be a reason, there always was. Aristocratic families never did anything on a whim, too much was at stake.

And so I dreamed often, in the darkest recesses of the night, when nothing but stars peeked in at the window and picked out a lock of hair sprawled across my pillow and I, wide eyed and sleepless, would see it and ask if that star had chosen me for something special, something outstanding; something magnificent. Childish thoughts that somehow came true. It is indeed true that everyone should be careful what they wish for.

The Kathryn Henry cast his covetous eyes upon had carnal knowledge of men, knew what to do and how to do it and had a constant ongoing need for it, provided it was done well. Thomas knew how.

The Kathryn Henry desired was well aware of what her body could do but not what her mind could do, for none had encouraged actual learning outside of being able to read with difficulty, to write well in a fair hand and not splatter the vellum with ink and thus ruin the work, to dance well and play the lute with faltering fingers. I longed with all my heart to play the harp well, for I so loved the sound of its plucked strings. It seemed to pluck at my heartstrings, as if I had at some time known what it was to be Celtic and know this music in my very being.

The Henry that Kathryn knew then was a bloated giant of a man. He had bad teeth, bad breath, troublesome headaches that incapacitated him for hours and left him surly and suffering as if he had too much to drink.

I have to divert here for a moment and talk of the one thing I have not mentioned, nor has anyone else as far as I can see, the fact that Henry did not drink very much. He looked as if he did, he looked as if he tossed back flagons of ale and horn cups or goblets of fine wine but in truth, if you watched him closely as I did, you would see he took but a sip sometimes, a mouthful other times and would contrive to spill most of it on the ground at his feet or into his trencher. He said once, in our private talks, that to drink too much meant losing control and at no time did he wish to lose control. Only when he had one of his violent headaches that rendered him all but blind did he allow others to guide him. The rest of the time this proud strong determined man knew well at every moment what he was doing; who he was with, what they were saying to him and more importantly, what he was saying in reply.

The Henry I knew had troublesome bowels and stomach, emitting horrendous smells at times. It was hard to pretend this did not matter, that I was not bothered by this, for of course I was. At the same time I knew well he could not help it. If what you call a 'diet' had been known then, he would have benefited, instead the apothecaries came with potions and powders for wine and water and none of it made one bit of difference to him. They only plagued him with their bad taste which often lasted for some time. For a man ever on the edge of temper, that was not a good thing.

Henry's ulcerated legs were the real reason he was short tempered with many, for they gave him constant pain and even more constant rancid smells which no amount of powdered pearl or any other noxious aid could control. 'My body rots, sweet Kathryn,' he said once with great bitterness. For Henry this was the ultimate insult of being a living being, he could not control his ageing and his many health problems. If he were to live today, there would be what seems to me to be magical cures for this and for that which troubled him but nothing can stop the ageing process and that he rebelled against all the time.

And so, in his later years, he sought a young woman, someone to share the carnal secrets of life with him.

And now we talk of something none knew and only now will I say it. And only because I am honour bound to do as my liege lord asked, to be totally honest about him as a king and as a man.

I spent more time talking with Henry about sexual matters than I ever did practicing it with him.

If you think again on what I just said, 'if he were to live today' – he would be watching sexy films in the comfort and security of his inner chambers. He would have a library of them and demand that none touch them but him. This I can well imagine. He would delight in them, for the king was a sexual man in every way. Sex dominated his thoughts and his body, he had bedded countless women, he told me, he rejoiced in the intimacies and the secrets of women's bodies. And so, when the urge is there but the body refuses to respond, what do you do but seek and rely on outside stimulus. Is this not right? And is this not what the king did in asking me to talk with him on all matters sexual? I say this to stop the outrage that some will throw at this book at my words. Think before you condemn. How much sexual content is there in your films, how many sexual films are made for the titillation of men? Then relate that to a time when film was not known, when what you call 'sex aids' were not known either, and ask yourself what did a king do when he needed 'help'? If you had the chance to look into the lives of the rich and famous of that time, would you not find others doing the same task as I? The earls, the dukes, the lords of the land…

The agreement for our marriage was drawn up, the date set.

The unsigned, unwritten agreement for our marriage was agreed between us. I would renounce all activity with Thomas Culpepper for the duration of our marriage and cleave only to him. The Howards had assured me that the king had not many months left to live. With that firmly in my mind, I agreed.

His Rose without a Thorn. His Kathryn. God send me relief from the regret I suffer still that I could not hold to my word all that endless time.

Let me not divert yet.

From then onward, Henry and I would talk of sexual matters. He would sometimes become aroused, other times he would not, but this was a man who had enjoyed countless women, had used every position, every trick, every potion, oil, salve, whatever was available, to ensure that he had maximum pleasure – and so did the woman he laid with. And so, to him to talk of it freely and openly with someone who was already aware and willing was a pleasure for him. He relived many encounters, many affairs where it lasted longer than a quick roll in the bed, and there were more of those than the historians have realised. Any of them could have become serious, the woman become a contender for the role of Queen, for he had a discerning eye for the right woman. I know this from the names he gave me. I will not share the names, for these women need their blushes spared. They did no more than go along with the king's command and even at this long space of time between then and now, their names could be traced and known and it is best that I keep silent on that aspect of our discussions. It is enough I have his word that I can talk of this part of our relationship.

I will tell later how these talks affected me.

For now the question is asked, did I love this man? I say fair to you; no I did not. I admired him, his strength of mind, his intellect; his incredible grasp of humanity, his ability to absorb and retain minute details of someone's life and give it back to them when needed. The court was full of people, more than could be counted in a single day yet he knew every servant, every stable person, everyone involved in any of the sports at which he once excelled – need I go on? Imagine now in your time and your place a huge towering building of hundreds of people all coming and going, could any one person know them all by name, their families, their status, their financial needs? I think not and doubt you would know anyone who did. But Henry did. I also tell you he rated their financial needs more important than anything else, for that, he said, dictated whether they were loyal or just greedy. Those who were in need were the ones most likely to thieve from the store rooms, for they would reason that it did not matter, there was enough for all.

They made the mistake that so many did, of under-estimating Henry's ability to know all that went on. Often someone was dismissed and when asking why, were told because of their thieving and they would ask, how did you know? The response was always, 'there is nothing the king does not know.'

And you can hold that thought for the time being, my description of the man I married, for there are more revelations to come about that marriage which may shatter some of your preconceptions on that, too. I am here to shatter the mirror you have long held up to reflect the Howard/Tudor marriage. And in truth I delight in doing it, for you – the vast majority of you – have never tried to find out what really happened.

Be patient. I will tell all. Kiss and tell indeed…

And for those who said I was unlearned, not fit for being a Queen, read this and know that I had a wide education, could talk on a few subjects with the king, was able to write well, would he really have taken someone to Queen who was not reasonably intelligent? It is not a position for those who are incapable of holding a conversation with anyone! This again proves that all of you, historians in particular, took the stereotype image of an ageing king with a small bit of a girl to **** and ignored the rest, the man, my abilities, my feelings, his feelings… all thrown away to fit that which you want him to be. And how you want me to be, if we are being honest here. You know it; you are guilty of it, all you who write of the king's Queens. You make so many mistakes and that is not limited to us, I am sad to say. I have seen the mistakes you make about other people, I think it fair to say ALL other people you write of, for again you come with preconceived ideas and will not allow the truth to get in the way of the 'facts'. May I make a suggestion? In future, before you begin yet another biography on yet another historical figure, you give a lot of time to thinking about them and asking yourself, does this make sense?

I must move on or this book will never be finished. I could rant against you for hours.

And so we were married. And so by course of time I became Queen of England. And so the Howards were forced to bow and curtsy to me, for protocol was rigid in court. And did I not delight in that, for so long they had bullied, pestered, argued and pleaded with me to do their bidding, even though they admitted, in their more honest moments, not a one of them would be in the king's company for too long for the smells and his sudden switching of mood would be something they could not cope with. But oh were they happy for me to be there… doing their bidding, becoming queen of England.

And so I oft turned away from them and denied them audience with me or with Henry, as my personal revenge for all I had to suffer for their sakes.

This is where it becomes a little difficult and I have to formulate my thoughts clearly before I can go on.

I have taken time to consider my thoughts.

I had everything, or almost everything. I was queen of England at a very young age. My king and husband did not seem to mind that I had no knowledge of government, of the geography of our country, of the location and geography of our neighbours in Europe or who their heads of state were, or even who the current Pope was, not that it mattered any more after Henry's triumphant and well publicised break with the Vatican. I relished the jewels, the homes, the horses, dogs, cats or any other animals I cared to have around me and travel with me. I had my own entourage of ladies in waiting. I had my family where I wanted them for the first time ever, on their knees mostly before me. It was a thrilling outlook.

But – the man I had at my side was not young, slender, handsome, fit and capable of satisfying me. And that is something I wanted more than anything. My bedroom talks with Henry did nothing to help that condition. It left me wanting and desperate and finding all sorts of substitutes for the times he was incapable – more often than he was capable, as his health was rapidly declining. And still I lied; still I told him he was the only one I wanted.

And wondered sometimes how much I was lying to keep him content and how much I was fabricating to cover my traitorous thoughts.

For I did want to be with him, sometimes. I did want to listen to him, sometimes. I did like to walk with him in the grounds, as best he could for as long as he could, because everyone deferring to us made me feel as if I was as tall as the buildings surrounding the gardens. I know, I know well it was nothing but my pride but would you not be the same, if you had come from an aristocratic but impoverished family, struggling to provide new outfits to attend court and not be scorned, hoping no one noticed the age of the mounts we rode or the parlous condition of the harness or – any of the other unforgiving signs that we were short of money?

It was then I began to feel a tremendous sympathy for Anne Boleyn and Jane Seymour, both pushed before the king by their families, both families in the same state ours was until I reached those giddy heights. As they were until their chosen puppets were pushed so hard they too reached the giddy heights.

It was then that my fears began to take over. For each of them did not live long to enjoy that position, that wealth, that fame and fortune. Did Anne come to the point I had soon come to, the need for satisfaction which was withheld but not disposed of, did Jane tire completely of not having her own estate, her own family; her own servants? I can only follow what they said and hope that one day they would reveal yet more as we talk in the Realms, for there is always more that has not been revealed than has been revealed. I know that well. I know some of how much of Henry's life has remained a state secret, taken to the grave with him and that is just one example. How many secrets did Cromwell take to his grave, or Thomas More? What knowledge of state affairs did they conceal beneath the calm placid faces of acceptance of His Majesty's orders?

I only caught glimpses, very small parts, of the many goings-in in Henry's life, when I saw this envoy or that counsellor arriving to talk with him and I would hastily summon a lady in waiting to walk with me or a musician to entertain me or even Henry's jester to make me laugh, which he did most of the time, so I did not hear what was being said. If Henry wanted me to know, he would tell me.

And so I began to fear that my life would not be a long one and yet – and yet the pull of the thought of Thomas Culpepper outstripped those fears completely. At night, when the palace was silent, when nothing moved but the endlessly revolving stars and the occasional nightjar which, disregarding royal commands, dared to fly over the roof and call to its mate, I would find work for my fingers and memories for my mind and I would, for some hours, shut out the sight of my husband's face and body.

I know well Henry deplored what age, disease and accident had done to his body and went on doing it, as well. He admired that Hans Holbein painting, to him it depicted a king in full regalia and control of his country and his destiny. Indeed it is, in many ways, a triumphant stance and a very accurate painting.

What Holbein could not see, for which I for one am eternally grateful, is what was beneath those jewel encrusted clothes. Held tightly in corset and bandage was the bloated troublesome stomach, which defied even the rigid corset which he so hated, and the ulcerated legs which he loathed with a total deadly loathing. If it had been possible, he would have had the ulcers cut from his flesh and suffered the torment of healing but at least they would have been gone. Unfortunately no surgeon or physician or even alchemist had the skill, the knowledge or −in truth − the nerve to do such a thing to the king. What if anything went wrong? It would be an immediate death sentence for both of them.

And so Henry suffered. It was not that long before he had two walking sticks to assist him on his regular exercise, which he knew he had to do or his legs would get progressively worse.

For all of us who were close to Henry, this was difficult to cope with. His inability to move easily, his stomach, his bowels, his bad breath, his teeth which were rotting because of his problems, or so we were told, his hair going thin, which he bewailed to me in the sanctity of his rooms or mine. Nothing was right. He was perpetually in a bad mood, until we could sit into the night hours and talk of his sexual conquests and bring back a smile to the bloated face and in that smile I could see, so clearly, the handsome man he had once been. The handsome man the fortunate Katherine and the fortunate Anne got to see and love and be with. Jane had some of his youthful time, but he was ageing by then and the two years he lived through waiting for another wife to be chosen added to the ongoing deterioration to his health.

The courtiers and others never made the mistake of thinking that if his body was failing, so was his mind. It seemed to me - and I told him so – that his mind seemed to sharpen in direct contrast to the failing of his body. He was, if anything, sharper than ever, cutting through the rubbish some people tried to foist onto him and ensuring that they knew at all times he was in complete control of his government, his finances and his country.

We were married in July. The sun warmed our bones and our relationship; we had flowers by the thousand to look at as we walked and talked. We had sunshine and summer rains to dampen the dust and let us ride in majestic glory, both of us glittering with jewels and gold thread on our clothes. Those who rode with us were outshone by our glorious reflective outfits. At times like this I could believe I was queen, for even after the marriage I could not always believe it to be true, that someone would tell me Queen Anne needed me and I would hasten to her chamber to attend to her.

By then Queen Anne had been gone from court for some time and there were many who missed her gentleness and fractured English, her winning winsome smile and delicate ways. I tried, I tried hard to fill her shoes but they were too big for me.

And so I concentrated on being what she called me, that plump pigeon who had captured the king's attention. Now I know to call it lust and you can, too. That lust carried us for a while, but riding the mountain of his stomach grew tedious and unsatisfying – for me – and so I resorted to other methods to keep the king happy and give my stretched thighs a much needed rest. As long as his rose without a thorn was there, doing something to keep him satisfied, she could get away with a good deal.

And I did.

And now we come to the part you may find difficult to comprehend but believe me, trust me, it makes sense of the whole Howard/Tudor marriage and its sad and inevitable end. For there has to be logic in all things, reasons for all things. Nothing happens without a reason, nothing can happen without a reason.

It's just that the reasons are often hidden. In this case, they have been hidden for 476 years. It is time they were brought into the open for all to see and read, so that the nonsense written about this marriage can be laid to rest. I am long tired of being thought of as of no consequence, no intelligence and of Henry being blind to all that went on when all of us queens have made it clear that he knew everything that went on all the time, no matter where or with whom or what. He knew. His spies were the best there were, his knowledge vast and all-encompassing and yet your historians, you historians, insist he knew nothing of what happened next.

Let me tell you that apart from one time when Henry was ill, sick to his bones, with fever, we were never apart.

At no time did I learn to love the king but at all times I respected the king for what he was, what he knew, what he did and in his secret sexual moments, how he reacted. For one such as me, a mere Howard, to know you had brought the king a moment of pure ecstasy was reward enough but he showered gifts on me anyway.

I also need to add something here that you probably didn't know. It's like a game, *name ten things you didn't know about Henry VIII.*

He was a consummate actor.

Friends and enemies alike never knew of his true feelings about them. They thought they did. It is because of that small fact the world sees a different picture than the one that was actually painted at the time, by life, by people, by love, by lust and by sheer longing to turn back the clock and be young and golden again.

He was a consummate liar. That was part of the acting but whereas a mummer has a script to follow,

Henry wrote the script as he went along. And never slipped up, ever.

And so it was he used information to re-form his court into the way he wanted it. When he grew tired of someone, who had plagued him, bothered him, probably lied to him, the one thing he could not tolerate. For him it was on a par with treason and he would find an excuse to have them removed or executed or both.

This is the key to what happened to our relationship, right there in those lines.

There was a greater degree of honesty and openness between Henry and myself than with anyone else that I know of. No, let me say it was a different degree of honesty and openness. They have not once hinted at the sexual side of the relationship. For me it was everything. It was the relationship.

I doubt the other queens had the confidences I had, very much doubt it for he – and they - would have said if he had discussed these matters with them. The truth is, of course, that with the other queens, he was still slim enough, handsome enough and virile enough to bed others and have his fun and variety that way. By the time I found favour in his covetous eyes, he was well past most of that.

So let me get into this part of the story by saying all the rumours of my supposed pregnancy were just that, rumours. By the time I was part of the king's life and a welcome person in the king's bed, his virility had subsided to a level where it was hard to arouse him, let alone have him impregnate me.

And so we concocted a ruse between us, one that would satisfy both of us. I used the word carefully. It was chosen to let you know this was a joint ruse. It was Henry's idea, because nothing happened in court that was not Henry led, either openly or behind a hand, or muttered over a goblet of wine, that I recommence my relationship with my beloved Thomas Culpepper and report back, in great detail, to the king.

Thomas did not know it was all being done with the king's connivance. My ladies, my relatives, the many servants who saw me coming and going from Thomas' apartments, did not know. They thought they were taking part in a giant conspiracy. In many ways, they were. The whole thing was fraught with as much danger as if I really was going behind the king's back. We dared not let the world know it was planned.

We hid the secret well. No one has ever discovered it. But then, ultimately, Henry ended it with his usual signature, have everyone permanently removed, but we will get to that soon enough. In truth, even that was part of the conspiracy and the story we set up between us.

Oh the nights we talked this through, the nights we laughed over it! In that time I came closer to Henry than at any other point in our marriage. My respect for him grew in proportion to the ramifications of the whole outrageous idea.

Because, thinking it through and I had to, at his insistence, it was the perfect solution for both of us to go on enjoying ourselves.

Thinking it through meant accepting that my role in history as his fifth wife would be one of an adulteress, I would go down in history as the one person who defied the king. The person who made him a cuckold. He in turn had to think on that too, did he want that as part of his reputation? He said he cared not, because there were countless elderly men who were jealous of what he had anyway and if they laughed at him for being a cuckold, would know in their hearts he still had far more than they had ever had in their lives. No plump pigeon for them.

Not that I was so plump at that time. I was getting thinner all the time and blamed it on the stress of being with Henry, being Queen, being part of a highly dangerous escapade, deception, call it what you will. It involved acting and I was not as good an actor as Henry, who could in a moment, a mere blink, put on a face of pure blankness which none could penetrate. And equally, flare into the most appalling temper as if someone had struck a flint and a spark had ignited a fire.

Did I care what history thought of me? At the time I said no, it mattered not, for I would at some point be dead and buried in a shallow grave somewhere within sacred walls for as queen I was entitled to that. I did not consider the afterlife and my ongoing resentment at the way people have depicted me. Had I known, though, would I have acted differently? Told Henry this was not a good idea and could he please think of something else? But then, who dared defy Henry Tudor when he wanted something?

Only those who had nothing to live for.

In those heady days of intrigue, of affection, of lust and love and conspiracy and hours of swapping stories with Henry, I had much to live for.

It didn't last.

Everything didn't last.

Too much went wrong.

First, Henry got jealous, more than either of us thought he would. Talking sex with him was not enough any more and he was not capable of making it with me. Not if he wished to avoid crushing me with his weight.

Second, despite bribes and threats, people began to talk. Human nature says if you have a secret, you have to share it.

Third, Thomas became unhappy with sharing me. His ultimatum was, all of you or none of you. That's putting it the best way I can. He wanted me – or did he just want my body? I know not and I have not asked him since, either.

Fourth, the Howards began putting pressure on me to become pregnant, to secure my position. It couldn't happen. I couldn't tell them that. Some things were too personal to share with a bunch of relatives who would immediately spread it around the court. And the country, no doubt.

Fifth and possibly the most important part of this, for me anyway, was in discovering I was, from time to time, losing blood. It was obvious something was very wrong.

I could not share this with Henry; he hated illness, disease, surgeons, physicians, nurses; anything that spoke of less than perfect health. I was supposed to be the epitome of perfect health. On the days the blood flowed, I made sure I was covered when I went to his bed and he, for some reason, never questioned this. Maybe he thought it part of my seduction of him, I don't know. It was just easier than trying to tell him that I believed the blood loss and the weight loss were connected in some way. I felt ill, dizzy, tired, lacking any motivation and had to work very hard to retain the bright cheerfulness he wanted from me. When I could, I escaped to the sanctuary of whatever rooms I had in whatever great palace we were in. There I would sleep for as long as I could and try to gather my energy together for the next occasion we were together.

There came a time when we talked into the night hours. I sat by while he watched and recorded the moving of the stars and heavenly bodies, slowly realising how wonderful it was that anyone could understand what was going on, having wonders revealed to me I never dreamed of. To see Venus in full glory was something I would not forget and never have.

We talked of how we had to get ourselves out of the mess we had got ourselves into. We talked and we decided…

That the moment someone handed Henry a report of my 'activities' he would be shocked, horrified, upset as only he could act it out and would immediately order my arrest. I asked to be confined to Synon House, I loved it there, and he agreed. He said he had to have Thomas and others arrested too, this I knew and this I had to agree to.

It was with the most incredible sadness imaginable, the sheer misery of what he had to say to me writ clear all over his great body and his face and almost broke his voice when he spoke, he told me that I would be executed.

And then I told him of my blood flow and the pain which had begun and how I feared a long drawn out death, of losing more weight – he said he had noticed and worried about it – and wished only for it to end. And his order for my execution would mean that I would leave this life with dignity.

If this great king had cried at any other point of his life, I knew not of it. But he cried that night, staring up at the mass of stars, which seemed brighter and clearer than ever after we had talked. There was no disguising the tears and I did not think he wanted to, either.

I left him there, looking at the stars, trod gently down the stairs and back to my rooms. I went as a ghost would, not really there, not really knowing what was coming, what I had left, what I would lose, what I would gain. Everything foggy, misty, white, black, everything confused, everything cold, so very very cold.

There were those who saw me but who said nothing. What could they say? They knew I had been with the king, they knew not whether I had been ordered or invited to be there and it was not for them to know anyway.

Only when I got to the sanctuary of my bed did I allow myself to cry, for Henry, for Thomas, for Francis Dereham, for he would surely be one that would be arrested, and for the Howards, their dream was dead and they knew it not.

I cried for the remainder of that night but I did not cry for me. I knew, without any physician to try and tell me, that if I did not go with this plan, I would die a solitary painful death. It was in that moment I knew I was also crying for sweet gentle loving Katherine, who had suffered so badly at the end of her life, separated from the man she loved, the daughter she loved, crippled with the disease that distorts the fingers and gives great pain and with the broken heart she surely had.

Selfishly I wished for it to be over, so my suffering was ended.

And for Henry's sake, too. He could then find another queen to accompany him to the end of his life. I did not think it would be that long, for he had difficulty walking anywhere without his heart pounding so hard it hurt.

Regrets. Oh yes, many regrets.

That I had become involved with Francis Dereham and Thomas Culpepper in the first place. Francis had given me pleasure, it is true, but did he have enough pleasure from it in return to counter being hanged, drawn and quartered? For I knew well that was what his death would be. It always was for a traitor.

And my sweet Thomas. Oh, I had such pleasure of his body and his love which, real or not, seemed to wrap around me. Regret that I had not been strong enough to say to Henry I would not be part of the masquerade that was our strange relationship, with my bringing him stories of what I did with Thomas and Thomas being the victim here, for he had no idea what was going on but knew that what we were doing would be considered treason – and it was. I dragged him into a situation and I was directly responsible for his execution.

But then, did he not have the right to say he did not wish to lie with the queen, for it was treason against the great king?

Yes.

So were we both to blame?

Yes.

Did this make the thought of his death any easier?

No.

Would anything make the thought of his death any easier?

No.

Did I think Henry loved me?

Yes.

The questions went on all night, around the tears, around the aching in the heart and the body, the sore eyes, the dry mouth, the racing heart which was nearly as fast as that of Henry's when he walked too far or tried to move too fast. I hoped it would burst out of my body and end it all there and then. Nothing happened but I felt ill.

And so we move to the end.

As we anticipated, a report was handed to my husband the king. He acted out his part, shocked, hurt, upset, angry; I heard he went through the entire range of emotions and I smiled deep inside at how good an actor he was. I was arrested, politely and treated with the most courtesy imaginable and taken to Syon, as I had asked.

I asked for news of Thomas but it was refused. I had not made an agreement with Henry over that, more fool I.

So began the countdown to the end of my days. Dignity, we had decided on dignity so I asked for a block to be brought to my rooms so I could acquaint myself with it and not find myself repelled and do something utterly stupid and ruin my execution in the eyes of the world.

All the stories of my kneeling and putting my head on the block are true, true as the words I give you here. What is not said, what is not known, is that every time I did that, I was wishing it were over. I was bearing more pain each day, more blood flowed and I found it hard to disguise it, to lose the rags into the midden so none would know of my silent sorrow that my body should so betray me. I wanted it over. Being separated from those I loved, my dearest Thomas, my friends, my ladies, from those I respected, Henry and some of his advisors, his jester, his musicians whom I had come to care about from their consideration for me as a young queen with no experience. The loneliness was intense and I cared not for the company of the cleric come to shrive me before my death. Oh I said the right prayers, said the right words, but the real ones came from me to Almighty God in the dark hours of the longest nights I had ever known, longer and darker even than the ones I endured when knowing I would be married to the most powerful man in Europe and that he wanted me, little Kathryn, above all others. That is something I thought I would never live up to, his expectations of me. I never ever expected, dreamed or believed our relationship would turn the way it did. But it did and there it is, laid out for you.

And so I was executed, cleanly and swiftly and I was released from a body that was betraying me and a heart that was dying.

And so I draw my section of this book to a close. Tis shorter than the testimony of the other queens, but holds more revelations, I do believe, and I trust you will have sympathy with me. The historians have been unkind to me over the years and I am grateful for the chance to set the history right. When I watched the libel being spread by others through the years, I thought I would never have the chance to tell my story to the world and have the true balance of our marriage shown, lit by lanterns so the world can see the truth. Does it not all make sense to you that such a virile man should want to have titillation in his ageing years? Of course. Has anyone considered that aspect of Henry VIII, king of England? No.

And now it is done. My channel, thank you. Henry, I trust you are content with all I have said about you in trying to bring your true self to the world stage.

My liege lord, my respect, my affection, my loyalty remain yours and will do so for the rest of time.

Treasured Memories

The many times at the table when I found him looking at me, more with wanting than lust, as if he craved me, little Kathryn, rather than my body.

The gentle way he taught me so much about the stars and the planets, the movement of the moon, the mysteries of the night skies.

The slow meandering walks through the gardens together, arm in arm, ignoring those who clustered around us, doing nothing more than absorbing the beauty of the flowers.

His sighs of ecstasy and satisfaction when I had pleasured him.

The boyish excitement with which we concocted our ruse to keep him pleasured and I to find satisfaction too.

Being Queen of England alongside the greatest king England has ever known, or ever will.

Expressing Henry in one word: Lustful

Ten questions about Henry:

His favourite colour: blue
His favourite sport: archery

His favourite animal: hawks
His favourite interest: astronomy
His favourite meal: quail with cranberry sauce
His favourite sweet: medlars in syrup
His favourite time of year: Autumn
His favourite home: Grenewich
His favourite gem: emerald
His favourite musical instrument: lyre

Katherine Parr

Henry's wives, divorced, beheaded, died, divorced, beheaded, survived

Henry's sixth queen, nursemaid and carer (survived)

Shall we go on now, into the story of the final Queen of this great king? If we do, we go with tender footsteps for by this time the king was a man of much substance and standing in the physical sense but much distraught and desperate in the heart for he suffered that most terrible of afflictions: loneliness.

I know not even now whether Henry actually loved me. He talks to all of us in the same way, for he has an intense feeling for each queen, no differentiating, despite treating us all differently when we were alive and walking the gardens of the homes with him, or listening to his sweet music or comforting him when the pain was too much. For though we did the same things for him, his needs were individual to us which is why we were chosen, of course.

Now we are all the same, queens who are always delighted to see their king. For to us nothing has changed, we live as we did then, for it is the way we know and what we feel comfortable to do.

That is for you to know, for you may have wondered why we were and are talking so freely about our husband, giving away bedroom secrets that some might consider best kept in the bedroom. The king asked us, in turn, if we were prepared to talk freely and openly, to tell the world what he was truly like, to make sense of supposition and often outright lies. To put the record straight for all of us, for all of us have been misrepresented, slandered, libelled, discussed as if we were no more than Henry's marionettes, dancing when he pulled the strings.

And do we not know that we, in turn, are creating a vivid picture of the king you have also misrepresented, slandered, libelled and discussed as if he were a new toy on the market for the children to play with. No thought of him as a living breathing human being, who walked this earth like a Colossus for fifty seven years.

You have here the combined wisdom of six queens, six ladies who were chosen to be the Queen Consort of Henry VIII and, believe me, he knew what he was doing when he chose us.

Do we not know, from the records, all that the first Katherine did for him?

Do we not think that the first Anne was more in love with him than he was with her? 'The Lovers' indeed: any who were there at the time knew it was a one way relationship but he had enjoyment from it for a while. And she got to be with the one man she loved above all others.

Do we not know that Jane, slender, beautiful, would not bear a child easily for the king, but did we think – as I believe – the surgeons and others would take it upon themselves to cut her open and get to the child to please the king? Did any consider he might want his queen instead and for her to try again to bear a child? Rumour has it that he ordered what became the murder of his queen. My opinion is this was and is false, that they did it to please the king and blamed it on him. It did not stop them being banned forever from the palaces and thus they lost their livelihood and were soon gone from this life.

Do we not know that the second Anne would have been a fine companion for Henry, had he looked further into her than her appearance?

Do we not know that the young, seemingly flirtatious and foolish Kathryn actually had more to offer than mere looks and youth? Only if we were sensible enough to look past the obvious and ask ourselves, what did an intellectual intelligent all powerful king see in a flighty little one like her? The hidden depths of sensuality that he knew how to delve into and satisfy himself with her stories. We know too that she is right about his drinking and yet none have commented on it in the many, many books written on this outstanding man and not a one of them coming near to pinning down his complexities and his intellect and his appeal to women.

I say here the once and will not repeat it again: Kathryn was good for him, she gave him the elixir of youth, sex; gave it to him with her body and her tales. Gave it to him in the sure knowing that it would rebound on her and she be defiled for eternity as a wanton and later as adulteress. Now perhaps they will think differently of her. I sympathise and sorrow at her physical problems and admire her dignified way of dealing with it. I know of his tears at her departure, we spoke of it once and then never again.

And so we come to me, the final queen; the final helpmeet for a great but suffering king. And so I say, we come to me, a different person from all his other queens, for I came twice married and twice widowed and knowing what it is to suffer grief beyond bearing at times. When you become 'famous' the world thinks it knows you and thinks it owns you. So it is known my third choice of husband was Thomas Seymour and I would have been wedded to him much earlier had the king not made it clear he favoured me as his queen.

When the request came, I admit it was a shock to my senses for I did not truly believe I would ever be elevated to such high office. My first reaction was 'no, I can't do this,' my second reaction was 'Queen? Of course I can.' But then the ramifications hit me, not marrying my beloved Thomas, not living my own life – I was well aware a queen lived the life of the king, not the life she wanted to lead – and of coping with a very difficult sick man. Would I be wife or nursemaid?

There was no gainsaying the king. I could not say to him, 'Your Majesty, I would prefer to be married to your devoted servant Thomas Seymour' for what would that say to Henry? That I preferred a mere aristocrat over a king? Not this king, not this proud man who fought his endless pain and disabilities to carry on his studies and his governmental work and his writing and composing, even when spending whole days abed and taking copious amounts of laudanum and other pain killing substances.

I was torn for a while, for I longed for Thomas Seymour in a way I had not longed for my other husbands. Oh, I would have you know I was happy, content in those marriages and had wished them to last much longer than they did. Becoming a widow once is hard enough, twice is too much. I told myself that 3 was a lucky number and I would have a husband with which to share my old age. But that was not to be. It was made clear to me by Henry's courtiers that he had admired me for some time and that he wished we could walk and talk together with the ultimate aim of my becoming his sixth queen.

So I found myself confused, unhappy, indecisive, wanting Thomas but also not able to say no to the king. And here I confess I found it in my heart to have utter sympathy and concern for him, I found that I ached to help in some way, to ease the pain of the legs and his many other ailments, to share my life with him for a while. It did not take a soothsayer to let me know it would not be a long marriage. If Thomas would but wait, we would be together before our lives were through. The Seymours knew how to live in close proximity to the crown, they had been there already, although they made it clear their sorrow for Jane was far from over and still sought the answers to who and where and why the order was given or the decision made. I found that foolish, for those responsible were long gone and there was no way they could find out. I believed eventually they held to the long unsolved puzzle out of bitterness that their first choice did not stay queen for long, did not have the big coronation they longed for, did not garner the estates, titles and wealth they longed for but would not admit to. And I say to them, even now, let go. Jane played her part, gave our king the son and heir he so desired and a fine boy he was too, with a Tudor look about him but with the softening influence of his mother's looks and personality. We had the phrase 'gentlewoman' in our time, it suited Jane well.

I find I am confusing myself. That in turn is a reflection of the way I was at the time, a-dither with myself. My ladies urged me to become Queen, as if I had any real choice in the matter, as I told them. Thomas urged me to say yes, for the benefit of the Seymours and of himself, of course. My heart said no, my mind said yes.

Truth was, there was no decision to be made – by me. Henry had made it for me.

I need you to see Henry as he was at that time. I need you to see him, the great king, Supreme Ruler of the whole of England and anywhere and everywhere else he set sights on. I want you to see him raging against his illness and condition, tossing his great body around the bed so the ropes creaked and the boards clattered together and his retinue of favourites, doctors, nurses, cooks and scribes were always on the verge of fleeing for their lives. I want you to understand his frustration. There was always a quantity of papers to be read, a group of people to be seen, a stack of decisions to be made and all he could think of was the pain racking his body and the potions and mixtures baffling his mind. 'Delegate' was a word he did not know.

He was still in grief for Kathryn at some level, for he loved her so. Your historians say 'obsessed' and 'cuckold' but they knew not of what happened – until now. He was not obsessed; he loved her in his own way, as far as Henry was ever capable of loving anyone as they wanted. Henry really loved – not Henry the man, but Henry the king, the all powerful, the influential, the controller. All the queens have said how he controlled everything and that is so, he did. He controlled his appetite; it was not through over-eating at the table which caused the weight to materialise in places he did not wish it to be, but the lack of exercise. He went from someone capable of riding horses into the ground on a hunt to someone who could scarcely walk. Then the weight goes on, whether you wish it or not.

You now have to dismiss the over eating, drunken Tudor image and see someone who tried to moderate everything but physically was incapable of riding or walking to lose the weight. You see how easy it is to mis-read someone?

He needed a helpmeet, the only word which describes our relationship and a right good word it is too. For I would have gone into another marriage in the hope of what? Not being lonely? Knowing that made it easier for me to give Henry the affection he craved, the attention he sought, the loyalty he desired and the soft breast to lean on when it all got too much.

Think you I exaggerate? Then you have not taken in the message of this book. The message is simple, not a one of you understands Henry Tudor or ever will if you will not listen to those of us who had the honour, the challenge, the romance, the heartbreak of being his queen consorts.

And so, after what seemed a very short time, I had distanced myself from Thomas Seymour, having to overcome the thought that I would possibly lie with the king and then with Thomas. And the thought was compounded by the names – again. For we have the proliferation of Katherine/Kathryn/Anne/Anne and Kathryn with her Thomas and I having a Thomas awaiting me. And Henry with his Thomases – it becomes confusing for all.

So we must separate my feelings about Thomas Seymour for the moment, a marriage suspended for a time, for the needs, wants and orders of the king came before everything else. I longed for security, for someone who would perhaps outlive me, having gone through grief twice already but when I saw the king close up, when we met to discuss our marriage, our future life, I knew well it was not for long. I also knew in all conscience I could not refuse him, for his loneliness, his unhappiness was so obvious – to me – that my heart went out to him.

What basis is that for a marriage of such high standing, you might ask and you would be right to question it, but we made it work, Henry and I, we were a loving couple for the time he had left on the earth.

I just had to ask my Thomas not to come too close to me during that time, to speak with Henry when he needed to but not to me. It was not easy for me, I know not how difficult it was for him; we never spoke of it, not even when I was his wife after Henry died. Some things are best not spoken of if there is to be a future.

I found it easy to develop deep affection for Henry's son Edward, a fine boy, a handsome boy, as I have said, with the look of a Tudor about him. I built a relationship with both Henry's daughters, prevailing upon him to reconcile himself with them. They were both headstrong, determined young women, having learned the hard way that life was not handed to them on a gold plate or any other kind. They had to fight for their role in life in the court hierarchy and they did, both of them. This made them stronger in will than many other women in the court, some much older than they were.

This all sounds easy, I have written it as if it were easy but there was a good deal of diplomatic pressure needed to change Henry's mind about his daughters. For Henry only the son mattered, the true heir to the throne, all women were dismissed as of no consequence. I think and believe even now that this way of thinking made it easier for him to walk away from marriages, no matter how they ended, and seek another woman to be by his side. Ever did he desire change, challenge, interest; nothing to remain the same. It was this which drove him to the Progresses around England, the seemingly endless journeys that required so much planning, so much money and demanded even more of the many homes at which he stayed with his vast retinue, all of which had to be catered for. I heard the complaints, whispered mostly, over the years I was in the employ of the court.

As always, Henry only concerned himself with Henry, as supreme ruler of the country he was entitled to do just that, and he did. None could gainsay anything he ordered or even asked, for he had a trick of asking and making it clear it was an order which could not be disobeyed or argued against in any way, without risking incurring the wrath of the king.

So it was when Henry decided to make me his Queen consort.

And so we were married in a private ceremony and, for the first time, I saw true happiness in his eyes and on his face. He was much taken by the fact I had been named for his first Queen, for he held a deep affection for her still. Somehow that made it even more interesting that I was his Queen consort. 'I will have no difficulty remembering your name,' he jested once, as if he could! Our celebrations after our wedding ceremony were delightful, musicians playing all the music Henry had composed up to the day before the wedding, the finest lightest confections imaginable, mulled wine because he knew I liked it. Just to sit with him as his wife, admiring the heavily jewelled doublet he had commissioned for the occasion, smoothing the silk of my deep blue gown, also heavily jewelled, that he had paid for, because he wanted everyone to see how he favoured me. He presented me with a jewel on a chain; a heavy perfectly cut sapphire of the lightest blue, so it showed up against my gown. It was worth a king's ransom, I do believe. For the first time since the proposal had been made, I was able to be content within myself and with Henry. He was soft spoken with me, his eyes twinkled, something I never thought anyone's eyes ever did, he smiled often, he encouraged the musicians and those who danced to his music, utterly delightful music, lilting and melodic. I noticed he only sipped at the mulled wine and took tiny bits of the confections. I did ask him if his legs or his head pained him and he told me he was at that moment feeling very good. It showed in the way he held himself, upright, regal, every inch the king, where at times he walked or sat with slumped shoulders and a mask of pain on his face. Sometimes his hands were not still, they quivered and trembled and tapped out a silent melody of their own on the arms of his chair, but this time they were still.

And they came, the courtiers, the envoys, the messengers, with their good wishes for our happiness, giving me their loyalty as Queen.

And for the first time I realised how wonderful these heights of power could be. And how dangerous, for so many came to woo me for my contact with the king, trying to bribe me with jewels, coin and promises if I would but put their name before the king. Henry told me to take the jewels and coins and dismiss the promises and forget the names the moment they were spoken. He said he had done that throughout his reign and it hadn't caused any harm, just enriched him even further. For those who did not get what they sought came back with more jewels, more gold and even more promises. 'And,' he told me with a serious yet laughing face, 'there was always the chance that a promise might be kept, even though that was as remote a possibility as our travelling to the Moon, dear wife.'

His honesty was a reason for laughter between us in the sanctuary of our rooms, either his or mine; knowing well that if the courtiers knew of our mirth they would be highly offended, but though he cared nothing for that, he was still careful not to let them know. It would diminish his power over them, he said: absolute power meant absolute control and that is all he sought at all times. And had it for himself, too.

It is hard to convey the impact this man, this king had on my life. I had seen him from a distance, had very few words with him during my time in court and yet every part of him seemed imprinted on me in some way. I knew his habits, the little things he did, how he turned his head so little but saw so much, how he walked so slowly because of his ailments but used that to ensure he viewed everyone from head to foot to gauge what they were wearing. He could assess their fashion, their jewels; their footwear, in a single sweeping glance and, I would swear too, he knew which barber they went to for shaves and hair trimming. He never said that, I just knew it.

The women he assessed on a different level; were they interested in him as king or as a man, for his ego was still huge and his needs immense, his need to be admired, revered, accepted as supreme ruler of both them and of the country. I understood, on a deep level, that this was more important to him than anything. Sick and old and tired, yet he still sought to be the ruler of his land, his kingdom, his court and his courtiers and women.

This made me feel very proud at times, that I had been chosen as Queen consort. It also terrified me at other times, was I capable of living up to the standards he imposed on his queens?

History must judge me there, for Henry did not live long enough to persuade me I had done enough to care for him, despite all I did do, I always felt I should have done more.

The question has to be asked, could I have done more? No doctor am I, no nurse either, but I took on the role of both for almost immediately Henry bid his doctor and nurse to go through me to him, rather than go to him. He said he was sick to his bones of the medics who had done nothing but give him increased agony and no respite for the ulcers on his legs. And so it fell to me to bathe the ulcers and bind them and I did this with the herbal scented and enriched oils he had in his room or in his robe for use in sexual practices. We found they were very good for the ulcers and, properly attended to, he found a degree of relief from them whilst he was my husband.

I have to say here it continued to be passing strange to call the king 'my husband.' I was named for his first wife, as I said before in this piece for this revealing book, so there was something of an age difference between us. I arrived in this world when he was married to his Katherine, his Spanish princess, the one who meant so much to him. To ultimately be married to him was a twist of fate, of life, call it what you will, that continued to gently amuse and interest me for some time. Henry, on the other hand, dismissed it as his being 'fortunate' and 'nothing to dwell on, dear wife' and continued with the life he had, that busy one of attending to government matters, to accepting visits from envoys from Europe, to sitting up half the night studying the movement of the stars or creating alchemic potions which might or might not prove to be the elixir of life he sought to extend his years. I believe he knew then that the time was getting shorter, that he would not have many more years in which to study, to work, to read, to do all that he had wanted to do throughout his life. It drove him to more intense and demanding work, if you can call it that. For him it was all pleasure, even though he defined it as a task to be done, to be achieved and to be conquered, as with everything in his life.

Henry was ever the perfectionist in all he did.

If we were conceited women – and is there a reason why we should not be? We could say, he chose the perfect women.

Where one man chooses a wife and that young person grows into a middle aged person and into an old person, Henry chose different women for each stage of his life.

Consider: for twenty three years he had the exotic, devoted, intelligent Katherine of Aragon at his side. We will, for the moment, discard and forget the many he bedded in between lying with his lawful wife, for he was king and he could have whatever he wanted when he wanted it.

When his middle age began to approach, when he began to realise he was not the young golden prince any more, the beautiful Anne Boleyn became his partner, his consort, his next wife. When he realised she loved him more than he loved her and he desired someone quieter, gentler, more adaptable to his ways, he moved on to Jane Seymour. She at least fulfilled one of Henry's needs and gave him a son. Unfortunately and sadly, she gave her life for her son – or is it more correct to say her life was taken to give life to her son?

A partner is needed for the king, the net is cast wide, Anne of Cleves is caught in its snares but the reality does not match the image. I would ask now of you, how many times has that happened? Someone seen from afar is everything you want, seen closer they are not. And so it was with poor Anne. But she became the cherished sister and friend, all was not lost.

And so we find an ageing king who needs to be reminded he is still young at heart and sometimes in body, too. So he fastens his attention on the young, sexy Kathryn who is happy to play his games, to keep him interested. But life, illness and reputation put an end to what was a goodly partnership for a while.

And so it came to me, the twice widowed, the one able to cope with a king in his final years of life, ill, sick at heart and in body, and together we found a level of happiness neither of us truly thought we would find. Think you not Henry and I talked of this during the long nights as the stars moved on the infinitesimally slow pathways the Lord God set them on? We did, many and many a long night.

And so I say to you, Henry chose well, for even the mis-choosing of Anne of Cleves gave him a friend, a non confrontational friend, who was happy just to be in the country he ruled.

I would just qualify these statements by saying to get the women he wanted, Henry did some radical and drastic things. I have to ask you now, would you be content to still be ruled by and influenced by and controlled by Rome, or is it your liking that he broke away from the yoke of Rome and gave you that most singular of things, a Church of England?

Before we move on, let me say what is in your mind, what has always been in people's minds: Was he capable? Yes, at times. Not often, not as often as I would have wished. After two husbands I was ready for more but someone as severely afflicted as Henry by both outward and inward problems, his bad heads were astonishingly awful to witness and none of us could ever begin to understand how they felt, how they could be endured, could not perform at will. But… when the body was ready, so was I and so we were as man and wife on occasions. I cherish those occasions and hold them close to my heart in memory even now. I say to myself, on those occasions I was bedded by the greatest king England has ever known. The honour is all mine.

It was in that closeness, those special times that we shared when he spoke freely and openly to me about his other queens, his women, his life. I believe he liked to share, for he shared much of this with his Kathryn, maybe for a different reason, that I cannot say. I wondered if he sought approbation for the women he chose, the decisions he made, the acts he put into motion which had far reaching consequences, sometimes I believe consequences further and more far reaching than he envisaged when they began.

But leaders lead, that is what they do. If it goes wrong, the resulting chaos is loaded upon them and rightly so. History has not been kind to this king, blaming him for so much and at times blaming him for events which had spiralled away from him, other people's obstinacy; other people's determination to be martyrs. I say this from my heart for I know of or actually knew these people and mourned their passing.

And so where do I go from here, what else can I tell you about this great king? I was honoured to be named Regent when he went to France, I was worried when my arrest was pending, but not so worried that I lost sleep over it, for I knew somehow Henry would support me and he did. I need not spell this out for you now; it is all there in the history books and has been turned over many times. What you seek from this book are the truths which never made it into your time, those forgotten, overlooked, conveniently dismissed or, in our case, never told for us queens knew when not to speak. We only speak now with his consent, his urging; his insistence that for once the truth be put out there, to be vilified or accepted as you will. It will be your choice.

What we ask is that you read this book in its entirety and consider the overall picture we have given you of the man each of us called husband, whether that be for years or a very short time. You now have the truth about each marriage, each queen, each decision made by Henry which affected that queen and her passing. You will know now that for some the decision was welcome, for others there was intense sorrow but once we are on the other side of life, all is forgiven, forgotten and relegated to the past where it belongs.

Henry's passing was a relief to Henry, for at that time his fifty seven years weighed heavily on him, caused him much sorrow in his heart and mind, and even more so in his body. That great heart had laboured long enough, that great head had suffered more than enough and we need not speak of the ulcers or the illness or disease or whatever it was eating his body.

He died knowing he had produced at least one heir and two fine women. I know from all I have seen from my side of life that Elizabeth became a queen fit to stand in her father's great shoes.

My sorrow is I did not have longer to live with him but I was released to go to my Thomas and I did. I found happiness for a short time until, just like poor quiet demure Jane, my child took my life. Oftentimes us women traded our lives for the new one. It was something we all had to live within our age.

I thank you, dear channel, for receiving these words, for working so well with me, for the music you found which pleased me.

I now leave you to close this outstanding book, in the hope that our words will put right all that is wrong in people's minds about their great king,

Henry VIII.

The channel writes... of what she knows.

Katherine of Aragon

I have had confirmation several times over that I was Katherine of Aragon in one of my past lives. I visited a qualified respected hypnotherapist on two occasions for regression and went back to Katherine's life both times, even though I fully expected to go elsewhere. No one was more surprised than me when on the first session I went back to Aragon and experienced the certain knowledge of having to leave the land I loved to go to that cold wet place called England. The second time I was pacing the stone floor of my chamber, demanding to know why Henry loved 'her' more than me. I remember well the bitterness that pervaded me. Later, the wonderful mediums at Silver Moon Psychics in the north of Scotland confirmed I had indeed been Katherine of Aragon and that the guide of the main medium there, Crystal Green, knew me from that time. As he is Thomas, a cleric, my guess is that he was my cleric then. He visits me from time to time.

Katherine first came to visit me in August 2005 when we spoke for some time. She said then:
"I want my story told, for my story is one of great interest to many and is not known from my viewpoint, any more than any of the other people who would seek to come to you. But before then, you and I need to reunite into the person we once were, in that far off time which is yesterday to me and a lifetime of history to you."

This we did when I channelled the life of our husband, Henry VIII. I had many flashbacks during the writing of that book: often he would ask me a question about our marriage and I had the answer in an instant. Some of it surprised him.

Katherine is a fine, proud lady who suffered much during that lifetime. Her inability to bring living children into the world caused much deep sorrow and regret, her inability to keep her husband at her side also brought her much sadness. She suffered greatly in her confined quarters away from Henry. She felt she had lost her daughter through separation, they were like strangers, so the one person who could bring her solace was not able to do that.

She died at the age of 50, very much alone, racked with rheumatism, cancer and a broken heart. It was a difficult life but she was dignified and proud throughout, no matter what anyone did or said to her.

When she died, her spirit was released to return to Aragon, the place where her heart had long been, from the very first. She comes from time to time to talk with me about our husband, for we both love him still, but the call of Aragon is strong and she is ever there, walking the palace corridors and gardens, at peace at last.

It has been an honour and a pleasure to channel her story and have her friendship.

***

Anne Boleyn

Meditation time but before meditating I realised someone was in the room, someone saying 'Katherine, I am so sorry. So very sorry.'

Anne Boleyn was there, in what looked like the clothes she wore when she went to her execution.

I had been watching the TV programme of the dramatisation of her life with Henry. At the end of it the historian mentioned what Katherine had been through, devoting twenty years of her life to Henry only to end it in cold and damp and misery, shut away from her daughter and her life. This seems to have prompted the visit from Anne in November 2014.

Anne returned in June 2015, when this book was first proposed by Henry himself, to say she would willingly take part and tell the world the truth – that she was innocent of all charges. She is a proud, independent and most of all, dignified lady, the kind of person any king would have been proud to have as queen consort.

Anne says her execution set her free to pursue her life's work. There are many who have their heads cut off for whatever reason; in our time it is terrorism at its worst. Those who died that way are there to help and console the spirit which returns to its home after such a death. You know who they are. Many and many are there who died that way. In this remembrance Anne joins Antony Woodville, who dedicated a section of his book to ten people we knew of who were beheaded by terrorists. We know there are hundreds more. Our hearts break for each and every one of them.

***

Jane Seymour

One night I swung round from my desk and burst into what can only be described as hysterical tears. I was thumping the chair and myself and shouting 'I did not want it!' and tears were pouring down my face. I realised immediately this was not me, it's not something I would do, that it was a spirit working extraordinarily hard to get my attention. For a fleeting moment I saw Jane Seymour and then the image was gone and I was left with her presence, distressed, determined and demanding I write her story. I wrote it exactly as she dictated it. The other side of the demure calm Jane, the person who wrote that narrative was someone full of fire and passion which was killed by having to be the calm consort Henry craved at that time. Her story is one of 'if only's' – if she had only she had lived, would she have retained his affection? If only she could have borne children easily for him, would she have been his most treasured queen? Henry would say yes but life was cruel and we cannot say it would have happened that way. All I know is; Jane is a spirit now at peace with herself, her story having been told.

Jane gave me only her rage at not being listened to, saying she did not want to be queen and horrific details of her birth experience. A few weeks later this book was proposed by Henry and Jane came back to say she had plenty she wanted to pass on, so… we took the original short narrative and built it into the chapter we have here. It's a tragic story of someone going through the medieval equivalent of a nervous breakdown, culminating in inept surgeons killing her to save the child. The question hangs, even in Jane's mind, did Henry give that order? None of us will ever know for certain but the possibility, the probability, is very much there. For Henry only the son and heir mattered.

***

Anne of Cleves

When this book was proposed, I asked if Anne would come and she said yes immediately. She (rightly) said no one had asked for her side of the story before and she was pleased to have a chance.

When the time came to work with Anne, I formed a level of friendship with her that had not been there with Katherine, Anne or Jane. We talked like old friends and she had no problems discussing her sexual experiences with Henry for the book.

It must have been heartbreaking, devastating for her to be cast aside in such a way but she overcame it with dignity and good humour, to the point when she became a trusted friend and was able to visit the court and be with Henry. She is a fine lady and it is sad how many historians continue to dismiss her as of no consequence. As she rightly says, she was Queen of England for a while.

***

Kathryn Howard

When working on Henry's book (I Diced With God) I took time out to look through my portal into the past to see what could be revealed to me. I saw a great hall, Henry stomping along with a walking stick, his gentlemen with him. A line of men and women were waiting, bowing or curtsying as he walked past. I saw Kathryn make her curtsy and then break with protocol to leave the line, flashing her ankles and a big smile as Henry turned to look at her. She was taking a calculated risk; he could easily have been very displeased that she did this, leave his presence without his permission. Instead, as she says, he saw her breasts bouncing and her skirts lifted to show her ankles and in that moment he was captured. He was hers.

It is the middle of February, 2016. I worked with Kathryn all evening and we accomplished a good deal. I said my thanks and began to prepare for bed, then realised the bedroom was full of spirit visitors. To my amazement and overwhelming pleasure, all six queens had come to visit me. They came with their sincere thanks and assurances of friendship. Katherine Parr spoke briefly with me; she is ready and willing to give me her story. I can almost see the end of the book… it's all so good, so very good.

Kathryn proved to be a brilliant narrator, full of stories and regrets, determined to have her voice heard as she, like Anne of Cleves, is very much overlooked by many who write of this time. The truth is they really only want to write at length about the first three queens, for there, they say, is the real story. How wrong they are… Kathryn's stories would have hit all the tabloid papers had they been there in her time, had she released press statements in her last days, 'Read all about it! This is what your king is really like!' It isn't hard to imagine…

***

Katherine Parr

The call went out for the queens; it was answered by Katherine on the 4th June, 2015. She said she will be here later to tell me her story. Again, she says she is very pleased to have the opportunity.

And here we are, March 2016. Katherine's part of the book is finished. She came with light, a delicate and lively vibration; it is not difficult to see why Henry was enamoured of his sixth wife. She was a perfect choice for him at that time, sick, ill, suffering daily and needing a helpmeet and nursemaid and finding a wife alongside his other needs.

Katherine has been a perfect narrator, full of confidence and insights into this enigmatic king, casting light in dark corners. It has been a true pleasure to work with her.

257

I find it difficult to cope with some 'historians', no matter how many degrees they have or what studies they have attempted, the results are the same. Ego-led books that bear little or no resemblance to the truth or even to commonsense. It seems often the 'facts' are not allowed to get in the way of commonsense. There are few who get it right and their reputation is sullied by those who don't.

So incompetent has the generality of historians been for the province they have undertaken, that it is almost a question, whether, if the dead of past ages could revive, they would be able to reconnoitre the events of their own times, as transmitted to us by ignorance and misrepresentation
Horace Walpole, (1768)

History is the version of past events that people have decided to agree on.
Napoleon Bonaparte (1769-1821)

It has been said that though God cannot alter the past, historians can: it is perhaps because they can be useful to Him in this respect that He tolerates their existence.
Samuel Butler (1835-1902)

It is surprising how few people are willing to support the truth, and how many people are willing to accept the deceit.
(Found on a motto calendar.)

History is the distillation of rumour.
A comment found whilst reading:

Propaganda, thy name is History.
'Medieval Lives' by Terry Jones

Historians are like deaf people who go on answering questions that no one has asked them. *Leo Tolstoy*

Herodotus says, "Very few things happen at the right time, and the rest do not happen at all: the conscientious historian will correct these defects.
Mark Twain

To give an accurate description of what has never occurred is not merely the proper occupation of the historian, but the inalienable privilege of any man of parts and culture.
Oscar Wilde

All historical writing, even the most honest, is unconsciously subjective, since every age is bound, in spite of itself, to make the dead perform whatever tricks it finds necessary for its own peace of mind.
Carl Lotus Becker, The Heavenly City of the Eighteenth Century Philosophers

Some historians hold that history is just one damned thing after another.
Arnold Toynbee

To seek in the great accumulation of the already-said the text that resembles 'in advance' a later text, to ransack history in order to rediscover the play of anticipations or echoes, to go right back to the first seeds or to go forward to the last traces, to reveal in a work its fidelity to tradition or its irreducible uniqueness, to raise or lower its stock of originality, to say that the Port -Royal grammarians invented nothing, or to discover that Cuvier had more predecessors than one thought, these are harmless enough amusements for historians who refuse to grow up.